NEW YORK TIMES AND *USA TODAY* BESTSELLING AUTHOR

VICTORIA ASHLEY

BEAUTIFUL SAVAGE

2nd edition 2022

Cover design by Dana Leah | Designs by Dana
Edited by Charisse Spiers
2nd Edition Edited by Virginia Tesi Carey
Formatted by N. E. Henderson

JAX

I CAN'T FUCKING BREATHE... I don't want to. With every breath that fills my lungs, I feel the rage building inside of me, making it hard to think straight.

If I don't find out where this son of a bitch is within the next thirty seconds, I know without a doubt I'll be taking a man's life tonight.

I'll stand here, my rough hands wrapped tightly around James' throat, squeezing until I see the last sign of life drain from his eyes.

And I will feel nothing.

Which is exactly what I've felt for the last three days; since I showed up at Alexandra's house to find it littered with pills and cocaine.

I'm numb to every emotion other than fury.

My grip around James' throat tightens as I hold his head above the bathwater, giving him a few moments to catch his breath.

The prick can hardly remember his name at this point from

the lack of oxygen to his brain, but I don't give a fuck. Either that or he's not talking. One way or another, he has answers that I need and I'm not leaving here without them.

"Where is he?" I ask again, my voice gruff as I lean in close to his bloodied and swollen face. "This is your last chance."

He coughs and digs at my hands when I give his throat a firm squeeze and lift him higher out of the water.

"I don't..." he coughs. "...know—"

"Tell me, before I rip your fucking throat out." Anger courses through me, making me see red when I don't get the answer I need. "Fuck this."

Growling out, I shove him back into the water, watching with dead eyes, all the fucks in the world gone as he gasps for air and slaps at the porcelain surrounding him.

It's hard to see him through the bloodstained water, yet I keep my gaze on him, not wanting to miss a second of his suffering.

It's this piece of shit's fault that Alexandra got mixed up with Jasper to begin with.

I kept her in the dark when we were kids, not wanting her to ever know who that sick fuck was; even though he'd been at my doorstep more times than I could count while growing up.

I couldn't protect my mother from him, but I made damn sure he never set his eyes on Alexandra to chance ruining her too.

Even when I was too young to fully understand how that part of the world worked, I still knew he was bad news.

I'd seen how dangerous and greedy he was through his careless eyes.

With my hand still around James' throat, I step into the water and kneel above his body, so I can get a better grip. Looking him dead in the eyes, I reach into my boot and pull out my knife, placing it to his cheek.

"Tell me where the fuck he is, before I start cutting you into pieces, starting with your tongue. Now!" I scream in his face, before releasing his throat with a shove.

I keep my body above his, not giving him a chance to escape even if he had it left in him, which he doesn't.

We've been at this for over twenty minutes now.

"I don't know..." he gasps out, gripping at the bathtub. "I swear! I swear! Please, don't. Please..."

Letting out some pent-up anger, I slam my fist into his face, knocking him out cold.

I still need him alive, so I grab him by the shirt and pull him above the water, before walking across the room to grab another cigarette from the sink.

"Fuck!" I smash the box in my hand, before tossing the empty package at the wall. This is not a good time to run out of smokes. They're about the only thing keeping me from killing this asshole.

Yelling out, I grip my hair, before reaching for the closest thing to me and breaking it against the wall. I don't stop until everything in this small bathroom is broken and out of place.

When I stop to catch my breath, I look into the mirror, staring long and hard at the monster I've become for her. She is the only girl I'd kill for. Always has been.

I slam my fist into the glass repeatedly, not stopping until my skin is hanging from my knuckles.

Blood covers everything.

My fist.

The sink.

The floor.

And I know more blood will spill until I get what I need, because I won't stop until I'm standing above Jasper's lifeless body and he's paid for hurting the person I love most in this shitty world.

And I'll kill any motherfucker who stands in my way...

ALEXANDRA

PRESENT

THE HEAVY BREATHING BESIDE ME lets me know that James is still sleeping. We've been screwing for almost a year now, and even though I've told him numerous times I'm not capable of settling down and having a normal life, he decided to follow me here anyway.

He may pretend he's cool with us not being exclusive, but I can tell it bugs him I'm still refusing to commit after all this time.

I remove his heavy arm from my waist, before I reach over into the nightstand and pull out a random bottle of pills, popping the last two into my mouth.

I've stopped reading the labels and trying to keep track of what I put in my body, because honestly, none of the labels match what the bottle contains.

I've gotten into the habit of just grabbing and popping,

needing just enough of something—anything—to numb me throughout the day.

"You're up early." James kisses my neck, a gesture that should make me feel something, but it doesn't.

"Couldn't sleep. It's weird being back here."

And really... it's not early. It's already past noon but considering we were up past three A.M. drowning ourselves in whiskey, while doing lines of cocaine, I suppose it is considered early.

He brushes my hair away from my neck, before running his fingertips over it. "Well, it's been a long time. I'm sure it'll feel weird for a while."

I close my eyes and roll onto my back as he reaches over me and into the drawer. He moves around a few bottles, but I don't hear any pills move. "Are there any left?"

"No. I took the last one," I lie, which is something I've become good at.

"The last two, Alex. There were two last night after you passed out. I know because I counted them after I popped two."

"All right, so I lied. One doesn't do shit and you know it, James." I sit up and reach for my thong, slipping it on. "What does it matter? We need to get more either way."

I can feel his eyes on me, as I stand here half-naked, lighting up a joint. "Come smoke that with me while I smash you."

"No." I take a long drag and hold the smoke in for as long as I can, before I blow it in his direction. "I don't feel like fucking, James. If I did then you would know, because I'd be on your dick already. I need to go into work early today. I need the money for bills. Plus, I need to keep busy before I go stir crazy in this hellhole."

"Well, I hope you plan to shower first, because you smell like booze and weed. No one is going to let you work if you walk in looking and smelling like you've been at a rave party. Not even the shady bar you serve at."

"And no one else is going to want to fuck you if you keep busting your load within the first ten minutes." I lift a brow and place the joint between my lips as I reach for my bra and a clean pair of jeans. "Don't tell me what I need to do, because you know damn well I'll do the opposite."

"Okay, so then don't fuck me. Will that get you over here and on my dick?" He sits up, his muscles bulging as he looks me up and down.

He's hot as hell. Probably one of the hottest men I've ever slept with, yet he does nothing for me.

"I'll pass. Like I said, I'm not in the mood."

"What the shit? You haven't been 'in the mood' since I got here a week ago. Is there something I should know about? Maybe some old boyfriend I need to kick the shit out of?"

I clench my jaw and throw the joint at his head. "I'd watch what you say, James. The only person I've ever truly cared about calls this place home, and if you touch him, I'll kill you myself."

He quickly grabs the joint, places it between his lips, and throws his hands up. "Whoa. Dick that good? He must've tore that pussy up for hours on end or else you'd hate him as much as you hate me."

"Fuck you." I jump on the bed, straddle him, and grab him by his throat. "He gave me more than you can ever give me. And I was only twelve, you asshole. We never had sex. He was my best friend and he took care of me. That's more than anyone else has ever done for me, including you."

James smiles and blows smoke into my face. "So, he's the reason you're so angry all the time, huh? Your daddy made you leave him—the one boy who made you forget how messed up that piece of shit father of yours was." Disgust boils inside me as he slides his finger down my arm in a sexual way. "And didn't you say some of his friends even touched you and got off to you.

Do you really think this boy could've saved you from that? He was a kid, babe."

"He was a man," I grind out, angry that he's speaking of Jaxon. "He was a man because he would've protected me no matter what it took. Every other asshole I've ever met since him has been nothing but boys wishing they were men. He's more of a man than you'll ever be."

"Shut up." He grabs my head and pulls it down until his lips are against mine. "My dick proves I'm all man. You don't think I'd protect you?"

"You don't," I spit out. "If you did I wouldn't be popping pills and drinking until I pass out with you right beside me. This is exactly why we're not a couple. Go home, James."

With that, I push on his chest, before I jump out of his lap and disappear into the bathroom.

I lock the door behind me, so he won't attempt to join me like last time. There's no way in hell I'm letting that son of a bitch get near me right now.

It's been thirteen years since I last stepped foot into this town and I've been fighting hard to keep my head above water since being back here, afraid of drowning in the memories.

James just had to go and bring them up again, catching me off guard and fucking with my mind.

I was a complete wreck after we moved. I cried for weeks, maybe even months, because I knew I no longer had Jaxon Kade to comfort me. And he was the only person I've ever truly cared about.

He was the only person who ever made me feel safe and loved. I was never scared when I was with him.

The worst part of it all was that I didn't even know we were moving. I never got to say goodbye. We got up in the middle of the night and left everything behind.

If I had known my dad was going to force me to leave Jaxon, I would've run. I would've stayed hidden for as long as it took if it meant I didn't have to leave the one person I loved and trusted.

Trusting people isn't something I do easily, and it has proven to only get harder over the years.

I've been fucked over so many times that I've lost count. I've been lied to, cheated on, and emotionally and physically abused. I'm sick and tired of it.

I'm so mentally and physically drained that I truly have nothing left to give. It hurts just to wake up in the morning, because I know my day will only be as shitty as the last.

Once you're filled with as much hate and distrust that I have, everything good in the world dies.

And everything good in my world died the day I lost Jaxon.

But if he saw me now, he'd probably wish he'd never known me in the first place, because I'm just as fucked in the head as his mother was.

He was too good for me. Probably still is.

It pains me that he fought so hard to change his mother's lifestyle and save her from the damage the drugs were causing and I ended up going down the same path as her.

I need my medicine to escape this reality, and even the pills, cocaine, and liquor aren't enough to numb the pain.

If I found Jaxon and pushed my way back into his life, the only thing I would end up doing is ruin him just as I am ruined.

I could never do that to the beautiful, protective Jaxon I remember, yet the idea of being in the same town where he grew up somewhat comforts me, and that is exactly why I'm back after all these years.

Doesn't mean I plan to look for him. He's probably not even still here and maybe that's a good thing. At least for him.

After a few minutes, I finally jump into the shower and stand under the steaming water, scorching my skin.

It burns.

My flesh is red from the heat, and it's hard to breathe in here, but I don't care.

At least I feel something. Anything at all.

IT'S BARELY PAST EIGHT, YET I've already been tempted to strangle at least three people in the seven hours I've been here.

Okay, more like five or ten people, but I suppose it is better than most nights.

These assholes just don't get that I'm not interested in them taking me home for a good fuck as they call it. I'm only interested in surviving, and apparently, I'll do anything to do that or else I wouldn't have taken the first job offered to me when moving back two weeks ago.

This place is a dump. It's dirty and the liquor is cheap, which draws in all the lowlifes who think they're exactly what I need to loosen up so I'm not such a bitch day in and day out.

It's not surprising to say that I have a resting bitch face one hundred percent of the time and the attitude to back it up.

I'm not interested in changing that, and even if I were the men who come here wouldn't be enough to do the trick.

"Here's your tab." I drop the little white paper in front of the jerk that's been dropping pickup lines my way for the last fifty-two minutes.

Yes, I've been timing his idiotic ass.

He picks up the bill and balls it up. Then he flashes me what he believes is a charming smile and drops it down in front of him. "I'm not done here yet, baby. Not until you let me buy you a drink."

"No."

"Stop playing hard to get when we both know you're leaving here with me tonight."

Closing my eyes, I take a deep breath and slowly release it. I've been working on my anger as much as I can lately and being here really tests me and pushes my limits.

I lean over the bar and get right up in his face. "You can take your cheap drink and shove it up your ass. It's not happening. Now shut up and pay so I can go home."

"Damn, girl." He gives me a sour look and reaches into his pocket for cash. "Here. Keep the damn change."

I eye him over as he stands up and walks away. He's not a bad looking guy, but nothing lights my fuse more than a guy pushing himself on me when I'm clearly not feeling it.

"What an ass." My roommate Tessa slides in beside me and reaches for the small pile of cash the jerk left on the bar. "After this crappy tip, he's an even bigger ass. Wow. These assholes never cease to amaze me here."

I met Tessa after I got the job here. When she learned I was staying at a shitty motel, she offered me the spare room at her place.

"Yup. It's bullshit, but what can we do?" I don't even bother counting my tip. I grab the two twenties he left to cover the bill and shove the coins leftover for my tip into the tip jar that Tessa and I will split at the end of the night. "You good without me? That ass was my last open tab and I want to get out of here before I get stuck with another one."

"Yup." She quickly wipes the bar off and jumps right into helping the next person who pulls out a stool and takes a seat. "I've got it from here. It's slowing down now anyway."

"Okay, great. I'll see you when you get off."

By the time I make it out to the parking lot, all I feel like doing is popping a handful of pills and passing out right here in my shitty old Dodge Neon so I don't have to deal with anyone else today.

James has sent me six texts since he left my house earlier. The latest one said he's at my house waiting for me. I have no desire to go home and pretend I want him around, when really, all I want is to be alone.

Ignoring all my messages, I sit here with my eyes closed.

Twenty minutes pass—maybe more— allowing myself some time to unwind before I finally drive off, unsure of where I'm going.

It's dark and quiet out here, almost relaxing, so I'm not really concerned about my destination at the moment.

I just keep driving.

When a motorcycle pulls up on my left at the next stoplight, it's kind of hard not to look over at the noise to see who's causing it on this otherwise peaceful drive.

What I don't expect is for the guy on the motorcycle to catch my attention, but as soon as he turns my direction and I catch the way his dark hair falls over his eye, I can't seem to look away.

He's got this rough, edgy look that calls to me, drawing me in.

His eyes are focused on me, as if he's amused that I'm checking him out the way I am. Even with the dark facial hair around his mouth I can see that he's smirking, most likely enjoying having this moment of power over me.

It's enough to have me quickly turning away and looking straight ahead once again.

He may be sexy as hell from what I can see, but I'll never allow another man to have power over me.

Not again.

The light turns green, and for some reason, instead of driving off I look beside me at the mysterious motorcycle guy to see he's watching me, as if he's waiting for me to take off first.

Unable to stop myself, I rake my eyes over his body, starting at his black boots and slowly moving up his muscular thighs, all the way up to his leather jacket he wears so damn well.

This guy was definitely made for that bike.

Both seem to be dangerous and powerful at first glance.

It's not until the vehicle behind me honks two times that I finally manage to pull my eyes away from my distraction.

I'm about to drive off when the dick sticks his head out the window and screams at me. "Move, bitch! I'm going to be late because of you. Get out of the way!"

The guy beside me catches my attention again, when I notice him kick the stand down on his motorcycle and get off.

I don't know what else to do, so I watch him as he walks over to the car behind me, reaches into the window and slams the asshole's head into the steering wheel.

He doesn't even bother saying anything to the guy. Instead, he walks right back over to his motorcycle, as if nothing unusual just happened, and drives off.

I don't know what the hell has gotten into me, but when he takes a left turn, my eyes seem to follow.

My heart is racing in my chest at what just happened. It definitely has nothing to do with the asshole behind me, and everything do with the sexy, dangerous guy that just drove off.

Without giving it much thought, I finally give the jerk behind me what he wants and drive off, taking a left.

I find myself driving around for a bit, before I pull up at a place called Savage & Ink.

As much as I'd like to say I'm here only for the drinks, a part of me knows that's a lie. I'm curious about this man who lost it on some asshole at my expense not long ago.

There are a lot of motorcycles parked out front, but I can't tell if one of them belongs to him or not. I can only assume this is where he went once I lost him a few blocks over.

Jumping out of my car, I head toward what seems to be a tattoo parlor attached to the bar. It's been a while since I've gotten some ink done and knowing there's a shop in the area has me itching for one now.

When I step inside, I look around at the art on the wall, my mouth curving into a small smile. This is definitely the right place to get some ink done.

I don't see anyone in the tattoo room, so I push open the second door and step into the bar area.

It's full of bikers drinking and playing pool.

Most women would be intimidated by this scene. Not me. I taught myself years ago, when I turned sixteen, that the only way a man will learn what no means is by showing him.

I still remember the look on my dad's friend's face when I stabbed my steak knife into his arm after he grabbed my thigh during dinner one night.

He never touched me again and my dad started letting me make my own decisions after that. He must've learned that day too that I wasn't a scared little girl anymore and I'd learned to stand up for myself.

Then, by seventeen, I was living with some friends who were just as screwed up and unwanted as I was. That's when I got into pill popping, snorting cocaine, and drinking, looking for ways to escape.

I'll be twenty-six in a few months and I've only gotten angrier and more bitter with time—numb to any other emotions.

Most people don't know the true meaning of a bitch until they've met me and pissed me off.

I feel eyes settle on me from around the room as I take a seat at the bar and wait for the bartender to look up from the cooler.

He must be refilling it, because it's been a few minutes and he still hasn't noticed me sitting here.

"Mind giving me one of those beers? Actually, make it two."

He pauses for a second, as if he's surprised to hear a woman's voice, before he grabs two bottles and stands up.

His amber gaze lands on me, his eyes locking with mine as he pops the cap off the first beer and slides it across to me.

I swallow as I watch him pop the top off the second one and take a swig, as if I didn't just order two beers.

Well, shit. Motorcycle guy works here.

"Who are you here for?" he questions. "Blaine? Or one of these other assholes?"

I snatch the beer from his hand, right as he's about to tilt it back again. He watches me as I bring it to my lips and take a drink. "What makes you think I'm here for anyone?"

He smiles and reaches for the untouched beer. I'm not sure if he recognizes me from the stoplight, but he has a look no woman could forget even if she tried. "Because women don't usually come here alone. You don't see all the assholes behind you, eyeing you over while thinking up ways they can get you on the back of their bike and in their bed?"

I look over my shoulder, while taking another drink of beer. "I'm not worried about them. None of them can handle me." I bring my attention back to the man in front of me and the crooked smile on his sexy lips has me a little hot and bothered. "They can look all they want, but they won't be touching unless they want to lose a nut. I deal with assholes like them all day."

The crooked smile turns into a full one as he runs his hand over his short beard and leans against the bar. His confidence as he locks eyes with me has me looking lower at his firm chest in that black t-shirt he's wearing.

I couldn't see how toned he was when he was wearing that leather jacket on his bike, but I have to admit that his body is enough to make any woman sweat. He looks like a tattooed God.

He's definitely the kind of guy I wouldn't mind taking some sexual frustration out on.

I look back up to see his dark hair falling over his face while he looks around the bar, as if he's keeping an eye out for something to go down.

"Then maybe this is the right place for you to be. Some of

these dicks deserve to lose one…" he brings his attention back to me, his eyes becoming intense as they land on my lips around the beer bottle. "Or maybe both."

I smile and lower the bottle. "Does that include you too? You're looking at my lips like you wish this bottle was something else."

"I'm a man, love. It's only natural that I wish it were my dick. But it's because I'm a man that I won't slip it between those beautiful lips until you're begging for it. And since you're not I'm going to mind my own damn business."

He goes back to working but looks back over at me occasionally as if he's checking to make sure I'm okay.

I also don't miss that he gives a few dirty looks over my shoulder as if he's warning assholes to stay away or something.

Whatever it is that he's doing seems to be working, because even after being here for over an hour, not one guy has messed with me or has attempted to talk to me.

I have to admit I like the way he controls the room. It's been a long time since I've been able to go anywhere without being groped by some loser.

"People here are intimidated by you, aren't they?" I can't help but look him over from head to toe as he stands there, leaned against the wall, watching the room.

"What makes you think that?" He pushes away from the wall and the way his thighs flex when he walks toward me has me licking my bottom lip and watching closely. "I haven't done or said anything to make you believe that."

I lean over the bar and stop once our lips are almost brushing. The feel of his beard tickling my skin makes me want to yank him to me by it so I can kiss him, or maybe even bite him, but I don't. "It's in your eyes. All you have to do is look at people and they know not to fuck with you. I find it very intriguing."

When I go to pull away, he grabs the back of my neck, keeping me in place. "People still fuck with me. Just the ones who carry knives and guns. This is only the early crowd, love. This ain't shit compared to what I'm used to dealing with." I swallow when his lips move around to brush below my ear.

"You should go before I have to kill someone tonight for trying to put their hands on you. I've already broken a guy's nose over you. Don't make me do it again." His words have me swallowing. "The night crowd is beginning to swarm in. This is no place for you."

With that, he grabs the beer I am currently sipping on and tosses it into the trash.

I stand up and slap the bar, angry that he did that. "Hey! I wasn't done with that. That's a waste of my money."

"You are now. It's on me anyway, so really, it's a waste of my money."

"Fuck you," I say in his face. "I don't need someone telling me what to do. I can handle myself."

"Fuck you right back, baby. But even that won't make me serve you another beer." He nods toward the door, his eyes now dark. "Get out."

"You're an asshole."

"Maybe," he says as I stand up. "But I do what I gotta do. Always have. Always will. Now get the fuck out."

"Fine. Thanks for the beer, bossy asshole." Even though he said the drink was on him, I toss some cash on the bar, not wanting anything from him.

My entire body is heated with anger as I walk out of the bar and jump into my car.

It's been years since I've allowed a man to tell me what to do, yet here I am allowing this stranger to have power over me and I don't even know his name.

I take a few deep breaths to calm myself, before I drive off. I don't even realize where I'm going until I find myself sitting outside Jaxon's old home.

I sit here for a while, staring at the rundown house, remembering the past and trying to imagine what Jaxon must be like now that he's a grown man.

It has my chest aching because he will always be my best memory. The only good ones I have are filled with him, yet I know I can't go looking for him.

Seconds turn into minutes as I sit here, trying to calm myself down, before I head home and hope like hell that James is either gone by now or has found a new supplier to buy from.

After dealing with that hot asshole at the bar, I need an escape more than anything now...

JAX

THIS NIGHT IS GOING TO kill me if I don't get out of this bar soon and away from the chaos of Savage & Ink.

I'm on edge, my whole body covered in sweat as I stand out here in the cool night air, doing what I can to chill out before I kill someone.

I've already slipped up and lost my temper once today, thanks to some woman I don't even know. She's a sassy-mouthed, sexy as hell pain in the ass.

Leaning my head against the side of the building, I close my eyes and take another drag off my cigarette, holding it in for longer than usual before slowly releasing it.

I swear if one more fight breaks out tonight that I have to jump in and stop, I'm going to end up breaking someone's neck.

This is exactly why I made her leave earlier and pissed her off. No matter how tough she may claim to be, she'll never be ready for this shit. The last thing I need is some woman getting hurt here because she thinks she can handle these pricks.

I'm not even ready for it half the time. Plus, I doubt she'll be back. I've lived here my whole damn life and have never seen her. I'd remember if I had.

That's exactly why she caught my attention when I pulled my motorcycle up beside her at the light earlier. But it was her beauty and the way she was looking at me that kept me looking.

I never for one fucking second expected her to walk into the damn bar and take a seat as if she belonged there.

When I turned around and saw her fiery red hair, I about lost my shit right then and there. But when I got a good look at the piercing in her nose and the ink covering her right arm, I turned into one of those assholes I was wanting to protect her from.

My cock didn't only twitch at the sight of her, it about jumped right out of my jeans. It took a lot of restraint not to bend her over the bar right there in front of everyone.

My entire body stiffens at the sound of glass breaking against the front of the building. I know for a fact that wasn't a beer bottle. It sounded a lot thicker than that.

"Damn, these assholes."

I crack my neck, before running a hand through my messy hair and preparing for what I'm about to do. This shit never ends up being pretty.

Taking one more drag, I toss my cigarette against the side of the building and make my way around to the front of the bar.

My gaze immediately lands on Blaine grabbing his dick and yelling at some insanely huge biker. "The ladies find my cock irresistible. I can't be blamed for that shit!"

"Cocky son of a bitch! I'm going to kill you," the large biker growls, before coming at Blaine with a switchblade.

Blaine just smirks and opens his jacket, revealing his two pistols. "You were saying, motherfucker?" Keeping his gaze on the big guy, he reaches into his pocket, places a cigarette between his lips and pulls out his American skull Zippo.

He's standing there all chill and confident as he lights his smoke.

Just as I think the situation is under control, the door opens and three guys in leather cuts matching the big guy's, step outside. They look ready to fight, so I say fuck it and jump right in.

Swinging out, I connect my fist with the jaw of the closest one to me, knocking him against the building. He immediately pushes away from the wall and comes at me, tackling me into a row of motorcycles.

Damn this shit hurts, but I do my best not to let it slow me down. If I give these assholes a chance, each and every one of them will be reaching for their weapons, ready to blow mine and Blaine's heads off.

I ignore the pain shooting through my side and shove my knee down onto the dude's throat, before I reach for my pistol and aim it between his eyes.

He might've thought tackling me was a good idea, but clearly, he wasn't prepared to stumble himself.

When I look over to my right Blaine is in a headlock, taking blows to the stomach from one guy while his legs are wrapped around big dude's throat, squeezing him to death and yelling about how his girl loved taking his dick.

"Everyone calm the fuck down or I'll put a bullet right between this dickhead's eyes," I bark out. "Don't test me."

Everyone freezes and looks my way, before finally releasing each other and fighting to catch their breath.

I place my hand on the dick's face below me and push myself back up to my feet. He immediately begins gasping for air and mumbling fuck you under his breath.

"Blaine is an asshole who can't keep his dick in his pants.

Next time leave your girl at home. But I'm not trying to kill or be killed over this shit. Got it?"

Blaine jumps to his feet and spits out blood. "Hey. It's not my fault she showed up after close last night looking for me. Fuck, being a sexy motherfucker is hard."

The big dude punches the building a few times letting his anger out, before he bumps Blaine back with his chest. "Touch her again and you're dead. Next time it'll be more than just a threat."

Blaine smirks as the angry biker, along with his crew, jump on their motorcycles and speed off. "I could've handled them myself. You didn't have to jump in."

"There's no doubt that I'll always have your back, you're my boy, but I'm not trying to get myself killed so you can get your dick wet."

He grips my shoulder. "Then what kind of friend are you?" He lifts a brow and smiles. "I've got a tattoo to finish up, brother. You got the bar?"

I clench my jaw and nod my head, trying my best not to kill my friend my damn self.

He slaps my back and walks inside.

The next few hours seem to go by slow as shit with little to no action. But I know what I'm about to do next is going to cause a big shitstorm. It always does.

The place is full of broken bottles and wasted bikers that don't want to leave, they never seem to, and since Blaine is wasted now, it's up to me to get them all out.

"Out, motherfuckers," I shout. "Party is over. Don't make me tell you again."

"Suck my dick, Jax," Cape says before tilting his beer back and tossing a dart at the wall. He's a big dude. Almost twice my size. "Party is over when we say it is. Plug the jukebox back in."

The drunken bastard really thinks I won't shoot his ass right now to get him and his crew out of here.

He's mistaken. Those cuts don't scare me. I've already proven that once tonight with a different crew. He's been giving me hell all night and I'm two breaths away from snapping.

Knowing what I need to do to get this crazy crowd out, I reach behind me and pull my pistol from the back of my jeans.

Then I walk over and grab one of the rowdy assholes by the back of the head, slamming his face down onto a table.

This gets the attention of every drunk bastard in the room.

If this doesn't show them I'm serious, then I don't know what the hell I'm gonna have to do to get them out and I really don't feel like getting my hands bloody tonight.

With a growl, I raise my pistol and lift a brow when Cape turns to me with a clenched jaw. He's not used to many people standing up to him, but I'm not like most people. I've put up with scary motherfuckers like him my whole damn life. "I said the party is over. Now get your crew out of here before I put a bullet in someone's leg. Any fucking one will do."

Cape's dark eyes stay on me as he tilts back his beer, not stopping until it's empty. He's so damn wasted that he knows not to push me too far tonight. He can barely stand, let alone fight. He and I both know his gigantic ass will fall.

The same goes for his crew. One call to Royal and Mark and it'll end up being a shit night for them all.

After a few seconds, he finally laughs and slams his empty bottle down on the nearest table. "All right. Cool." He stumbles over, trying to keep his balance as he reaches for his leather cut. "Let's go before pretty Jax over there puts a bullet in someone's leg. I'm not sober enough to dig bullets out of any of your asses tonight."

His jaw clenches again as he gives me one last look, letting me know he's no damn pussy. I wouldn't mistake him for one, but doesn't mean I'm willing to back down and let him and his dipshits walk all over me.

Fuck that shit. I've been walked over way too many times in the past to let that happen now.

I release his guy's head and take a seat on one of the tables, watching closely as Cape and his guys gather their belongings to leave.

Once the bar is empty, I lock up and make my way to the tattoo room to find Blaine's ass passed out with the tattoo machine sitting in his lap.

His pants are halfway down his thighs as if he was ready to give his dick a tattoo or something.

You never know with this guy. Wouldn't surprise me one bit.

Just to mess with him, I step on the foot pedal and start the machine, digging it into his exposed thigh.

It takes me drawing a long, crooked line before he finally moves a bit, his eyes opening and then quickly closing again.

"Seriously, motherfucker," I mutter.

All right, if he's going to sit here passed out like a dumbass, exposed for me to mark his skin, the asshole can't complain.

Pulling up the leather chair, I take a seat and start working on the nickname Blaine got back when we were in high school.

I still haven't forgiven this dirty prick for what I walked in on. It was the last thing I wanted to witness.

Ever.

Truthfully, it made me want to bleach my fucking eyes out.

It's not until I get down to the final letter that he finally starts moving around again as if he's about to wake up. So, I push harder, hoping the dumbass does.

After what he put me through tonight, I hope this shit hurts like hell.

"What the fucking fuck?" He wakes up, scared, looking around the room in a panic as if he's being attacked.

He finally relaxes a bit, his wide eyes going back to normal once he realizes it's only the two of us in the room.

"All done, buddy." I slap his leg and spin the chair around to set the tattoo machine down on the table.

"What?" He sits up, mumbling shit that I can't quite make out. "Done with what? How long was my ass out for?"

I slap his thigh where I just tattooed it and laugh. "Long enough."

After blinking a few times, he finally looks down at the spot I just marked on him.

"Mother fucker," he reads. "Really. Shit, that was like seven years ago. Your mom loved it and you know it."

"Fuck you. Let's go." I toss his jacket at his face. "I'm tired."

"The bar is closed?" he questions, while practically falling out of the chair to stand up. "Did I miss any action?"

"Pull your pants up, dumbass."

Smiling like an idiot, he reaches for his jeans and fixes them. "Don't be jealous because my cock is bigger than yours, pretty boy."

"Yeah, sure," I say just to shut him up. "Oh, and since your dumbass can't drive your motorcycle home, I called Royal to come get you. I'm not driving you home bitch on the back of my bike."

"Shiiiit," he groans. "I don't need Royal to pick me up. He's going to kill my ass for dragging him out of bed. You know that, right?"

I smile and shut the door behind us, turning off the lights on the way back into the bar. "Hell yeah I do."

A few minutes later we hear an angry growl as Royal appears in the back doorway, looking as if he just crawled out of bed. "Blaine! I should kill you for pulling me away from my family at three in the damn morning."

"Wait a minute..." Blaine looks Royal over, walking around him as if he's looking for something. I have a feeling I know what too. "No pistol?" He begins patting Royal's back, feeling for one. "Good. Let's go then."

"Don't get too excited, dick." Royal lifts the front of his shirt, revealing his gun. "I'm half tempted to use it if you don't hurry the hell up so I can get back home. Your intoxicated ass is sleeping on the couch, by the way. The one in the damn basement. Let's go."

I laugh at Blaine's sour-ass face and begin cleaning up some of the bottles littered around the room. "I need to clean this shit up before I head out. I'll be good."

"Alright, brother," Royal says, while stopping at the door. "Appreciate it." He gives Blaine a shove toward the door. "Leave the rest for this drunken idiot. He can take care of it in the morning."

"Well shit..." Blaine mumbles, while walking out the door.

I laugh at Blaine's stupidity and get to making my way around the bar, dragging the garbage can with me.

About an hour later, I make my way out the door and straddle my bike, taking the long way home.

The cool night air hitting my face feels good, but it's not enough to take the edge off. I realize that as soon as I step into my house and shut the door behind me.

Taking a moment to chill, I fall back onto the worn-out leather couch and pull the half-smoked joint from my pocket, placing it between my lips.

I allow my gaze to scan over my new place, taking in the mess of boxes still needing to be unpacked. It wasn't until I began this moving process that I realized how much junk I've accumulated over the years while living with Royal.

Although Royal and Avalon both gave me their blessing to stay with them for as long as I wanted, I felt the need to give them space as a family. A place where they can be alone and not have to worry about Blaine and I coming in at late hours of the night drunk and high off our asses.

Blaine seems to hate his place, so he's been alternating his nights between staying here and Royal's, crashing on the couch downstairs. I have a feeling it's because he doesn't like to be alone in his fucked-up head. The kid has a lot of demons up there that he allows to swallow him whole at times.

I can't let that shit happen, so I keep my eye on him as much as I can before we end up losing him.

Closing my eyes, I take a few hits off the joint, holding the smoke in for as long as I can, before slowly releasing it.

It doesn't take long for me to get lost in my thoughts, allowing memories of Alexandra to take over. This shit always happens when I get high, but apparently, I enjoy the pain, because I always seem to light up another, knowing damn well where my head will take me.

If thirteen years hasn't been enough time to erase her from my thoughts, I don't think I ever will. Her pale blonde hair and bruise-covered skin created by her father is unforgettable. She looked to me for safety away from her hell and I gave it to her for as long as I could.

It only seems I think about her more with time. I'm constantly wondering where she is and how she's doing. There's so much shit I want to know, but can't seem to find the answers for and I hate it.

Just as I'm beginning to relax for the first time all night, my front door opens to Blaine and Madison letting themselves in.

"Miss me, motherfucker?" He grins and shuts the door behind them. "Told you I didn't need Royal to pick me up. I'm recharged and ready to go."

I know exactly where this is headed.

It won't be the first time Blaine and I have shared a girl, but it'll be the first time it's been Madison. Which surprises me since he's been so stingy with her, even though they're both fucking other people.

Truthfully, I don't think he's capable of claiming any woman as his. That's exactly why he's here now. He's getting too close and needs me to fuck some sense into their situation.

Shit, maybe I need this distraction right now.

The room is silent, none of us bothering to speak as Blaine comes up behind Madison and runs his hands down her sides as if he's admiring her curves.

Her gaze locks on me, her eyes filled with need, as Blaine lifts her dress and wraps both his hands around her thong, lowering it down her long legs.

On his way back up he bites her ass, before slapping it and grabbing the back of her neck as he stands, to whisper in her ear. "Turn around and ride his dick," he growls. "Fuck him good and hard and then I'll fuck you while he watches. We both know how long you've wanted to test drive his cock."

"You're not the only dirty one here, Blaine." She bites her bottom lip as she reaches down to undo my jeans and pull my hard cock out. "You look like you need this tonight, Jax—a distraction for all of us."

I clench my jaw and watch as she grabs a condom from Blaine, opens it, and slides it over my dick. "You're right," I growl, as she turns around to face Blaine before spreading her legs and straddling my thighs. "I do need a damn distraction right now."

Yeah, because now I'm so fucked-up that I have two women on my mind. One I'll most likely never see again and one that I'm hoping I never see again, because just seeing her once I know she'll be enough to shake my world up.

Blaine steps up to Madison and wraps his hands into the back of her hair, slowly pushing her down onto my cock until she can't go any further.

Madison lets out a satisfied moan, her nails digging into my thighs as I grip her hips and squeeze.

I wait until Blaine has a chance to pull his cock out and swipe it across Madison's lips before I begin thrusting hard and deep, taking my sexual frustration out on her pussy.

She opens her lips and moans around Blaine's dick as I take

her. Apparently, she likes it rough, because she takes his dick in deep, sucking it hard as Blaine tugs on her hair.

"Fuuuuck..." My fingers dig into her hips, most likely bruising her flesh as I guide her up and down on my dick, causing her to scream around Blaine's.

This has Blaine shoving her face further down his dick, making her gag on his length.

There's nothing gentle about the way Blaine and I fuck. It takes a down ass woman, just as crazy as us when it comes to sex to be able to handle both of us.

Me fucking her pussy while Blaine fucks her mouth has her clenching around my dick in no time, her whole body shaking above me as her orgasm rolls through her.

She screams out, gripping at the wall as I pick her up and slam her against it. My hands tangle into her wild hair and I pull back on it as I take her hard and fast.

It doesn't take long before I'm pulling out and running my hand over my shaft as I come into the condom.

Blaine barely gives her a moment to breathe before he picks her up, wraps her legs around his waist and pushes her down onto his cock.

This has her moaning out, scratching at his back as she fights to catch her breath.

I have to admit that a rough fuck is exactly what I needed tonight, but now I'm just ready to sit back and chill. It feels as if I haven't had a moment to breathe all day.

Sitting back on the couch, I pull the condom off and toss it, before lighting up a cigarette and watching Blaine knock over some boxes as he roughly fucks Madison.

As good as it felt being inside her, I can tell by the way Blaine is taking her now—his gaze on hers as he buries himself deep inside her—that he cares about her more than he leads on.

I thought it'd be us in the beginning, when I first met Madison a year ago. But every time I thought about getting close to her, I thought about the girl from my past that stole my heart and disappeared with it.

Maybe it's time I finally move on, but fuck, it won't be easy...

JAX

THIRTEEN YEARS AGO... THIRTEEN YEARS OLD

I'M PISSED OFF AS I stand against the wall and watch my mother crawl around the bedroom, looking for her precious pills; little white circles she calls Oxy.

She can barely even move right now without me helping her, but she wants more, as if she'll die without them.

How could she want more?

"Where are they, Jaxon?" she cries, slapping the floor in defeat. "Why do you do this to me? Give them to me. Now! I know you have them."

"No." My voice is strong, firm. It has to be to make it through moments like these with her. "You might as well give up, Jan. You won't find any lying around this shithole room. I flushed them down the toilet."

She looks up at me, her eyes wet and rimmed with red. Her brown hair is a tangled, sweaty mess as she tugs on it. "Get out!

Get the fuck out of my room you little shit. I hate you! I should've never had you."

I ignore her words because I've heard them all before. In the beginning, it hurt, but I'm numb to them now.

Years of dealing with a sick, drug addict for a mother will do that.

"You need to eat. You haven't eaten in days." I hold the plate out for her, but she uses what energy she has to reach up and slap it out of my hand.

"I don't want that shit. I can't eat and you know it." She lies down on the floor, curls up into a ball, and begins rocking back and forth. "I can't take this anymore. I can't. Just give me my pills, Jaxon. Please... just be a good boy for once and take care of me. Do this for Mommy."

My chest aches as I crouch down in front of her, grab the sandwich from the dirty carpet and set it down in front of her face.

It hurts me to see my mom this way, even though she hasn't been much of a mother to me. Not since I was eight. She gave me life, though, and that's a good enough reason for me to want to take care of her. "I'm not leaving this room until you eat."

She watches me as I take a seat on the floor and lean against the foot of the bed.

My mother knows me well enough to know that once I sit down with her there's no getting me out of her room unless she physically throws me out and we both know she's too weak to do that.

"Fine." She sits up and reaches out her shaky hand. "I'll eat the damn sandwich if it gets you out of my room. I want to be alone."

Keeping my gaze on her, I hand her the sandwich and make sure she's really eating it and not just hiding it like she's done in the past.

It takes her a good twenty minutes but she finally finishes the sandwich, all except for a few small bites that she throws onto the floor. "There... are you happy?"

I help my mom to her feet and get her situated in bed, just like I do most nights. "Yeah, I am, actually. Because now I can go to sleep tonight knowing that you have something in your stomach other than just pills and alcohol. You're going to end up killing yourself someday and I can't just sit back and watch you do this to yourself."

She doesn't say anything.

Instead, she closes her eyes and pulls the blanket up over her head. She's done listening to me and this is her way of hiding from me.

She's been doing it since I was old enough to argue back with her.

I stand back and watch her for a few seconds before I reach into her nightstand and pull out her bag of rolled joints, placing one behind my ear.

I'm so angry with her that I couldn't care less if she gets mad at me. Truthfully, she probably just doesn't care, because no matter what I do, I'll never be as messed up as her.

I close the door behind me as I leave her. Then I pull the joint out from behind my ear and spark it up, before falling back onto the couch.

I feel numb as I sit here, smoking and flipping through TV channels, looking for something to distract my mind from the mess in the next room over.

It's hard not to go back in there and scream at her. Scream at her to be a better mother... a better person. One that gives a shit whether or not she lives or dies.

But I know it'll do no good. It never does.

She's been this way since my piece of shit dad abandoned us.

My body is tense, my heart pounding mercilessly as I turn my attention to the front door, waiting for it to open.

As much as I hate to admit that I need Alexandra as much as she needs me, I can't deny it in my heart.

I can't deny that seeing her beautiful face makes the world seem a little brighter, in this otherwise dark place I've been swallowed up whole by.

But I haven't seen her for three days now and I hate it, because we usually see each other every day. I know it's because her father told her she can no longer hang out with me, but I figured she'd find a way anyway.

She always does.

"Jaxon. Come in here. I need something to help me sleep." My mother's desperate voice has me turning up the volume, showing her I'm no longer listening.

She'll eventually fall asleep.

She always does.

I'm tired of watching her slowly die because she's unable to love anything in this world enough to want to live. Not even me.

The only things she cares about are the drugs that alter her reality enough to make her forget I even exist. That she has a son who depends on her and needs her to be there for him.

She's a selfish parent, yet she thinks I'm supposed to help her when she needs it.

I refuse to help her give up on life and slowly kill herself.

I stare at the door for what must seem like forever, until I finally turn away and sink into the couch, wishing I could disappear from this world.

Not even this joint is enough to make that happen. I've learned over the months that it does help calm me though.

Maybe that's why my mom needs them so much, but what do I know?

I'm only thirteen... almost fourteen.

I don't have everything figured out yet.

My whole body comes alive; this small spark of hope filling me as the front door slowly creeps open to soft footsteps making their way across the carpet.

There's only one person I know who can walk so softly and quietly.

"Jax, I'm cold."

When I look over at the front door, Alexandra is standing there, holding a small blanket over her bare arms.

It's cold outside; so damn cold, and she's not even wearing a jacket.

It makes me so mad, but I do my best to stay calm for her.

It's something I've mastered, thanks to my mom.

"Come here, Lex. Hurry." I pull the thick blanket from the back of the couch and cover us both up once she crawls next to me and curls up into my side.

Her skin is cold against mine, so I take my hands and rub them over her arms to help her warm up faster.

We don't say anything for a long while as I hold her close to me and finish my joint.

We just sit here as Alexandra watches TV and giggles quietly once in a while at something she finds funny.

I can't help but to laugh too, even though I'm not watching TV, because the sound of her laughter gives me small tingles that tickle my heart.

The only time I feel anything other than anger is when she's around.

Now that she's here, finally, all I want to do is watch her smile so I can see that she's happy.

Her dad won't allow her to watch TV unless it's a show he's watching, so when she's here I let her control the remote.

But lately, I've just been keeping it on the few channels she seems to like the most. It calms me some, but not as much as her being here does.

"Why aren't you wearing a coat, Lex? What happened to it?"

She lets out a small breath that hits my ear, before she hides her face in my shoulder. "He took it away from me so I wouldn't sneak out after he passed out on the couch. But I had to come see you. I don't care if it's a cold walk."

I hate the idea of her dad being so mean to her all the time. I hate that he treats her so badly and never lets her go out and have fun.

"You're my only friend, Jax, and I missed your beautiful face. It always makes me feel better. Safe..."

"I like that it makes you feel better. It's my job to make you feel happy and safe." Leaning in closer to Lex, I wrap my arms tighter around her and make sure the blanket is nice and snug around her.

"Why is it your job?"

"Because I'm the boy and I'm older."

"Only by eight months. Soon, I'll be thirteen too and it'll be my job to make you feel happy and safe like you do for me."

"You do," I admit. "You're about the only thing that can make me smile anymore, Lex. You make me happy."

"Is that true?" Her voice is soft and sweet as she speaks up at me. "Do I really make you happy?"

I hold her tighter; to the point I'm almost pulling her into my lap. She's so tiny compared to me and I just want to protect her. "Yes. I'm not sure I'd know what happiness was if I didn't have you in my life."

"You make me happy, too, Jax. Ever since my mom took off..." she wraps her arm around mine and tightly holds onto it. "My dad has been horrible. I can't stand being at home with him all day. But when I come here after he's asleep, I forget about all the bad that's happened to me. I like it here with you. I wish I could stay here, always."

I kiss the side of her head, because I want her to know that I love her. I'm not sure in what way yet, but I know that I think about her almost every second of every day.

"I would love that, too. Because then I could take care of you, always. I'd make sure no one ever hurt you. Especially your dad. He's an asshole."

"You're the greatest, Jax." Her green eyes are soft as she looks up at me, taking me in. The way she's looking at my lips has me swallowing and licking them, nervously. When she leans in and quickly presses hers against mine, my heart beats in a way it never has before and in this moment, I feel more alive than ever. "Thank you for being you."

We're both silent after that, unsure of how to act for a few moments, before she stretches beside me and hides her face into my arm again. "I'm so tired. Will you wake me up in a little while, Jax? I can't sleep when I'm at home."

"Yeah. Get some rest," I say, my heart beating so hard it feels as if it's about to fly from my chest.

Exhaling, I close my eyes and get comfortable. I can tell by her breathing she's already fallen asleep, but the only thing I can manage to think about is how it felt when she just kissed me.

I don't know why she kissed, but it's the best thing that's ever happened to me and I'll be sure she knows this after she gets some rest.

I listen to her breathing for a while, my mind replaying our kiss until I begin to fall asleep myself.

I don't know what time it is, but I wake up in a panic when I hear something at the front door.

It takes me a few seconds to realize that it's someone knocking. The realization has my heart beating out of my chest with fear.

This is not good.

"Oh shit." I shake Alexandra awake. "Your dad is outside. Wake up, Lex!"

Another knock comes, causing her to sit up and look over at the door with wide eyes. "It's my dad! He's going to kill me, Jax. What do I do? I don't know what to do. He'll hurt me. I don't want him to hurt me anymore."

I can see the panic and worry in her eyes and it hurts me. I hate that she has to be afraid of him and I wish I could do something to take her away.

"Go home and pretend you were sleeping in the garage on the cot the whole time. You know he never looks for you in there. Tell him it was an accident because you were reading and didn't want the distraction of the TV." I grab her hand and help her to her feet, before giving her a quick hug. "Sneak out the back door. I'll keep him here for a few minutes. Hurry! Run as fast as you can."

She seems scared, but listens anyway and quickly makes her way toward the back of the house.

Her father knocks again, but this time I can hear him screaming at me to open up before he breaks the door down. I quickly mess up my blonde hair and rub my face, making it as red as possible.

I need to look as if I've been sleeping for hours. He can't know that Lex fell asleep here again.

I have no idea what he'd do to her and I can't let him hurt her again. I'd have to steal a gun and kill him myself.

Yawning, I reach for the baseball bat we keep on the wall and open the door, pretending as if I'm fighting to keep my eyes open.

"Alexandra!" he growls. "Where is she? I know she's here. I told her not to leave the damn house and this is the only place she comes to. Alexandra! Get your ass out here now!"

I yawn again and pretend I'm wiping the sleep from the corner of my eyes. "I haven't seen Lex in three days. Not since you told her she wasn't allowed to hang out with me." I shrug and cross my arms with my baseball bat, making sure he sees it.

"Maybe she's in the garage. She likes to hang out in there. All her books are out there."

He looks around me as if he's checking to see if I'm lying.

"You wanna come in and look, Mr. Adams? If not, then I'd like to go back to sleep. I have school in the morning and you're keeping me up past my bedtime."

He growls out and takes a step back. Actually, more like a stumble back. "No. I'll just check the damn garage. She better be there or you're both going to be in a shitload of trouble."

I watch as he stumbles back again, almost falling off the porch.

He's so wasted that he either hasn't noticed my bat or just doesn't care at this point. So much for intimidating him.

"Need me to walk you home?" I give him a cocky grin. "You can lean on my shoulder like my mom does when she's fucked-up."

This seems to piss him off, so I hold back from saying anything else, not wanting him to take it out on Alexandra.

It's another reason I haven't swung my Louisville Slugger at his head yet, but if he doesn't stop hurting her then I just might take my chances.

Once he leaves I sit here for thirty minutes, before I slip my jacket on and walk two blocks over to where Alexandra's house is.

Every light in the house is off, except for the TV, so I slip around the back of the house and stop beside her bedroom window.

I'm just about to knock, but freeze when I hear her screaming and crying out.

My entire body begins shaking and something takes over me that I don't quite understand, but before I know what I'm doing, I open the window and climb inside with my baseball bat in hand.

Alexandra's screams are so loud—as her dad towers over her beating her with his old belt—that he doesn't even realize I'm in the house until I accidentally knock something over on her dresser.

But it's not his looks to kill that scares me. It's the broken look in her eyes and the welts and scars all over her half-naked flesh that scares the shit out of me.

I've never been so terrified in my life, but seeing her this way will scar me forever.

She looks at me, shaking her head as her entire body trembles in fear.

"Don't ever touch her again or I'll kill you!" The words come out of my mouth before I can stop them, as I raise my bat up and squeeze it in my grip.

Keeping his eyes on me, he drops his belt on top of his daughter's bruised body and laughs. "You're going to kill me with that, boy?" He comes at me, and even though I know I should be afraid that he's way bigger than I am, I stand up straight and tall. "You think you're man enough? Huh!" He pushes me back and I stumble. "Huh?"

I scream out in anger and swing the bat at his head, knocking him down and into the side of Alexandra's bed.

He looks up at me with wide eyes and grabs the side of his head, but before he can do anything I come at him and repeatedly swing my bat, not caring where I'm hitting him.

I keep swinging over and over again, wanting to hurt the piece of shit who's been hurting Alexandra all these years.

She's broken inside and it's all because of him.

I'm still swinging the bat, determined to hurt him, when he somehow manages to grab my arm and stop me.

Then, next thing I know the bat is in his hands and I know that I've screwed up by letting that happen.

He stands up and the first swing he takes sends a bone-crushing sound through my right arm. I scream out in pain and fall to the ground as I feel the bone snap.

I can hear Alexandra crying out for me to run, but I can't, because the swings keep coming, until my whole body is in pain and I black out...

ALEXANDRA

I'VE BEEN SITTING HERE FOR over an hour now, numb, just staring at the wall while drinking straight from a bottle of my dearest friend: Jack.

The water has since turned cold, my skin now wrinkled and disgusting, but I can't seem to find enough shits to give, so I stay put.

Closing my eyes, I tilt the bottle back and take a long swig. The more liquor I consume, the more my thoughts lead to Jaxon and what he might be like now that he's a man. Especially since I'm back in town where he could very well still be after all this time. Questions tumble in one after the other.

Is he still caring and protective like he was when we were kids?

Does he ever wonder what happened to me?

Is he married?

Have kids?

Frustration takes over and I find myself setting the bottle aside to run my hands over my face.

Why does it bother me so damn much to think about Jaxon with a family?

I haven't seen or spoken to him in thirteen years. Surely, he's changed. There's no way he'd be able to make me feel like he used to.

We're both different people, living different lives now.

And from the looks of his childhood home last night, his mom is no longer around. With that thought, there's a chance he's not even here at all. What if he moved after what my asshole father did to him that night?

I'll never forget it. The vision of him bloodied and bruised still haunts me to this damn day.

I suck in a breath and hold it, before sinking under the water, keeping my eyes open.

I feel dead as I lie here, full of hate for this world that's done nothing but take from me over and over again until there is nothing left of me to give.

My lungs feel as if they're about to burst, but it's not for that reason that I finally sit up and gasp for air. It's because my thoughts suddenly change to the guy I met last night at the bar.

He made me angry. Lit a fire in me that I haven't felt in years. Actually, he made me feel more in just that short amount of time than I have since before we moved away.

I spent my night trying to pretend it was nothing, but it was far from it. When I walked out that door after he kicked me out, I was pissed, yet part of me wanted to climb his hard body and choke him as he fucked me hard against a wall.

There's nothing I hate more than a man telling me what to do, but shit if it didn't slightly turn me on when he did it.

I didn't even get to ask about that tattoo I went in there thinking I'd get.

My phone vibrating across the floor has me leaning over to reach for it.

"Oh, come on. Not now."

Releasing a long, slow breath, I open James' text.

JAMES

Let me come over tonight and we can spend the night having sex and eating pizza.

ALEXANDRA

No, James. I already told you we're not going to make this an every night thing. We're not a couple so let's not pretend to be something we'll never be.

JAMES

Why? What is so hard about being with me? We've been fucking for longer than I've ever messed around with anyone else before. Is that all I'm good for?

ALEXANDRA

It's not about you, James. You want something I'm unable to give. I don't know shit about love and I won't pretend to either. I was upfront with you from the beginning. You were fine with it then. You changing is not my problem.

JAMES

Come on, Alexandra. Let me come over for a quickie. You said it before… I don't last long. Then I'll leave.

ALEXANDRA

No. You know my limit. Two times a week.

JAMES

I scored some Xanax, Oxy, and cocaine…

I think about it for a minute; my need to forget considering it. But the part of me that tries to survive without the pills wins out… for once.

ALEXANDRA

Goodnight, James.

Before I can change my mind, I toss my phone down and sink under the water. When I come back up, I sit here for a while, looking at the random scars that cover my flesh.

Some are faint, barely noticeable, while others are so visible that it's hard to believe it's been almost ten years since my father placed the last one on me.

The more I sit here and allow myself to think, the more the craving for some kind of relief consumes me. I've been sick for some time now, relying on anything I can get my hands on to numb the bullshit of my life. But even I'm tired of my own sick habits.

If I don't get out of this damn house I know without a doubt I'll be messaging James back and giving him permission to come over tonight.

Standing up, I step out of the tub and reach for a towel, before I make my way through the house to find some clothes.

Thirty minutes later, I'm out the door and in my car, heading toward the only place I feel like being right now.

There's a small chance this sexy, bossy, and possibly even dangerous man might be the only thing able to distract me from my past long enough to feel something other than what I've been feeling since I lost Jaxon.

Maybe what I need is to challenge myself. Something to get my blood pumping and to make me feel again. He did that all within a couple of hours.

It's just past eight, so I have a feeling that sexy bartender isn't going to like me showing up past dark, but he doesn't get to make that decision this time.

If he wants to kick me out again, he's going to have to carry my ass outside to the parking lot himself. A part of me believes he probably would too.

When I pull up at Savage & Ink, the parking lot is so full that I have to park across the street, unlike last time.

A majority of the vehicles parked outside are motorcycles

again, which doesn't surprise me, given the crowd I saw here yesterday.

I smile as I run my hand over a shiny, new Harley parked right outside the door. It's so damn sexy that I can't help but want to straddle it, so I do.

A throat clears behind me, probably expecting me to get scared and jump off in a hurry, but instead, I turn around and straddle it so I'm facing some guy leaning against the building with a joint resting between his lips.

He looks me over while bringing his tattooed hands up to light it. "You like my buddy's new bike? It's pretty fucking powerful."

"Is that right?" I place my hands on the seat between my legs as I check him out in his white t-shirt and black jeans. His body is just as sculpted as the bossy bartender I met here last night. I think I could get used to this place. "I like powerful. Especially when it's between my legs."

"Well, fuck, baby." He reaches down and grabs his dick with one hand, holding the joint with his other. "I've got a lot of power right here, gorgeous." He releases his dick and takes another hit off the joint. "My buddy may not like it if you test drive his new bike, but I sure as fuck don't mind if you test drive my cock."

This man is gorgeous. Definitely enough to have me imagining how he fucks, but he still doesn't spark any emotions inside.

Not like the guy who I hope is inside right now.

I curve my finger at him, motioning for him to come to me.

He pushes away from the wall and comes at me, stopping at the end of his friend's bike.

With a small smirk, I run my hand up his hard body, before I pull the joint from his lips and place it between mine.

His lips tilt up into a cocky smirk, before he leans in and

places his lips close to mine, waiting for me to blow the smoke into his mouth.

Just as I go to blow the smoke out, he grabs the back of my head, holding me in place so his lips are brushing mine.

This has me leaning in and biting his bottom lip so hard that he pulls away and licks the blood from his mouth. But before I can tell him off, we're interrupted by a deep voice.

"Don't you have work to do or some shit, Blaine?"

I look over Blaine's shoulder to see another equally-as-hot guy standing by the door, looking aggravated.

He's blond, covered in tattoos, and has a beard just a little longer than bossy bartender's. With one look at him, you can tell he's someone not to be messed with.

"Can't a motherfucker get a break around here?" Blaine reaches up and wipes his mouth off, before turning behind him to look at blondie. "Those assholes can wait. They're not going anywhere anytime soon, Royal."

The blond shrugs and lights up a cigarette. "You're lucky Mark is here and decided to help sling some drinks for a bit since he's off duty." He turns his gaze in my direction, his gray eyes landing on me. "You here with this dick or the one whose bike you're on? 'Cause it's crazy inside. Might want to stay close."

I swing my leg over the bike and walk toward the door, passing them both up. "I'm not here with anyone. I can handle my damn self."

I step inside, realizing it's a different door than last time, because this one leads straight into the chaos of the bar.

It's loud, but seems to quiet down just long enough for gazes to land my way. I ignore them all, setting my attention straight on the bossy bartender.

The angry look he gives me is just enough to set me on fire. Damn, he's sexy when he's angry. Maybe even a bit beautiful.

His jaw clenches as he watches me make my way toward the

bar, while him and some other sexy guy continue to serve drinks. The other guy must be this "Mark" person Royal mentioned outside.

Bossy bartender is completely busy, but doesn't take his eyes off me as I find an empty spot up at the bar and take a seat.

My blood is pumping as his intense gaze stares me down, as if he's challenging me. It gives me a small rush.

"What are you doing back?" He slams a beer down in front of him and pops the cap off, before downing half of it. "Are you trying to make me rip someone's throat out tonight?" He looks past me, his jaw still clenched tightly. "These men are ruthless bastards who give no fucks about what you want or don't want. Unless you're here with someone then you shouldn't be here at all."

I smile and grab the beer from his hand, knowing damn well he'll probably refuse to serve me one. "Then we can say I'm here with you. The beautiful, bossy bartender that everyone seems to be afraid of." I tilt back the bottle, getting a tiny bit excited to place my lips where his just were.

"Well, if you want them to believe you're with me, babe..." He leans over the bar, grips the back of my hair with force, and sucks my bottom lip into his mouth, before releasing it with a growl.

My heart is hammering inside my chest and my legs slightly tremble; a feeling I've never experienced before other than when I kissed Jaxon that night back when we were kids. "You better damn well play the part while you're here. 'Cause everyone's dicks are about to jump out of their pants right now."

Pretending he doesn't have me all fired up inside, I smile and lick my bottom lip as he releases my hair. "Playing is what I do best, beautiful bartender. It's all I can do anymore. It's how I survive."

He lifts a brow and stands back as I crawl over the bar, jump down in front of him, and grab the front of his shirt. He smells so damn good that I could seriously eat him up right now.

"Is this what a girl with a man like you would do?" I tug on his beard and pull him closer, running my tongue up his lips. "Huh? Or would she do this?"

His jaw flexes as I run my hand down his stiff abs, before lowering it to the sizeable bulge in his jeans and squeezing.

It feels nice and big, full in my hand.

I'm not really sure what has come over me. Maybe it's the craving of how he makes me feel. I want more of what I felt when he pulled my bottom lip into his mouth.

"I'd be real fucking careful about messing with big toys unless you're able to handle them, because I don't play nice." He whispers the next part in my ear, causing me to slightly moan. "Never have, and I sure as hell won't start now."

Gripping my hand, he pulls it away from his dick and reaches into the cooler, setting a beer down in front of where I was just sitting. "Now sit and drink where I can see you."

I smile and grab the beer, placing it to my lips. "And by the way... I don't play nice either."

Ignoring his orders, I walk past him and the Mark guy and find an open spot in the room to dance.

It only takes fifteen seconds for some asshole to grab my ass, but as soon as I turn around and eye him over, not impressed, he mumbles bitch and walks off.

The bartender must've noticed, because the next thing I see is him slamming the asshole's head down onto a table and saying something in his ear before he throws him down and walks away.

Everyone around the room seems to keep their distance from me after that, because clearly this guy doesn't mess around when it comes to someone pissing him off.

Dancing, I tilt back my beer and watch as Blaine stops beside the bartender and they begin talking.

It's not long before both sets of eyes are trained on me, the sexy guy from earlier looking overly cocky, while the bartender suddenly looks extremely pissed.

I watch as he jumps over the bar and stalks toward me, as if he's ready to choke me up against the wall, but instead, he grabs my arm and pulls me through the crowd and out the front door.

Once outside, he immediately goes to the Harley I was sitting on and begins checking it out, as if looking for any scratches or dents.

Of course, the sexy bike has to belong to the one person who'll probably never allow me back on it again.

"Who gave you permission to sit on my bike?" He looks behind him just long enough to give me a dirty as hell look.

"There was no one out here to give me permission..." My heart speeds up as he walks back to me, stopping just inches from my face. "So, I didn't ask."

"That's a big mistake at a place like this. Do you just not give a shit about what happens to you?" He backs me up until I'm pressed against the building, his strong arms blocking me in. "Are you looking to fucking get hurt?"

"Doesn't matter what I'm looking for," I say stiffly. "Because I gave up on that years ago."

He closes his eyes and releases a breath as if he's thinking something over. When he opens his eyes again, the intensity behind his stare has me swallowing. "Why is it that I want to protect you so much? What is it about you that draws me in?"

I open my mouth, but can't think of a response. Honestly, I was wondering that myself.

I've never had anyone want to protect me so much before, other than Jaxon.

But this stranger... Ever since he pulled up beside me on his bike, he's been trying to keep me out of harm's way.

"Maybe it's because you know I'm broken, irreparable, and

you need a challenge to get your blood pumping." I push on his chest, but he doesn't budge. "Well, baby, I'm the biggest challenge you'll meet. Now move."

With that, I push him away from me and head back inside.

There's got to be one damn person in this bar able to give me that tattoo I so desperately need right now.

And since he's working the bar, I can only assume it's one of the other two men who can help me.

I could really use a distraction from this man who has a way of working me up unlike anyone else has in years...

JAX

WHAT IS THIS WOMAN DOING to me? I swear she came back just to taunt me and piss me off to the point I want to rip her clothes off, slam her against the closest surface, and fuck her until she goes limp in my arms.

I want to exhaust her mind, her body, and her sassy fucking mouth.

I ended last night thinking I'd never see her again, yet here she is, working me up once again.

Taking a few moments to cool off, I light up a smoke and hope like hell she doesn't manage to get into any trouble while I'm out here.

But knowing Blaine is inside, I don't really need to wonder. She's for sure getting into trouble.

That dirty son of a bitch. I'm not sure why but it pissed me off to hear he was close to kissing her on my bike before she came inside.

The thought alone had me wanting to rip his throat out.

After a few drags, I toss my cigarette at the building and

make my way inside to see Royal and Mark standing at the bar talking.

"Where's Blaine?" I ask stiffly, while looking around.

Mark gives me a small smile and pours himself a shot of whiskey. He's been hanging here a lot when he's off duty, and although most people know he's a cop, they still give no shits when it comes to doing what they want here. "That sassy redhead came barging in here asking for a tattoo. She's in the back with Blaine. She practically dragged him away by his neck."

"Shit!" I reach out and knock over a half empty glass, before I shove the door open and head toward the tattoo room.

My blood is boiling because I know without a doubt Blaine will try to fuck her before the night is over.

I really shouldn't give a damn and it's none of my business, yet for some reason I do and I'm making it my business.

Stopping at the window, I look inside to see her peeling her shirt off and undoing her bra, while Blaine is sitting in the chair, his eyes on her as he slaps a pair of black gloves on.

A few seconds goes by before she notices me standing outside the room, but instead of waiting for me to walk away, she locks her eyes with mine and pulls her bra straps down her arms.

The way she bites her bottom lip as my gaze roams over her body has my cock jumping with excitement.

She's doing this shit on purpose just to get a reaction out of me. I can tell, because she's paying no attention to Blaine whatsoever, as if he's not even in the room.

It's when she goes to slide her hand down her stomach that I barge into the room and throw Blaine a hard look. "Get the fuck out," I bark out. "I'll take care of her."

Blaine flashes me a surprised smile as he stands up, yanks the gloves off, and tosses them behind him. "I thought you couldn't do tattoos for shit?"

"It's not that I can't. That was a lie to keep me at the bar so I could keep an eye on things better. If I get stuck back here while you watch the bar, we'd probably end up having to replace all the damn windows."

He shrugs and pulls out a smoke. "It's all good. My hand could use a break anyway. She wants an angel with dream catcher elements." He smirks and raises a brow. "Starting low on her hip and stopping right under her left breast. It may take a while."

Well, shit. She definitely doesn't play around. This shit will take a good two sessions.

"I got it. Tell Royal I'll be occupied for a few hours. See if Mark will stay until I'm done."

"Good luck, dickhead." Blaine exits the room and my attention instantly goes to the sassy woman beside me.

My jaw clenches as I watch her undo her jeans, teasing me with her eyes as she slowly lowers them down her hips.

I've never had a woman work me up this way. And it pisses me off that she's able to.

"What the fuck are you doing?" I ask stiffly.

She lets out a sexy little laugh while lowering her jeans even more. "What does it look like I'm doing?"

"Pissing me off."

"Good," she whispers, lowering the strap of her black thong. "I'm getting prepared for my tattoo too. In case you're wondering what else I'm doing. You know... other than pissing you off."

My teeth are clenched so tightly watching her that it's beginning to hurt, but I'm not going to touch her just because she's tempting me to.

A woman like this is probably used to every guy giving into her, but she's about to get a wake-up call.

I catch her eyes lowering to my dick. "You're hard, beautiful bartender. Do something about it. Show me what it's like to really belong to you."

I growl and run my hand over my cock, watching her chest as it begins moving faster with each stroke above my jeans.

She's playing a game she won't win, but she wants to play so I'll play.

Locking my gaze with hers, I slowly undo my belt and jeans, smirking as she breaks eye contact to watch what I'm doing.

She lets out a desperate moan and squeezes her thighs together as I slide my hand down my boxer briefs and begin stroking my cock for her.

I can tell she's desperate to see what I have packing under these jeans, but I keep it put away on purpose just to tease her.

"Is this what you want from me? Huh? Me stroking my dick for you? I want nothing more than to come right now, but just because you want me to, I won't."

With that, I release my dick and walk over to grip the chair and lean down close to her face. She's breathing heavily, giving me a dirty as hell look, because we both know she was getting off to me touching myself for her. "Don't fuck with me, because I will win, babe. I don't even need to whip the big guy out to get the job done. Just the thought of it is enough for most women. Just imagine how it must be once it's actually inside of you."

I don't even give her time to speak before I walk over to the sink and wash my hands.

"Do you do this often?" she asks as I slip a pair of gloves on.

"Do what? Tattoo?"

"Tease a woman and then leave her hanging."

I turn around to face her. "Nope."

She narrows her eyes and relaxes in the chair. "I was only testing you to see how far you'd go. If I really wanted you to come... then I'd do it my damn self."

Her words have my cock hard again and me cussing under my breath.

"What makes you think I'd let you?"

"The way you look at me." She lowers her gaze down to the bulge in my jeans. "And the fact that you can't seem to keep your dick soft around me."

I grab the green soap and spray her skin, but it's when I go to wipe it off with a paper towel that I notice the scars on her body. They look to be older, but it's hard to tell for sure.

They're all over in random spots as if they were put there by someone. The thought has me clenching my jaw, reminding me of how Alexandra's father used to hurt her. It has rage rushing to the surface at the memories.

"Who hurt you?"

My question has her sitting up and yanking her shirt back on. "Someone from my past I'd rather forget about."

"A guy?" The fact that someone actually was the cause of all these scars has my blood boiling with rage.

"Doesn't matter," she says as she stands up and fixes her clothing. "I didn't come here to have you question me about something that is none of your damn business."

"Maybe I should make it my business so whoever fucking hurt you pays for what they did." I move in close and grab her chin before she can turn away from me. "No one should ever be able to hurt you this way and get away with it, so don't ever for one second believe that shit."

The look in her eyes tells me she's thinking about something deep.

"I should go. Forget the tattoo."

Just like that she walks away, leaving me alone, lost in my thoughts.

There was something familiar about the way she looked at me before she walked away a few moments ago, as if I've seen that look before. It's eating away at me. I'm trying to figure it out.

The anger consumes me for the next hour or so. The result

is slamming down bottles and glasses, practically scaring everyone off from wanting to order from me.

"You good, man?" Mark swipes his arm across the bar, knocking a bunch of empty bottles into the trash. "I've gotta stop by and visit Avalon before it gets too late so she can cut this mop of mine. I told Royal before he left that I'd be over no later than eleven."

I look behind me just as he's running his hand through his long hair. "Yeah. I'm good. Blaine will stay."

"All right, man." He pats my shoulder and slips on his jacket. "I'll catch ya later."

"Later, man. And hey..."

He stops walking to look back at me.

"Thanks for helping out here. It's not your job, yet you seem to be doing it a lot these days. Appreciate it."

"Family helps family." He smiles and begins backing up toward the door. "So, it's not a problem."

Once Mark is gone, I begin looking around the room to see who's all still here.

We're down to a handful of people, which is a hell of a lot better than the crowd I had to deal with late last night.

I'm hoping it'll be an easy close tonight. I might even leave early and let Blaine close up if he can guarantee he won't get into any trouble after I'm gone.

But we all know that's never guaranteed.

Blaine comes in from outside a few minutes later and pours himself a drink.

Tilting it back, he leans against the wall and looks me over before speaking. "What was that shit about? She getting under your skin already, brother?"

I nod my head. "Yeah. She's getting under my skin all right. Don't ask me how or why."

"She's feisty, so I can see why." He grins. "And entirely way too sexy to be hanging out here alone. You're used to protecting women. It's in your nature, and I think we both know she needs some help."

I reach for my leather jacket and slip it on. I'm frustrated and just need to get out of here. "Yeah... you're right about that. But that doesn't explain why I'm so fucking drawn to her after only two days."

"I know that feeling," he mumbles, before downing a shot. "You taking off? I can handle it from here."

"If you can promise not to fuck shit up."

From the distant look in his eyes, I can tell his thoughts are going to Madison, even though he'll try everything in his power to deny it.

"Madison wants me to swing by and take her for a ride on my dick again," I say to get a reaction out of him.

Blaine instantly grips the bar and squeezes.

"You're squeezing that bar awfully tight for someone who doesn't want anything serious with a woman."

He releases his grip and looks up at me, trying to seem unfazed. "I'm good. Now, get the hell out of here."

"I plan on it, brother." I pull my keys out of my pocket and grin. "But don't worry; I won't be taking your girl for a ride again, so you can relax over there before you end up killing someone or being killed before the night is over."

"I'm as relaxed as I can be, but I'll do my best to stay alive. I always do."

Shaking my head, I leave him alone and make my way outside, hopping on my bike to head home.

I need to sleep this shit off and remind myself that she's not Lex. I can't expect this stranger to want my help like she did.

Fuck... this is going to be hard...

ALEXANDRA

A HAND RUNNING UP MY thigh has me waking from a deep sleep and kicking at the intruder, before reaching under my pillow for the knife I keep hidden there. The room is pitch-black, so it's not until I hear James groan out in pain that I realize the asshole somehow found his way into the house.

I must have passed out hard after leaving the bar last night, because when I look over to check the time it's already close to two in the afternoon. I hardly ever have a solid sleep unless I'm completely obliterated, and after the bartender decided to point out my scars I needed an escape and turned to whiskey to do the trick.

I flip the knife in my hand around and stab it into the mattress, angry with James for appearing in my room uninvited. "What the fuck, James? Don't ever do that shit again." I fight to catch my breath, while focusing on his figure in the darkness. I watch as he holds his ribs in pain. "I could've killed you. How did you get into the house?"

"Shit, woman, that hurt." He walks over and yanks the dark

curtain open, the brightness causing me to squeeze my eyes shut. "I climbed through the damn living room window since you wouldn't answer your phone. I've been texting since last night. Got some shit from Jasper."

The mention of him getting supply from his new dealer has me wanting with everything in me to accept whatever he has to offer.

Fighting the need is so hard that it hurts, yet a part of me wants to be sober enough to go find the bartender and tell him to piss off.

He had no goddamn right.

He doesn't know what I've been through. No one does.

"Do us both a favor, James, and don't climb through any more windows. It's not your place to just let yourself in when you want to."

Biting his bottom lip in an attempt to look sexy—which he does, as much as I hate to admit—he takes a seat on the edge of my bed and moves his hand under the blanket and over my bare thigh. "Or you can jump on my dick like we both know you want to do."

"Aren't you quite the fucking comedian..." Giving him a stern look, I throw the blanket off, grab his hand, and pry it from my thigh. "That would be doing no one but yourself a favor, James, and I'm not in the favor-giving mood. Now give me some space. I've got a lot of crap going on in my head that I can't deal with when you're riding my ass. If I wanted you here I would've answered the phone."

He shrugs and watches me reach into the drawer for a joint. A grin spreads across his face as he watches me light it. "I brought you a little gift, so how about you give me a break, Alex."

I look down at my thigh as a plastic bag with a handful of pills hits it. I barely give myself time to look at them, not wanting the temptation, before I toss them into the drawer and close it.

"I've got to shower and get to work," I lie. The truth is, I need some time alone to think. My head is all over the place from last night and I'm not sure what to do. I'm not even sure why I care so much, when usually I don't care about much of anything. But this guy... ugh. He has ways of getting under my skin and I don't even know his name.

"I know I sound like a cunt every time I tell you this, but don't come over unannounced anymore. You know how much I hate it."

A crooked smile crosses his face as he crawls over me to grab the joint from my hand, before lying beside me on the mattress. "Yeah, but you're missing the point that I like cunts. Especially yours."

My eyes are closed, due to the massive headache I have, so it's not until he slides his hand down my panties and quickly shoves a finger inside me that I'm able to stop him from touching me, unwantedly.

"Fucking hell, James." I turn around and kick him off the bed, before I rush to my feet to grab some clothes. "Be gone by the time I get out of the shower. I mean it, bastard."

He looks up at me from the floor, a pissed off expression on his face. "This is bullshit, Alex. You still won't let me touch you when I want to. I could be with any girl I want to and she'd let me touch her whenever I want to."

"Like I said before... I'm not like most girls."

Before I can go completely manic on James, I rush into the bathroom and slam the door closed behind me, my breath coming out in heavy bursts. I'm so angry at him for thinking he can touch me sexually whenever he damn well pleases that it's hard for me to calm down.

I take what feels like the longest shower of my life before getting out and forcing myself to eat something.

Hours go by and still I can't get the guy at Savage & Ink out of my head. He's getting to me, whether he's trying to or not.

He's the first person to point out my scars, acting as if he actually gives a shit enough to want to help me.

Screw that. No one has truly ever cared other than Jaxon.

He's no Jaxon and never will be.

I'VE BEEN SITTING IN THE parking lot staring at that damn sexy bike for a while now; trying to think of what to say once I get inside.

I hate that he challenges me unlike anyone else.

What am I doing out here? This is stupid.

But even after telling myself that, I can't bring myself to leave, so I throw my seatbelt off and climb out of the car, slamming the door shut behind me.

I make my way through the parking lot, unable to resist running my hand over bossy bartender's precious motorcycle on the way to the door and I hate that I can't help but to remember just how hot he looked on it.

The moment I step into the crowded bar and my gaze lands on him—looking sexier than sin behind the bar—I have to convince myself I'm only here to let him know how pissed I am about last night.

Nothing else. Especially not sex.

But damn if he wouldn't be nice to test drive.

The heavy pounding of my heels on the floor as I head straight for him has everyone's attention on me, including the person I came here to see.

But the moment the tattooed, bearded beast cracks his neck and flexes his arms, most of the room goes back to minding their own damn business.

Just like I pointed out before, people know not to mess with him and that power he has draws me straight to him for some unknown reason.

"You owe me an apology for last night," I say, looking up at him once I stop right in front of his huge frame. "You can either do it here or outside. Your choice."

He tilts his head and looks down at me as if amused. His amber gaze stays locked on me, despite me shooting angry daggers his way. "Why outside? So you can sit on my bike without permission again? Maybe you're the one that owes me an apology."

"Maybe I already sat on it on the way in. Want to run and see if I left any scratches?" I say, hoping to agitate him like he's done to me.

It doesn't work, because he just turns and walks away. He doesn't bother saying anything as he opens the cooler and reaches inside.

I stand here, mouth clenched tightly as I watch him reach for two beers and then lean against the bar, looking chilled and relaxed as if me coming here to yell at him hasn't fazed him one bit. "Who says I'm staying long enough for a drink?" I ask bitterly.

He lets out a half laugh half grunt and pops the cap off both bottles, setting one of them down behind him. "Who said one of these is for you?" He tilts the bottle in his hand back, taking a swig, before wiping his arm over his wet lips. "Maybe seeing you requires two of these."

"Me?" I point at my chest, annoyed. "You know nothing about me. You had no right to say what you did last night. It's none of your damn business what I've been through. You don't know what kind of shit you've stirred up inside my head."

His jaw tightens, before he tilts back the bottle again, downing almost the entire thing in one gulp. "Yeah, well it's always been hard not to make shit like that my business. You don't know me either. Trust me."

I definitely need a beer now, so I reach out to grab the other one, about to bring it to my lips, but he stops me before I can.

His harsh gaze stays on me as he snatches the bottle out of my hand, before tossing the now empty bottle he was holding in the trash. He grunts, before bringing it to his perfect, annoying lips and takes a drink.

My entire body heats with need the moment he pushes away from the bar and moves in close to me, his body pressed up against mine. He's so warm and hard against me that it's difficult not to picture wrapping my fingers into his long, thick hair and riding him for hours. I've never craved a man sexually so much before, but holy hell, this man is something else entirely.

"It's my nature to protect women from abusive assholes that can't keep their hands to themselves. Don't like it..." The muscles in his arms flex against me, drawing my attention to the tattooed bulges when he tilts the bottle back again, almost finishing it off this time. "Then you're going to hate being around me, love."

He takes a step closer and bows his head. His eyes are so intimidating as he looks down at me that I swallow and take a step back. Usually, a man being so close makes me want to push him away, but him being close has me wanting to do the opposite.

Maybe coming here wasn't the best idea after all. I came here with every intention of giving him a piece of my mind, but the look in his eyes is making it hard not to hate-fuck him.

"Screw the beer. Give me a shot," I say, walking behind the bar.

I almost think he's not going to follow me, but when I look back, he's shaking his head and stalking toward the cooler to grab a beer.

When he turns to face me, the protective look in his eyes makes my damn heart skip a beat.

What is it about this guy?

He's a stranger; yet being around him feels so familiar. Staying might be a mistake, but I'm full of them, so why change that now?

"Did you come back here to put me in my place or to get back at me by making sure I'll be on edge for the rest of the night?" He holds the beer out for me to grab. "No shots for you. One beer and that's it."

"Does it really matter?" I grab the bottle from his reach and take a desperate swig. "And I will be having more than one of these."

He runs his hand through his dark hair in frustration, watching me as I turn and walk toward the pool table.

I hope the bartender doesn't believe I'll be leaving anytime soon, because pissing him off is already starting to make me feel better.

Not to mention that messing with him seems to be keeping my thoughts in the present and away from the last place I want them to be.

Maybe hating him is the medicine I need right now...

JAX

WELL HELL… IF THIS WOMAN isn't just as fiery as her fucking hair.

The moment my attention was brought to her stepping into the bar, adrenaline coursed through me just from seeing her again.

After the way she took off on me last night, pissed off for being concerned about her scars, I was almost positive she wouldn't be coming back.

That's what I thought I wanted—for her to stay away from this rough, dangerous place. But after finding out she's had some asshole roughing her up, I want her here where I can keep an eye on her.

After all these years, it still hits me deep that Alexandra went through years of abuse from her father and I wasn't enough to save her. Just knowing there's another female out there being hurt by some selfish son of a bitch has me wanting to help.

I don't know who this asshole is or if he's still involved in her life, but he better hope for his sake he's not, because he's going to regret placing his hands on her once mine are crushing his fucking throat.

I cross my arms and watch as the fiery redhead intent on making me lose my shit makes her way across the bar to one of the pool tables.

Concentrating on anything other than her bending over the pool table in those skin-tight jeans and heels is impossible.

It won't be long before a group of assholes make their way over to join her and the thought of them even thinking they have a chance to get in her pants has me on constant watch.

These dumbasses must be brave tonight, because it only takes five minutes of her playing pool by herself before two assholes decide to join her.

They're both regulars, which means they've been here more than enough times for me to already know they're both dirtballs.

Keeping my attention on them, I crack my neck and stand tall, ready to chase them away if they try any shit I don't like.

Blaine is too busy talking to a group of his old friends to even realize she's here, so I can't take my eyes off her for longer than a few seconds at a time.

"I'll take another one over here, Jax." I nod over at Casey, before fixing him another Jameson and Coke and dropping it off to him.

After I serve a few more drinks and get caught up, I bring my attention right back to the pool table to see the blond one getting a little too brave, placing his hand on her lower back while she's bent over taking a shot.

She's quick to shake him away and move to the other side of the table, but I'm already set on making him leave.

"Blaine," I bark out. He looks over from the table he's been chilling at, waiting for me to continue. "Handle the drinks for a bit."

He gives me a nod, acknowledging my request, before I make my way over to her and the guys. She's concentrating on her second shot, both of these dickheads now hovering over her a little too close.

I move in right between them and wrap an arm around her waist, pulling her ass against my dick. She stiffens at first, but the moment I lean in and whisper in her ear, she relaxes. "Gotta play the part if you don't want these assholes hounding you."

She stands up straight so her body is flush with mine, before slightly turning her head to speak. "Does that mean you're going to play with me, bartender?" Her breath hits my lips when she speaks, and it makes my cock twitch with need. "These two have offered to play and I don't feel like playing by myself. Besides, the blond one is cute."

Her sassy mouth has me pulling her harder against me and growling in her ear. She doesn't know how these assholes work. "The blond one also doesn't know how to keep his hands to himself and is at risk of losing them with me around," I say loud enough for him to hear me.

The seriousness in my voice has him and his buddy walking away. Sean has dealt with me enough times in the past to know not to get on my bad side.

I release her waist and walk over to grab a cue stick, before re-racking the balls.

She watches me in silence, her gaze raking over my body as I grab the chalk and apply it to the tip of my stick.

"Like what you see?" I question, amused by the fact she's still looking at me. "Should I break or you want to?"

She answers my question by leaning over the table and breaking the balls, sinking a solid in the far right hole.

A small smile takes over my lips as I watch her lean in again and confidently take another shot. She misses this time, but her posture and aim are good, telling me she most likely plays pool often.

That's one sexy as hell image to jerk my cock to and I have no shame in doing just that tonight.

I smirk and sink in my next three balls, feeling her gaze on me the entire time. She's watching me as if every ball I sink has her wanting to ride my dick more.

Temptation has me close to kicking everyone out of the bar so she can do just that.

"So..." she says, bending over once it's her turn again. "Which one of you runs this place? The blond one with the beard?"

"Yeah. My buddy Royal." I smile when she turns to look at me. "What gave you that idea?"

She lets out a small laugh, before taking her shot and missing. "He was growling at your friend Blaine the other night. I figured it was because he's in charge."

I shake my head and take my next shot. "Growling is what Royal does best. I've been dealing with it for twelve years."

"What about the other guy? It seems you've known him for a while too."

I look away from the table, my eyes instantly lingering on her plump lips. The bottom one is slightly fuller than the top one. It's got to be the sexiest bottom lip I've ever seen and I can't stop thinking about what it'd feel like to suck it into my mouth again.

"We've been friends for ten years. Royal and Blaine saved me from the shit road I was heading down. We keep each other in line as much as we can." I wave my arm around the room. "We've practically lived here since we were kids and when Royal's father got into a bunch of shit, he took over and brought me and Blaine in to run it with him."

She nods and clears her throat. "Must've been nice to have

friends that cared enough to keep you in line. Good friends are hard to come by."

"That's true shit."

She's quiet after that, barely saying anything until we start a second game of pool.

I almost forget I'm here to work until she nods toward the bar. "You're not going to help your buddy up there?"

"Nah, he's good." The dick does this shit to me almost nightly, so I kick back and enjoy him yelling at assholes to calm down and wait their turn. "I'll be back." I set my cue stick against the wall and give her a stern look. "Stay right here."

She hops onto the pool table and takes a seat on the edge. "I have nowhere to be, bossy bartender."

Her nickname for me has me grinning as I walk away to grab us a few beers.

"Oh, calm your fucking balls," Blaine says, taking his time to fetch the last few drinks. "And take your time drinking these because once I sit back down I'm not getting up for a while."

I lift a brow and nod when Blaine gives me the middle finger with both hands. "Fuck you, too."

I barely make it back over to the pool table when she jumps down and grabs one of the beers from my hand, keeping her eyes on me as she tilts it back.

She's eyeing me over hungrily, as if that beer between her lips isn't enough to quench her thirst.

It has my dick hardening for the hundredth time since she showed up here tonight.

I tilt my beer back, allowing my eyes to wander over her body, taking in every curve and tattoo, making it shamefully obvious that I'm just as hungry as she is.

When she doesn't turn away from me after a few seconds, I set my beer down on the pool table and step in close to her. I'm so dangerously close that I can feel her heart beating fast against me.

But just when I'm about to grip her hips and pull her even closer, Blaine arguing with someone has me flexing my jaw in annoyance and looking over to see what the deal is.

"I should get going," she says in a hurry. "Thanks for the drinks."

By the time I turn away from Blaine and Ryland causing a scene, she's already walking away, not bothering to stop and look back.

Well fuck...

Leave it up to Blaine to distract me at the worst possible time.

ALEXANDRA

I TRIED TO LEAVE; TRIED convincing myself to go home and forget about the way this stranger is making me feel, but I turned my car around anyway and came back.

There's something about him that reminds me of Jaxon Kade and I can't let that go. It has me drawn to him in a way I can't seem to fight, even though I want nothing more than to keep my distance.

It's what I should do. What I should've done since the moment I saw him pull up next to me on his bike the other night.

But then he went out of his way to look after me, and for as long as I've been alive, there's only one person who cared about me enough to do that.

Jaxon's hair was a lot lighter— almost blond—so it's not that I believe it could be him. It's more that a part of me wonders if he could make me feel the way Jaxon did.

Even just a small portion.

And apparently, that's something I crave, because here I am.

I'm looking down at the ground, but my heart about leaps out of my chest at the sound of the heavy door opening and closing.

Swallowing nervously, I look up and my heart stops when I see him watching me with an intensity that is making it hard to breathe.

He's so damn powerful—dangerous and edgy looking.

I expect him to yell at me for being on his bike, but he doesn't.

"I thought you left?" He leans against the building and kicks his foot back, while reaching for a joint. "What're you still doing here?"

Being sure not to scratch his new bike, I climb off and walk over to stand next to him. "I did leave." I reach over and grab the joint from between his lips, before he has a chance to take a hit. "I decided I wasn't ready to go home yet. There's nothing there for me."

"Good." He kicks away from the building and begins walking toward his bike. "Let's go then, since you seem so set on being on my bike anyway."

Watching him reach for his helmet, I take a few quick hits and join him at his side.

He looks at me and his jaw flexes a few times, before he steps in close and slides the helmet over my head. "Toss that shit and hop on. I have more."

He straddles his bike and reaches his hand out for me. He's so sexy—the way he's looking at me—that my body trembles as I grab his hand and jump on behind him.

He takes off and I don't even bother asking where we're going, because I really don't care. What I want is to get away and it seems like he might want the same thing.

We ride for a while, taking some back roads, before he finally pulls into a neighborhood and parks in the driveway of a brick house.

From what I can tell it doesn't seem to be too far from the bar he works at. In fact, I'm pretty sure I passed this street on the way there from my place.

He doesn't say anything as he helps me off his bike and slides the helmet from my head.

"Is this your place?" I follow him to the porch.

"Yeah." He unlocks the door, before turning back around to face me. "If you want me to serve you drinks all night, we might as well do it at a place I know you'll be safe and I won't have to kick some big fucker's ass."

"Oh yeah?" I laugh and look him over. I still can't get over how sexy he is in that leather jacket. "How am I supposed to know I'll be safe from you?"

A small smirk crosses his face as he places his hand on my lower back and guides me inside. "Do you really want to be safe from me?" he asks beside my ear. "Because I couldn't tell back at the bar. I think it's my safety I should be concerned about."

I don't answer his question, because truthfully, I don't know myself. My entire body ignites into flames whenever I think about him fucking me.

A man like him couldn't possibly be anything other than wild and rough in the bedroom.

I look around at the boxes stacked around the living room before I take a seat on the couch. "How long have you been here?"

"Not long." He disappears into the kitchen and comes back a few minutes later with a bottle of whiskey and two glasses. "I haven't had much time to unpack, as you can see."

"You're not worried about having some strange woman in your new house?" I lift a brow and wait for his response.

"Not one that I can take. No..."

"Who says you can take me? I could very well be a psycho killer just waiting for you to show me a bit of weakness before I strike. You never know."

He shrugs and takes a seat next to me on the couch, before filling up the two glasses and handing one to me. "True, but I'll take my chances with you." His jaw tightens as he looks me over. "Are you going to tell me your name or should I just call you hot psycho?"

The way he's looking at me causes me to laugh. "I'm good with that name."

"All right..." He sets his glass down and tops it off with more whiskey. "I suppose you don't want to know my name so you can keep calling me bossy bartender?"

Without thinking, I lean in closer and speak against his lips. "You're correct. I like not knowing your name. The mystery makes it exciting."

I get ready to back away, but he grabs the back of my head, holding me in place. "So, you like things to go by your rules? Is that how I have to play with you?"

His breath hitting my lips has me swallowing before I speak. "I'd prefer it that way, yes."

He nods and leans in so close that his lips brush over mine. "What if I don't play by rules very well?"

Before I can even register what he's doing, he empties his glass, and once he slams it down on the table I'm being pulled into his lap.

Excitement courses through me as his strong hands grip my ass and squeeze, while he slips his tongue between my lips, as if he owns me.

The smell of his cologne and the taste of his tongue has me moaning into his mouth and reaching out to tug on his long hair.

"Who said you could kiss me?" I question against his lips, before biting him.

The animalistic growl that comes from the back of his throat tells me he likes it just as rough as I do.

He reaches one hand up and tangles it in my hair, before he

yanks my head back and brushes his lips up my neck, stopping at my lips. "You didn't ask permission to sit on my bike. What makes you think I'd ask permission to take what I want? I'm a man that takes it."

I release a needy breath and close my eyes as he grinds his erection between my legs and growls again.

"And from what I can tell..." He slides his hand in between our bodies and removes a pistol from his jeans. I didn't even know he was carrying, yet it somehow only manages to turn me on more. "You like that I didn't ask permission. And you also like that you feel safe around me because you know I won't let some asshole fuck with you without answering to me."

"Maybe..." I reach between our bodies and grip his dick through his jeans. It's so damn big and hard and knowing it's because of me has me all hot and ready to ride it hard. "All I know is I'm drawn to you and I need you to fuck some sense into me." I swallow and lower my gaze to his lips, while removing his leather jacket. I need him to remind me he's nothing like the person I lost so many years ago, because Jaxon would never be rough with me.

"That's what you want?" He bites my bottom lip, causing me to dig my nails into his arm because it hurts. "For me to be rough with you... because my version of rough is on a whole different level than what you're probably used to, love."

My eyes must say all he needs to know, because he reaches up with both hands and rips the front of my shirt open, before unsnapping my bra and pulling it out of his way.

A surprised gasp leaves my lips as he reaches behind me for the bottle of whiskey and pours it over the top of my breasts, before he leans in to lick it off.

The feel of his tongue as he swirls it around my nipple, then bites it, has me grinding in his lap, needing to feel him against me.

This must work him up more, because he lifts me up and

throws me down onto the couch, his jaw steeled as he hovers above me and works to undo my pants.

Without hesitation, he yanks them down my legs, along with my panties, before he tosses them aside and reaches for the bottle of whiskey again.

I squirm and bite my bottom lip as he pours a little of it down my inner thigh, before spreading my legs apart and running his tongue over the liquid.

It's when his tongue moves its way to my needy pussy that I let out a little moan and dig my nails into the couch cushion.

"Holy shit..." I thrust my hips toward his face and move my hands up to grip his hair. "Keep going... keep..."

Just when I'm on the verge of an orgasm, he slips two fingers inside me and finger fucks me so hard that I crawl up the back of the couch and scream out my release.

My heart is beating so fast as I watch him yank his shirt off and reach for his belt buckle that it's actually causing me to lose my breath.

He keeps his intense gaze on me as he tilts back the bottle of whiskey and then leans in to pour some into my mouth, licking off the excess liquid as it runs down my neck.

"Fuck, I could lick whiskey from your body all night."

I reach for his jeans and yank them down, my eyes widening as his hard dick springs free. "And with a dick like yours..." Wrapping my hand around its long length, I yank him to me by it. "I'd let you lick anything you want from my body as long as you can keep up with me."

With a deep growl, he grabs me by my ass and picks me up, wrapping my legs around his waist. He takes me through the house and begins digging through his bathroom drawer for a condom and opens it.

Next thing I know he's slamming me against a wooden door in the hallway and biting my neck as he slides it over his erection before slamming into me with one hard thrust.

I scream out and grip his hair, pulling it hard as he moans against my neck. "Pull it harder and I'll fuck you harder."

I want it harder, so I do just that. I yank his hair so hard that his head tilts back and he releases an angry growl into the air.

With force, he grabs my free wrist and slams it above my head, before he begins fucking me up the door so hard I'm pretty sure I just felt it crack.

A man who fucks like this is going to go through a lot of doors if they're all as cheap as this one.

Holy hell how that turns me on like nothing else.

With every hard thrust he growls into my ear, the vibration sends chills down to my core.

I've never heard a sexier noise in my life, and I can't help but to pull his hair harder, wanting more of it.

More of this man and his hard body taking me wild and rough as if his only goal is to fuck me until I can't walk out of here.

"Come on, sexy bartender." I pull his face up so I can run my tongue over his lips, before biting the lower one. "Is that all you got?"

"Fuck no!"

With that, he drops me down to my feet and spins me around to smash my face against the door. He grips my hair with one hand and pulls my head back so he can bite my lips as he slams into me from behind.

The combination has my pussy clenching around his dick within five thrusts and I find myself screaming against the door as my orgasm rolls through me, causing my legs to shake.

He pushes inside of me as far as he can and moans out as my muscles clench his dick.

"Don't challenge me, love. You won't last very long."

As soon as the words leave his lips, he lifts one of my legs against the door and begins moving again.

The sensitivity from my orgasm has me pulling my bottom

lip into my mouth, trying my best not to cry out as he moves fast and hard inside of me.

I've never been fucked so hard in my life and I've never had an orgasm that's been able to bring me to my knees.

Not until the sexy bartender, and I don't even know his name.

A few more hard thrusts and he bites into my shoulder, releasing himself into the condom.

The feeling of him filling me has me coming undone again and I moan against the broken door, gripping onto anything I can get my hands around.

We're both breathing heavily, fighting to catch our breath, when he leans in to whisper in my ear. "That was me taking it easy on you. If I had given it to you how I wanted to... I would've broken you in half."

His words have me swallowing as his body moves away from mine. "That's bullshit..." I bite out. "You don't think I can handle rough?"

I watch as he yanks the condom off and tosses it down the hallway. "No. I know you can't handle my level of rough."

His words have me heated and reaching for my clothes so fast I almost give myself whiplash.

"Fuck you. Don't tell me what I can and can't handle, bartender."

I'm just slipping on my jeans when he says the one word that is enough to stop my heart mid-beat and rip it straight from my chest.

"My name isn't bartender. It's Jax... Jaxon."

I can't breathe. I literally lose my breath at the sound of his name and I find myself grabbing at my chest as my gaze roams over his face, taking him all in.

He's so different from the Jaxon I remember as a kid, but now, looking into those eyes, I know why he's felt so familiar this whole time.

This can't be Jax.

My Jax.

"I... I have to go."

He looks confused as he watches me scramble for my ripped shirt and head toward the door. "Wait a minute."

Right as I reach for the front door to open it, he places his hand on it above my head, stopping me from opening it. "Why did you look at me like that?"

"Move! I told you I didn't want to know your name." I grab the handle and begin pulling on it, just needing to get away so I can breathe. "Now, let me leave!"

As soon as he hears the panic in my voice, he backs away from the door and watches as I make my escape.

My legs are shaky and I find myself falling to my knees and gripping the porch as I fight to get a grip on my emotions.

I know I won't be able to, though, so I search through my purse for the few pills I have hidden and pop two into my mouth, swallowing them down the best I can without water.

I'm just shoving everything back into my purse when the front door opens to Jaxon looking down at me.

"Don't," I growl up at him as he hands me his shirt. "I don't want to talk. I... I just need to leave." I throw his shirt on and shove my ripped one into my purse.

"I'm not going to let you walk away in the middle of the night. Let me drive you back to your vehicle."

I stand up and begin backing away as he takes a step outside. The thought of him touching me has me fighting for air again. "No. I can handle myself. I don't need anyone to take care of me."

"Then at least take my damn keys." Steeling his jaw, he grabs my hand and forces me to grip onto his keys. "Take my truck and leave it at the bar. That way you'll never have to see me again if you don't want to. Deal?"

I swallow and look down at the keys. Here he is... taking care of me like the old Jax and I don't know if I can handle it.

Especially not after the way he just fucked me so hard that my legs are still shaking.

He stands still and watches me as I make my way off his porch and over to his truck, jumping inside.

I'm a total mess right now and the only thing I need is to escape before my mind drives me insane with thoughts I know will ruin me for good.

Frantically, I pull away, nearly sideswiping a car parked on the other side of the road. All this does is work me up even more, making me grab my chest as I fight to catch my breath.

I shouldn't be behind the wheel right now, and even that knowledge isn't enough to make me stay and admit the truth. He doesn't need to know who I am.

All I want to do is get as far away as I can before Jaxon sees how much of a wreck I am.

Before my old best friend can see I'm a lost cause not worth saving anymore.

As soon as I pull up at the bar, I jump out of Jaxon's truck and slam the door shut.

I notice Blaine outside smoking a cigarette, but the last thing I can do right now is socialize or even be around another person.

"Where's Jax? Everything okay?"

I hear his footsteps on the pavement behind me, so I turn around and throw Jax's keys at his head, before I dodge into my car and drive off in a hurry.

I don't bother to look back at him to see his reaction. I just drive, trying my best to concentrate on the road the best I can before the pills kick in.

Once that happens, mixed with the alcohol I won't be able to function. That's what I'm depending on, at least.

When I pull up at the house and park in the garage, I notice my roommate's car is gone and I don't see James' vehicle either, which means I'm completely alone to ruin myself in peace.

And that's exactly what I do.

A few more pills, mixed with more whiskey, and the next thing I know I'm waking up to my roommate's fingers down my throat.

"Let it out, dammit!"

I barely make out her yelling at me as I begin to come to a bit.

I gag as she shoves her fingers down my throat again until I'm puking all over them and the floor I passed out on.

"Good… good. There you go. We need to get this shit out of your system." She pats my back, while shoving her fingers in one last time, making me puke out more of the liquor and pills.

I'm not really sure what happened after that, because after puking my guts out I passed out again.

But in the midst of it all, I still somehow thought about Jax and what he would think if he saw me this way.

That's enough to make me wish I'll never wake up at all…

I'M STILL STANDING HERE MINUTES after she took off, trying to decide on my next move. My mind is racing from what the hell just went down.

The last thing I want is for her to feel threatened by me, but I also feel uneasy about her being out there alone, driving around upset.

I should've picked her ass up, threw her into my truck, and drove her home myself, but the look in her eyes told me she most likely would've ripped my head off for trying.

"Shit. Fuck it."

Grabbing my jacket, I slip it on and reach for the keys to my bike, before heading out the front door in hopes I can catch her before she leaves the bar.

As soon as I step outside, I take a moment to pull out a smoke and light it. I'm looking down at my cigarette as the flame lights when I notice something white on the porch step.

I slip my lighter back into my pocket and bend down to pick it up. I can tell right away the thick plastic card under the random receipts that must've fallen from her purse before she left is her ID. But since I'm in a hurry, I slip it into my pocket and rush over to my bike, straddling it.

I want to try and catch her before she gets too far away, because chances are, she might not even be heading to the address on the card and I need to make sure she's safe out here.

There are so many assholes on this side of town that I barely even feel safe being out here at night, and I can take care of myself.

The only reason I got a place over here was to be close to the bar in case Blaine screws up and I need to get there in a hurry.

I take off and head toward Savage & Ink. I make it a few minutes from the house when some asshole at a stoplight begins revving his engine at me, wanting to race.

Usually, I'd drop everything I'm doing at the chance to show some dickhead up, but the thought of not getting to her before it's too late has me feeling anxious. So, I give him the middle finger and take off, making a left turn toward the bar.

When I pull up, my eyes instantly land on my truck. My heart speeds up at the thought she might still be here, but it only takes me seconds to realize her car is gone.

"You missed her." Blaine's voice has me looking toward the door where he's locking up and reaching for a smoke. After lighting it with his Zippo, he tosses a set of keys at me. "She threw these at my head and took off. What did you do to the girl? Fuck, that shit hurt."

I steel my jaw and my first instinct is to give Blaine an earful, because usually when a girl throws something at his head it's because he fucked them and broke their heart. But unless he somehow screwed her against my truck in under two minutes, she most likely threw them at his head because she's mad at me.

"I didn't do shit. She ran off after we fucked."

He laughs, clearly amused by my current situation. I should kick the dickhead's ass. "I'd give her time to cool off, unless you want your dick ripped off." He smiles at me, while placing his smoke between his lips. "Were you that bad?"

Needing to calm my nerves, I reach into my jacket in search of a joint. Relief hits when I realize there's one left. "Hell no. She wanted me to be rough with her, so I was..." I walk up next to Blaine and lean against the building, beside him. "I warned her first that my rough might not be what she's used to. But I don't think that's what made her run."

He gives me a confused look before reaching for the joint as I pass it to him. "Did you say something stupid that pissed her off? We both know how easy it is for assholes like us to say the wrong thing."

I shake my head and release a frustrated breath, remembering the look on her face before she left. "Nah... I just told her what my name was. That's when she freaked out and stormed out of the house like she couldn't get away from me fast enough. I can't say I've ever had a woman run off on me after sex or hearing my damn name before."

"I can't say the same, brother." He slaps my shoulder and pushes away from the building, heading for his motorcycle. "I've got some shit to take care of. I'll catch you tomorrow."

I take another hit off the joint, watching as Blaine jumps on his bike and takes off.

I remain for minutes after, cooling off and trying to convince myself to just go back home and forget her for tonight when I remember her ID is in my pocket.

I toss the joint down and reach into my jacket, pulling the plastic out.

I'm already making my way to my motorcycle before I can even get the chance to see where it is that I'm headed.

Except it isn't the address on the card that has my world feeling as if it just imploded.

It's the name.

The one name that's enough to shake my whole fucking existence and leave me fighting for air.

"Alexandra Adams." I whisper the name a few times to be sure I'm not just imagining shit.

It's not until her name leaves my lips for the fifth time that I finally begin to believe my mind isn't playing tricks on me.

"Fuck!" I punch my motorcycle, letting my aggression out, before I kick it over and begin pacing around the parking lot, feeling as if I'm about to lose it.

She was right there in my house and I just let her leave. I let her walk out my door and watched her drive away.

The worst part of it all is the way I fucked her. I pounded into her as if she was nothing more than a hole to stick my cock in.

I was rough with her; when years ago I promised her I'd never be anything but gentle when it came to her.

Rage fills me and before I know it, I'm repeatedly slamming my fist into the side of the building, not giving a shit that I might've broken a finger or two.

I can't breathe or think right now.

And I can't take back tonight.

I can't take back the fact I carelessly fucked the one person I promised I'd always take care of but failed.

After I've calmed down enough to get my thoughts in order, I take another look at Alexandra's ID, hoping it'll lead me to her.

Instead of making progress, I drop to my knees and run my hands through my hair, feeling helpless, because the address on the card is an old one.

There's a good chance I won't see her again for a while, because now that she knows who I am, I doubt she'll be coming back to the bar or to my house.

For some reason she wants to hide from me and I want more than anything to find out why.

"Fuck this. I'm not letting you hide from me, Lex."

Ignoring my busted-up hand, I jump on my bike and take off in a hurry.

I drive around for a good hour, looking for her red car, but can't find it anywhere.

It sets me on fire with rage; angry with myself for not realizing it was her all along.

I need to get to her. I can't let her go again. It hurt way too much the first time and back then I was too young to do anything about it.

Not anymore.

The thought occurs to me there's a chance she's hiding her car, so I decide to give it a rest for the night and head back home.

I'm a few blocks away when the same car from earlier pulls up on my left side, fucking with me again.

"Come on, pussy. Show me how fast that piece of shit is!" he yells. "Unless you're chickenshit."

I have no shits to give right now, so this asshole is at the wrong place at the wrong damn time.

Kicking my stand down, I hop off my bike and walk over to his car, yanking the passenger side door open.

"What the hell! Are you crazy?"

"Yeah… something like that."

Before he has the chance to come up with the bright idea of driving off, I shift his car into park and grab him by the throat, squeezing as I get up in his face.

"Fuck with me again and I will snap this twig of yours in half. Got it, motherfucker?"

He nods, gripping at my hand, attempting to pull it away.

"Say it!" I yell in his face, while squeezing tighter.

"I got. I got it." He begins coughing as soon as I release his throat.

"Now fuck off," I growl out, before slamming his door shut and straddling my bike.

With the way I'm feeling right now, this asshole is lucky I gave him a second chance.

The beast inside of me is ready to take out anyone who stands in my way of getting to Alexandra. Or anyone who even so much as looks in my direction while I'm trying to get to her.

I'm going to find her, and once I do, I won't let her get away. Not for a third damn time...

JAX

FOURTEEN YEARS AGO... TWELVE YEARS OLD

I ASKED ALEXANDRA TO MEET me here tonight as soon as she gets a chance to sneak out of her house.

I've been waiting for over an hour now and even though it's getting cold and late, I don't want to leave until I see her.

I would've had her meet me at my house like she usually does, but my mom's dealer, Jasper, has been hanging out there a lot lately and I refuse to let him take advantage of Alexandra's weakness and twist her up like my mother.

There's an old school bus in the woods that's been here for as long as I can remember, so I decided it'd be the best place for us to hide where no one would come looking.

I'm pretty sure she remembers how to get here.

I hope she does, at least, or else I'll worry about her the whole night and not be able to fall asleep again.

Finally, I sit up from the seat and look toward the front of the bus when I hear Alexandra step inside and close the door behind her.

"Hey, Jax." She shivers and takes a seat beside me, scooting in close, until her long, pale hair is hanging over my jacket. "I almost forgot how creepy it is out here at night. I kept hearing noises that scared me."

I yank my hat off, feeling like an idiot. "I should've met you outside the woods. I'm sorry for being such a jerk. You could've gotten hurt because of me. That's the same as me hurting you, Lex."

"You're not a jerk, Jax." She grabs my arm and holds it against her. "You're never mean. You're really nice all the time. You're the nicest person I know and I know you'd never hurt me. Ever."

The thought of me ever being rough or hurting her makes my heart sink. "I could never be rough with you or hurt you. I'd hate it and myself if I was ever anything but kind and gentle with you, Lex. You mean too much to me."

She gives me a saddened look and squeezes my arm tighter. "I'd hate it too, Jax. Because you're the only one who takes care of me. If that ever changed then I wouldn't have anyone left in this world to keep me safe. Or anyone who probably even cares about me."

Hearing her say those words makes me want to puke. I feel physically ill at the thought of not taking care of her and always protecting her from assholes who want to hurt her.

"Shhh, Lex. I'll always be gentle and keep you safe, so let's not talk about it anymore. Okay?" I grab her head and pull it down onto my shoulder. I can't stand to look at the bruise on her face that still hasn't gone away. It hurts my chest. "Do you want to talk?"

She shakes her head.

"Then we don't have to for a while. We can just sit here together."

"I'd like that."

"Me too."

We sit here in silence for a while, just enjoying being with each other, until Alexandra stands up and grabs my hand. "Let's go play on that old tire swing down by the river."

Keeping ahold of her hand, I stand up and lead us off the bus and toward the river.

It's so dark I can barely see where I'm going, but we've been to the tire swing enough times I could probably find the place with my eyes closed.

Once we reach the spot, I stop and look over at Alexandra's face just so I can see it light up like it does every time we come here.

"It's all yours, Lex."

She lets out her cute little laugh and runs toward the old tire. It's been a few weeks since we've been here and I hate it, because I know it's one of her favorite spots.

I always push while she swings, because no one else ever has. When I'm with Alexandra, my goal is to make sure she's happy, because I know she's unhappy at home and it's not fair.

Her shitty dad should know her happiness is supposed to always come before his.

I'm not even thirteen yet and even I know how girls should be treated. Boys are supposed to take care of girls and protect them.

"Come on, Jax!" She leans her head back to look at me. "Give me a good one this time. You don't have to be afraid of me falling. I'm not eight anymore."

She's the bravest girl I know and probably even the bravest eleven-year-old I know.

"Okay, Lex. Hold on tight, okay." I grab the bottom of the tire and pull it back as far as it will allow me to. "You holding on?"

"Yes! Let it go!"

I run forward and let go of the swing once it's above my head.

We stay here for a while, until I begin to worry that her dad will wake up. "I think we should go now, Lex. I don't want your dad waking up and finding out you're not in your bed."

"What about your mom? Do you think she's worried?"

I shake my head and grab for her hand. "No. She doesn't really worry about me."

She gives my hand a squeeze. "Is your mom still high?"

I nod my head. "She's sick and probably always will be."

"I never see her come out of her room or leave the house to go shopping. My dad is drunk all the time but always leaves the house to go to the store and stuff. He's there almost every day because he needs more beer."

"When she needs something from the store, she sends me. It's only a few blocks from the house, so I walk there. Have been since before I met you."

"Isn't the stuff heavy to carry?"

I shrug. "Sometimes."

"You'll just end up being strong from carrying things all the time. So, I guess that's not bad."

"Not really. I'm used to it now, so I don't really think about it."

When we get to her house, I stop and hold her back from walking. "I want to make sure your dad isn't awake. Let me go to your window first. Stay here."

She nods and stays back at the street as I quietly make my way around the back of the house. I always tell her to leave her window open after she climbs out so there's less of a chance of her closing it too hard and waking her dad up.

I poke my head inside her window and listen for any noise. When I don't hear any, I walk back to the street and grab Alexandra's hand. "He's asleep."

"Are you sure?" She pulls me back from walking. "Last time

he woke up he beat me with his belt. I don't want him to hurt me again."

I hate her dad so much. I would hurt him if I could.

"I'm sure." I tug on her hand to get her walking again. "Do you trust me?"

She nods. "Yes."

It feels good hearing her say yes.

"Good, Lex. I promise I'll always look out for you."

Luckily her bedroom window is close to the ground and really easy to climb into without making too much noise.

Once she gets inside, I carefully close the window most of the way, before I lean down and talk through the opened part.

"I'll meet you here tomorrow night once I know it's safe. Okay?"

"You promise?"

"I promise. No more meeting me in the woods. I'll come to you."

"Okay." She gives me the same saddened look she gives me every time we have to say goodbye. "Bye, Jax."

"Bye, Lex."

I close the window the rest of the way and then stand outside for a while just to make sure her dad doesn't wake up before she falls asleep.

"Goodnight, Lex," I whisper, before walking away.

Saying goodbye to Alexandra is just as hard for me as it is for her, but I have to stay strong for her. Always...

JAX

THREE DAYS HAVE PASSED SINCE Alexandra ran off on me and despite me spending countless hours searching for her, I've yet to find her.

There's a weight on my chest getting heavier with each passing second that I'm left wondering where she is, and I'm not sure how much more of the pressure I can take before I lose my shit and explode.

The fact that she doesn't want to be found hurts like hell. It's fucking killing me and I'd do anything to change that. I'd do anything to have her want to be near me like when we were kids.

It's been a long time since she moved away and I know a lot has changed, that she has changed, but so have I. That doesn't mean I still wouldn't do anything and everything to keep her safe. That hasn't changed.

I need her to see this.

"You good, brother?" I look away from the fireplace and up

at Royal as he takes the spot beside me and looks into the flames.

I came here for dinner and still don't feel like leaving, because I know it's only going to lead to more disappointment.

"Not at all, brother," I admit. "I'm far from it." I squeeze the glass in my hand, before looking down to realize I've finished off my sixth glass of whiskey in just under an hour. I used to think I was good when it came to dealing with hurt and disappointment, until it came to Alexandra. I learned then that I'm horrible at dealing with it; a complete wreck. "She's out there somewhere and I have no clue how to get to her. I'm about to lose my shit on every breathing thing. I'm only holding on by a thread."

Royal releases a long breath and grips my shoulder for support. He knows all about Alexandra and how deep my feelings for her go. I met Royal less than a year after she disappeared, so he was lucky enough to listen to me constantly bitch about her absence for the first two years of our friendship. "You'll find her. You're like me; we don't give up when it comes to something that means everything to us, and it's clear she's that one for you." He squeezes my shoulder harder. "We're destructive when we're hurting and it may be painful as shit, but that only pushes us harder. Me, you, and Blaine are all the fucking same."

"I don't disagree there. Not one damn bit."

My attention is pulled toward the door at the sound of tiny footsteps slowly approaching. On the inside I may be dying, but the moment my gaze lands on Kylie's sleepy face, I put all of my pain and anger aside and smile down at her. "What are you doing up, beautiful?"

She shrugs tiredly and begins walking to Royal with her arms up.

His face lights up as he bends down to scoop her into his arms and hold her close. The wholeness and happiness he feels when around his family makes my chest ache with longing for the same thing. I only ever felt that when Alexandra was around and the day she got ripped away, all hope of feeling that way again died.

But she's back now.

I just don't know where and it hurts so fucking bad.

"You can't sleep, angel?" Royal asks in a whisper, before kissing the top of Kylie's head tenderly. "Daddy will lay down with you until you fall asleep. Say goodnight to Uncle Jax."

Kylie holds her arms out and grabs my face when Royal brings her in close to me. "Goodnight, Uncle Jax. I love you."

I smile and kiss her nose. "Love you, beautiful girl."

Royal pulls her tight against his chest and begins rubbing her head to relax her. "I've gotta take care of my family." He gives me a stern look, his gaze lowering to the empty glass in my hand. "And that includes you too. Sleep on the couch."

I nod as he walks away, because I know there's no arguing with Royal. Twelve years of friendship has shown me that.

Pouring myself another glass, I take a seat on the couch and stare off into darkness. I don't know how many more drinks I pour, but I keep them coming for a while, until I finally manage to black out.

BOWING MY HEAD, I SQUEEZE the thick white plastic in my hand and swallow thickly. I've been staring at this thing off and on for nearly ninety-six hours and the look on Alexandra's face still haunts me to my fucking core each time.

She looks broken; ripped apart by the fucking world and I can't help but to think I could've somehow prevented that look if I had been around to take care of her like I promised.

I hate that.

"Can I get another beer?"

Without looking up to see who's been trying to get my attention, I slam down the bottle of whiskey I've been drinking from and step out from behind the bar.

I walk around in a daze, feeling completely out of it as I hold out Alexandra's ID and begin questioning everyone in the bar, hoping someone has seen her.

I'll do this every damn night if I have to, because apparently driving around and looking for her car isn't doing the trick.

With every "no" I feel the anxiety inside me build, getting closer and closer to becoming explosive.

"Are you sure?" I ask gruffly as I move on to the next person. "Take another look. She was just in here four days ago."

"I said no, Jax. Calm the hell down and let me enjoy my beer. Shit." Max has told me this three times now, but it still doesn't seem to be good enough.

After pushing a bit more I move on, making my way around the room, but apparently all of these assholes are just as clueless as I am when it comes to her.

Frustration takes over as I make my way back to the bar; about to grip the bottle of whiskey I so desperately need right now.

"You said she was in here four days ago?"

Pulling my hands out of my hair, I turn behind me and look toward the guy currently bending over the pool table. "Yeah, that's right."

A tiny smirk pulls up at the corner of his lips right as he takes his shot. "Red hair... sexy as sin with tattoos and a sassy mouth?"

My heart slams against my chest at the description of her and I find myself stalking over to the pool table, ready to choke any answers out of this asshole if necessary.

Once I'm standing in front of him, I grab him by the shirt and pull him in close, desperate as hell to find out what he knows. "Where the fuck did you see her?"

"...another beer up here, asshole. I'm tired of asking nicely," the guy at the bar says, continuing to try for my attention.

I ignore the prick waiting for a drink and grip the guy's shirt tighter, pushing for an answer. "Tell me!"

I have no patience left.

I'm two seconds away from going murderous on this roomful of people. It's taking a lot of restraint to keep my cool right now.

"Chill... okay. I'll tell you. Just take it easy, man."

"Can I get that damn beer? I'm thirsty over here."

Growling out, I release the shirt of the guy in front of me and walk over to the bar to get the thirsty motherfucker a drink.

I pull a beer from the cooler and set it down in front of him, before elbowing him in the jaw and slamming his face down onto the bar. "Interrupt me again and I'll shoot you in the fucking dick."

He groans out in pain and grips the bar.

"Are we clear?" I growl beside his ear.

"Okay... got it. Got it. We're cool."

"Good." I release the back of his head and look over to see the guy at the pool table watching me with wide eyes. "You got a fucking answer for me or am I going to need to shoot it out of you?"

"Midnight Joe's," he says on a swallow. "She bartends there. Saw her there tonight before I came here."

The whole room is spinning as I exit the bar to find Blaine. I can barely see straight because all I want to do is get to Alexandra.

Blaine is finishing a tattoo on one of his regulars when I poke my head in the room. "Watch the bar. I'll be back."

His head shoots up as I'm about to back out and shut the door. "Dude, I'm in the middle of a—"

"I don't fucking care!" I yell. "Watch it."

"Everything good?" He drops the tattoo machine and jumps to his feet, as if ready to leave with me if I need him.

"Yeah. I just have something important to do." I put my hand out, stopping him as he takes a step toward me. "Stay here, man. One of us needs to watch the bar. Don't. Leave."

"Shit," he growls under his breath. "You better call me if you need my ass. I'll get Mark here if I need to."

I nod and step out of the room, anxious to get to Midnight Joe's as quickly as possible.

Once outside, I straddle my bike and take off, nearly crashing into a passing truck. "Son of a bitch!" I stop and place my feet down, taking a few seconds to compose myself before I take off again, being sure not to almost kill myself this time.

I get to the bar in record time, due to weaving through traffic and rolling through as many stop signs as I can. Excitement and anxiety course through me at the possibility of seeing Alexandra again, but the moment I realize her little red car isn't in the parking lot, an ache hits me in the chest.

Just ten minutes ago I thought I had the answer I needed to see her tonight. I'm not sure I can handle not seeing her now.

I stand here with my hands in my messy hair and cuss under my breath, before I reach for a smoke, my hands shaking from my nerves.

I didn't prepare for her not to be here, and leaving here empty-handed is the last thing I want to do. I've waited too long to get to her for it not to be tonight.

Taking a few quick hits off my smoke, I watch the door as if I expect her to come out any second, which is ridiculous. I need a new plan.

I don't care if it takes me roughing someone up to get her address, I'm getting to her any way I can and I'll destroy anyone who stands in my way.

My attention goes back to the door when I hear two drunken idiots talking loudly as they step outside. One of them

I recognize from Savage & Ink. He used to show up nearly every night but I haven't seen him there in months.

"Can you believe that shit?" the familiar one yells out in anger, holding his hand over his nose. "That redheaded bitch hit me."

My ears perk up at the mention of red hair and it has me flicking my cigarette across the parking lot, ready to listen to what these pricks have to say.

"I warned you to keep your hands to yourself, dumbass, but you had to go and grope her anyway. I told you she's a crazy bitch."

This asshole chose the wrong person to discuss this shit around. I take wide strides toward the door, pausing just long enough to slam this prick's head into the building and give him a word of advice. "You should listen to your friend next time."

"Shit! You're going to pay for that." He pushes away from the building as if he's about to come at me, but stops once he sees who I am. "My bad, Jax. I won't touch her again. It was stupid and—"

I give him a hard look, stopping his stupid mouth from saying anything else that might piss me off. I don't have time to waste on him.

With a small growl, I yank the door open and step inside. I tense as I look around, taking in all the rowdy assholes filling the place. The idea of her waiting on these pricks has my blood boiling and the urge to take her away from this dump strong.

Desperate to get to her, I push my way through the crowd, not caring who I have to remove from my path.

"Hey, watch it, prick," the big guy I just pushed past growls out. "Yeah, that's right. Walk away like a little bitch before you get hurt."

His words have me stopping mid-step and turning around to face him. What this sorry motherfucker doesn't know is he's slowing me down from getting to Alexandra and I have no shits to give right now. I'll rip his world apart without batting a fucking eye.

Trying to be tough for his little friends, he tosses his beer down, rolls up his sleeves and comes at me. "You're going learn not to dis—"

Before he can finish what he's saying, my elbow connects hard with his jaw, knocking him back and into a table. He doesn't have time to even see me coming before I'm over him, gripping his throat tightly. "I'm not going to learn shit. Learn that, motherfucker."

He begins coughing and fighting for air as I squeeze tighter and lean in close to his face. "Get in the way of me getting what I want again and I'll come find you and end your life before you ever know I'm there."

He stares up at me with wide eyes, clearly not expecting someone around here to be crazier than he is. He may be used to being the big guy here, but that's about to change.

After releasing his throat, I stand up and look down at him as he grabs his throat and fights to catch his breath.

I flex my jaw and watch him for a few seconds, before fixing my jacket and walking away so I don't make the mistake of killing him.

I'm on fire, rage coursing through my veins, and when it comes to Alexandra I've never been able to control the beast inside.

I push my way past a few more drunken assholes, before my gaze finally sets on Alexandra behind the bar, talking to some guy.

Holy fuck...

I can't breathe as I stand here looking at her. She's so painfully beautiful, and seeing some other guy talking to her has me wanting to kick everyone out of the bar so we can be alone.

I want the world to know I'll protect her until my last

breath, and at a place like this, she's going to need me to, even though she won't ever admit it.

I'll take on this whole fucking room for her, before carrying her away kicking and screaming if I have to.

She's gotten feisty as hell over the years, but that won't stop me from throwing her over my shoulder if that's what it takes.

Even if that means I have to deal with her kicking my ass all the way to my bike, because there's no way in hell I'm leaving her in this dump.

Especially since some asshole at the bar seems to think he's allowed to put his hands on her.

He's about to find out otherwise...

ALEXANDRA

THE ONLY THING I WANT to do is forget about the last few days and make it through this shift without having to take my heel off and shove it through some asshole's throat for being handsy with me.

These dicks don't seem to be getting the memo tonight, because I've been fighting them off since walking through that door a few hours ago.

The last one hitting on me actually had enough balls to grab my ass when I went to reach for a pen for him to sign his credit card bill.

If it wouldn't be hard for someone like me to find a better job—a decent one that doesn't involve drunken assholes—I would walk out that door right now and never look back. I despise this place.

I can't do that, though. I need to save enough money to get a place of my own, where I can be alone when I want. A girl needs to have her own space to escape when necessary.

I've never had the luxury of a hideaway from the outside

world that I can exist in without someone being in the next room over.

That's why I'm here. This is the only place I've imagined that possibility, because the only time I ever felt peace, even for just a few hours a night, was here, with Jax—the place he grew up.

I was certain my assumptions were right and Jax had taken off. With nothing to keep him here, I figured he had moved on to another town after all these years. Finding out the guy who had been making me feel something since the moment I walked into Savage & Ink was him, sent me into complete breakdown mode.

The rawness of my throat from Tessa having to shove her fingers down it is a harsh reminder of how far gone I was to numb the pain.

The sad part about that is it's not the first time I've needed saving from myself, and it won't be the last.

Lying in bed the next morning, it took me hours staring up at the ceiling to get my head on straight and remember the details from the night before.

Savage & Ink.

A motorcycle ride.

Rough sex with the bartender.

The bartender that was in fact Jax...

My Jax.

As soon as the last thought popped into my head, I leaned over the side of the bed and tossed up whatever was left inside my stomach.

It smelt and tasted like whiskey from the night before, which only had me wanting to vomit even more, but there was nothing left to throw up. It left me dry heaving, which hurt like hell.

But that pain was nothing compared to the ache I felt in my heart when I took off to get away from Jax.

That night was never supposed to happen. I was nowhere near prepared to see Jax again. Not when I already made myself believe I'd never see him again.

When I went home with the bartender and asked him to be rough with me, it was supposed to help take my mind off Jax and remind me the man I was about to sleep with was nothing like him. That he wasn't sweet and caring like my Jax always was when it came to me.

Instead, all it did was show me that Jax is now a rough, dangerous man who fucks like a beast in the bedroom.

As good as it felt physically—trust me, it was the best sex of my entire life—it was never supposed to be that way with him.

When I was younger, I always imagined a life with a happy ending, where Jax and I would grow up and get married and he'd be kind and gentle with me just like he always promised.

But that didn't happen.

My father tore me away from him.

Now, the only thing I've been able to think about is Jax, and the more I think about him... the more I want to go to him and break down in his strong arms.

I can't do that.

Jax had it hard his whole life taking care of his depressed, junkie mother; trying to save her when no one else gave a shit, and it killed him every second of every day.

I can't and won't be the one to hurt him like she did. My depression runs just as deep as hers, and sometimes I can't get out of bed for days. Why put that on him? Why make him go through something that difficult again when he doesn't have to?

He deserves so much better than what I've become and I'm terrified of the way he'll react if he ever finds out who I am. That I was the girl he slammed against the door and fucked hard until my legs gave out.

What if he hates that he took me home with him?

What if he hates himself for having sex with the girl he used to protect?

And worst of all, what if he hates the person I've become and wants nothing to do with me?

Jax hating me is the worst possible thing that could ever happen to me.

My thoughts have me panicking, so I reach in my pocket for another pill and wash it down with the shot of whiskey in front of me. Doesn't matter how many pills I've popped over the last few days, because nothing seems to be working other than passing out, which unfortunately, I can't do right now.

Closing my eyes, I take a few deep breaths, trying to gain control of my thoughts, but they're going haywire.

Images of Jax slamming me against the door keep overriding everything else, stirring up my emotions all over again.

His hard, muscled body thrusting me up the polished wood. His perfect teeth digging into my lips as he growled out his need for me.

The way it felt when he first slammed into me, his thickness filling me to the max.

Jax Kade was inside of me and I'll never be able to erase those memories, no matter how hard I try. No amount of drugs or alcohol will ever be enough to make me forget him. I know this because I've tried everything in my power to.

If I care about him as much as I used to I'll stay out of his life before my depression and sick habits drag him down with me.

I'm just not sure I can stay away, though. I've never been able to, even when I knew my father would beat me for sneaking out to see him. And he beat me good and hard, making me bleed at times from the blow of his belt.

I don't know what makes me think I can do it now.

But for him… I'll try, because he means more to me than anything in this entire world.

Beautiful Jax... the name still suits him after all these years, except now he's a beautiful savage.

Pouring myself another shot, I swallow it back and set the empty glass down in front of me. I don't know how I'm going to do this. I don't know how I'm going to go on when everything inside me hurts.

And it's not the same deep ache I've been feeling over the last thirteen years. It's so much more now; now that I've had him in a way I never had before. It's that feeling of everything inside of me being crushed over and over again until there's nothing left of me.

I know where Jax is. I know where he works, where he lives, yet I can't go to him. Talk about dying a slow and painful death.

Grabbing a towel, I distract myself by cleaning up, but a couple customers causing a scene has me cussing under my breath, and hoping I don't have to call the cops to force them to stop fighting.

I'm in no condition to deal with the law right now, so I ignore it and hope it fixes itself. It usually does.

"Right here, babe." When I look over Jim is holding up his empty glass. He's been here since before shift change and I don't like the way he's been looking at me since I walked behind the bar. "One more and I'll take the bill."

I nod and grab a new glass, filling it with his choice of beer, before quickly dropping it off and printing out his tab.

When I give it to him, he touches my arm in a way that has me feeling sick to my stomach. I know that touch and what it means, because I've felt it from many guys before.

"Don't fucking touch me," I grind out, yanking my arm from his reach. "Keep your hands on that beer where they belong."

"My bad," he mutters, bringing the glass to his lips. "You shouldn't look so sexy if you don't want me to notice, bitch."

I bite my tongue and walk away, wanting to make it through this shitty night the best I can.

I really need some air right about now. Releasing a frustrated breath, I reach into my purse for a joint and step out from behind the bar. When I look toward the exit, I notice it's crowded with people stepping outside.

"What the hell is going on?"

I look around, trying to figure out what the deal is, and that's when my eyes land on an angry Jax, standing in the middle of the room. He looks on edge as his eyes scan behind the bar until they finally set on me.

I can't breathe and my chest feels as if it's going to explode from the pressure of emotions bursting inside me.

With each step he takes toward me, my heart beats faster and faster until the only thing I can focus on is the pounding of my heart.

Why is Jax here and why must he be so painfully beautiful? I can't take it.

His gaze stays locked on mine as he continues to come toward me, and I know from the hurt look in his eyes that he's figured out who I am.

I don't know when or how, but he did, and the knowledge of that has me fighting to breathe.

The screeching of the stool beside me, moving across the floor as Jim stands up to leave, isn't even enough to have Jax and me looking away from each other. It's not until Jim opens his mouth to say something stupid that Jax brings his attention to him.

"Here's your tip, you dumb bitch. Not that you deserve one."

"You want to repeat what the fuck you just said?" Jax stops and cracks his neck once he's standing right behind Jim.

The sound of Jax's intimidating voice has Jim spinning around to look at him. The lethal look in Jax's eyes as he stares him down almost has me worried for Jim's safety, and that's saying something, because I hate that piece of shit. But anyone who has the pleasure of pissing Jax off is one unlucky bastard.

I've witnessed his wrath a few times already and it isn't pretty.

"I called her a dumb bitch for talking to me as if she's b—"

Before Jim can finish his sentence, Jax is in his face, pressing a knife to his throat. "Finish that sentence and it'll be the last thing that ever leaves your mouth."

"Oh shit... take it easy," Jim mutters, his eyes pleading with Jax not to cut him. "I'll leave. I'll go right now. It's just drunk talk. That's it. It didn't mean shit."

"Good fucking plan," Jax says on a growl, giving him a shove so he's up on his feet. "Learn some manners when speaking to women."

Jim nods and scrambles to grab his wallet, before rushing toward the door.

As soon as he's out of sight, Jax's attention suffocates me again, his eyes taking me in as if he can't stop looking at me. "We need to fucking talk."

The moment Jax pulls off his leather jacket, revealing the two pistols in his shoulder holster, I'm completely done for.

Holy hell, he makes that holster look sexy.

As much as I know I shouldn't want to see him, the sight of him has everything inside of me coming alive just like when we were kids.

He's always been able to make me feel so many things, and the fact that all these years haven't changed that is terrifying.

It's terrifying because I know losing him again will hurt just as much as the first time, if not more, and I barely survived it back then.

I want to go to him. I want to run into his arms and hope like hell that he still wants me there, but I fight the urge as he turns around toward the exit.

"Everyone out!" he yells, his voice deep and intimidating, getting the attention of everyone still left inside. "Now!"

From the way the rest of the room rushes to do what he

says, I'm guessing they notice the guns strapped to him. They're hard to miss.

"What are you doing here?" I question once he turns back around. "How did you find me?" My voice cracks as he comes toward me, but I manage to get the words out.

He ignores my questions, his jaw flexing as he backs me against the wall and places his hands on my face. "Did you really think you could hide from me, Lex?"

I swallow, unable to get any words out as he bows his head to look down at me.

"Did you?" he questions, firmer this time. "Fucking answer me."

"Yeah," I whisper. My answer has him moving his arms around to cage me in. It's as if he's showing me that there's no escaping this time. "I didn't think you'd find out who I was or even care."

He lets out an angry growl, before reaching into his jacket and pulling something out. "You dropped this on my porch when running from me." His eyes stay on me, watching as I grab the plastic from his hand and look down at it. I hadn't even realized my license was missing. "Thirteen fucking years I've waited to have you here in front of me and all you can do is run from me?"

The sound of hurt and betrayal in Jax's voice has me wanting to lose it. "I can't do this, Jax." I attempt to push him away from me, needing some space to breathe, but he doesn't budge. He just moves in closer, until there's no space between us. "Jax, move. Now. I mean it."

"No," he growls. "I'm not moving so you can run again, dammit."

"Fine." I push his chest again and grunt. "I'll move you my damn self then." I continue to push at his hard chest, but he refuses to budge. Frustration takes over that he won't let me go.

"Fuck you!" I scream, my emotions getting the best of me. "Get the hell out of my way and let me leave."

His eyes soften as he looks down at the emotional wreck in front of him and I expect him to move so I can walk away, but he surprises me by pulling me into his arms.

He holds me tight. Tighter than he ever has before, and I find myself falling into him, wanting the comfort and safety he's always provided.

"I'm not going anywhere without you," he whispers into my hair. "Either you're coming home with me or I'm following you home. Which is it?"

I can't breathe in his arms, because every emotion I've been fighting to keep in over the last thirteen years comes rushing out, and I feel like I'm about to have a panic attack.

"Neither, Jax." I shove his arm out of my way and attempt to walk away, but he pulls me back to him, pressing his hard body against mine again.

"Which is it?" he growls against my lips. "I'll make the decision if I have to, Lex."

The fierceness and determination in his eyes tells me he's not letting me go without a fight, so I make the better decision of the two. The one that will still allow me an escape if needed. I'm not ready for him to know where I live. "I'll go with you."

"Good." He nods, his gaze lowering to my lips. The way he licks his bottom one while looking at mine has my insides heating up with need. "I'll call Mark to make sure this place gets locked up for the night, because you won't be coming back."

Clearly, this man is nothing like the Jax I remember, and I have a feeling that's going to make it even harder to stay away...

JAX

THE ONLY THING I CAN think about at this very moment is how it would feel to taste her lips, knowing that it's her this time. It's damn hard not to lean in and pull her bottom lip between my teeth to find out.

"You don't need to call your cop friend. I think I can handle locking up for the night. I've done it plenty of times without any help, Jax."

The sound of my name leaving her lips makes my heart speed up just like every other time she's said it since I walked through that door looking for her.

It's been so long since hearing it come from her. She was the first one to ever call me Jax and the only one for the longest time.

Until Royal came along.

"Yeah…" I pull my gaze away from her lips, needing to get her out of here as quickly as possible before she changes her mind and decides to fight me on leaving again. "But with all the unpaid drinks you're leaving behind, I think it's best if Mark deals with the owner. Let's go."

She doesn't look pleased, but reaches for her purse and heads toward the door anyway. "Looks like the bossy part of your nickname still applies. Let's go then, bossy bartender."

My lips curve into a small smile at her sassiness. It still makes me want to exhaust her body; except more now that I know it's her.

It may be wrong for me to still want her sexually, knowing she's Lex, but the savage in me wants to make it so that I'll be the only one to ever be inside her again. It should've only been me to begin with, and would've been had she not been ripped from me.

I adjust my erection and exit the door before she can get too far out of sight. Once outside I send a quick text to Mark asking him to take care of this place.

When I look up from my phone, Alexandra is standing in front of a little black car, watching me, while smoking a joint.

She never used to get high when we were kids, but we're both different people now, grown up, and I'm dead set on finding out who she is after all these years; even though she seems determined not to give me that option.

Looks like I'll have to take it.

Shoving my phone into my pocket, I walk up to her and grab the joint from her hand as she goes to take another hit.

She gets ready to say something, but me moving in close and studying her lips as I bring the weed to mine has her watching me in silence.

After a few seconds her gaze moves from my mouth to roam over the rest of me. My dark wild hair, beard, and tattoos. I know she's taking them all in, trying to figure out how I've changed so much since the last time we saw each other. I look savage and wild. Dangerous to most. I know that.

It's amazing what years of struggle can do to a boy when the one person he can't live without is no longer around to keep him level.

"We'll take my bike and come back for whoever's car this is tomorrow," I state, blowing the smoke up into the air, before looking back down at her.

With her eyebrows scrunched together, she takes the joint back from me and laughs. "Tomorrow? No one said we'll be together tomorrow. I only said I'd leave with you. That's it."

I tilt my head down and move in so that when I speak, it'll be against her lips. "I did."

She swallows and takes a quick breath, before stepping back. "I'll follow you in Tessa's car and I'll leave when I want."

Her fighting me has frustration kicking in. "I haven't set eyes on you in too fucking long, Lex. The least you can do after asking me to fuck you and running off when you realized it was me is to give me tonight."

She doesn't say anything for several seconds, and I can't help but wonder if she's thinking about how good that night felt just as I am.

"Fine." She snatches the joint from me, takes one last hit, and tosses it on the blacktop. "But I don't want to talk about the past. I can't."

"We don't have to talk about shit tonight as long as you're with me."

"Okay," she whispers, nodding her head. "I think I can handle that."

When we get across the parking lot to my bike, she runs her hand over the scratches in the side from when I kicked my bike over.

"What happened?" she questions, worry in her tone. "Were you in a wreck?"

I shake my head and straddle my bike, before kicking the stand up. "Nope. You happened when you ran off on me."

She doesn't say anything, but I can see the guilt in her eyes, before she turns away and climbs on behind me, wrapping her arms around my waist.

It feels good having her wrapped around me on the back of my bike. Feels natural, like she was meant to be there all along. I could get used to this feeling. Which is going to make it even harder that she's set on pushing me away.

I'm careful when pulling out of the parking lot this time, taking it slow back to my place, wanting to keep her safe since I left my helmet at home this morning.

Truthfully, I wasn't expecting to have her on the back of my bike again for a long time. I was almost starting to believe that she left town again.

We pull up outside of my place, and although Alexandra is taking her time getting off my bike, probably not wanting me to notice, I do.

For a moment, it felt as if she didn't want to let go of me. I could be wrong about that, but I'm choosing to believe otherwise.

"You do realize I can handle that place, right?"

I flex my jaw and turn around to face her. "That's not the point," I say, before walking away.

She quickly follows through the grass behind me, stopping once we reach the porch. "Then tell me what it is then."

I ignore her long enough to shove my key into the lock and push the door open. "You shouldn't have to handle a place like that, Lex, and I don't want you dealing with the assholes that drink there."

She pushes past me and walks inside, before she tosses her purse down on the couch and angrily turns around to face me when I close the door behind me. "You have no idea about the shit I've had to deal with over the years, Jax. I've been taking care of myself since I was sixteen."

"Is that when you got away from your shit father?"

The mention of her father has her reaching over to the

coffee table for the bottle of whiskey I left there last night. She unscrews the cap and brings it to her lips before speaking. "Seventeen. I left when I was seventeen, but that asshole finally left me alone when I turned sixteen." She tilts the bottle back and takes a long drink. "I haven't seen or spoken to him since."

I walk over and grab the bottle from her, needing a drink my damn self. That was three more years that she had to deal with her asshole father mistreating her and I wasn't there to stop it. Had they not moved away, I could've put a stop to it sooner.

I might've been too young and too small when I first attempted to save her with my bat, but I would've kept trying until I could get him to stop.

Closing my eyes, I tilt the bottle back, taking a long drink.

I have a feeling we're going to need a second one to make it through the night now that her piece of shit father is in the back of our minds.

"Let's go out back and get some air." Before she has time to argue, I take off through the kitchen and snatch up a second bottle, before making my way outside.

I pull up the only two chairs I own at the moment and take a seat in one, before setting the bottles down and running my hands through my hair.

The last thing I want to do is be a dick to Alexandra and tell her what to do, but being firm with her might be the only way to keep her here longer.

She's hiding from me.

A few minutes later, I look up at the sound of Alexandra opening and shutting the door.

Her eyes are laced with guilt as they meet mine momentarily. Almost as if she's done something she's not proud of and is too ashamed to look at me. It has my stomach twisting into knots.

"Everything good?" I question warily as she takes a seat in the chair beside me and reaches for the second bottle.

"Yup. Good. Everything is good."

"Don't lie to me, Lex. You never did in the past, so I don't know why you'd start now."

"Jax, don't," she says sternly. "I said everything is good and I meant it. I've had a long night and I'm just tired."

"Okay, sorry." I run a hand through my hair, looking at her as she takes a sip from the bottle. "You know it's always been natural for me to worry about you."

"I know," she says quietly. "But can we just sit here and look at the stars? I just need to relax and clear my head."

I nod and sit back, getting as comfortable as I can.

We sit here for a while, not saying anything at all. It reminds me of old times when all we needed was to be together. There were times when we sat in silence for hours, feeling happy and at peace knowing that we were together.

This almost feels like that, except there's so much to be said it has my chest aching each time I look her way, but I won't push her tonight. She's here with me and that's enough... for now.

The vibration of my phone breaks the silence, and as late as it is, I know without looking who it is.

"Everything good, Blaine?"

"For now, man." His voice comes through tired and stressed. "Just leaving your mom's. Her place is a disaster and there's barely any food in the fridge. Want me to run to the store?"

"Goddammit," I growl, running my hand over my face in frustration. "It's only been a few days since I was there. I stocked her fridge and cleaned up. Was anyone there with her?"

"She was alone and passed out on the couch. I didn't find any needles or pills, just weed and alcohol. Your mom must be throwing some wild parties or some shit."

"I'll go in the morning and take care of things. Thanks for checking on her, man. Appreciate it."

"Anytime, brother. Talk later."

I toss my phone down in anger, cussing under my breath. My mom has managed to stay clean for six years now. She was doing great until about two months ago.

As far as I know she's just been partying and drinking herself to sleep each night, but there's that part of me that worries she's using again.

"Your mom?" Alexandra questions.

I nod and tug on my hair, fighting to keep my cool. "She's still a mess, except now she's out partying, stressing me the fuck out."

"Some people will always need saving," she says on almost a whisper. "I've seen a lot of messed up people over the last few weeks at the bar. Makes me wonder if she was one of them."

My heart stops at the mention of three weeks. I hadn't even stopped to think of how long she's possibly been back. "How long?" I question.

She takes another sip, before turning back to face me. "I just told you how long."

"No." I shake my head and grab the bottle from her. "How long have you been back in town?"

"Almost a month. Does it really matter?"

"Fuck yes it does." I pause to gather my shit and keep cool. "And did you know?" I ask stiffly.

She looks me over before finally answering. "I thought you were gone, Jax. I drove by your old house and it was empty. You look nothing like when we were kids, so no... the answer is no."

My heart speeds up as I ask the next question. "Were you planning to ever look for me?"

My heart sinks when she shakes her head and stands up. "I need some sleep. I can't do this anymore tonight."

I sit here, my chest aching as I watch her walk to the door and disappear inside. There's no way in hell I wouldn't have looked for her if I had known she was back in town. Hearing that she never planned to find me feels like I've been stabbed through the heart.

Angry, I make my way to the door and shove it open, before quickly grabbing her arm before she can try and run from me again. "Why the fuck not, Lex?"

"Let go, Jax!" She yanks her arm from my hold. "What is this, Jax? Why did you bring me here? You want to sit and talk about feelings like when we were kids? You want to hear about all the fucked-up shit I've been through over the years or how damaged I am? Is that it?"

"Is that how you see yourself?" I question, angrily, before moving around to stop her from walking away. "Fucking damaged? You've been through some messed up shit, but you are not damaged. Never were and never will be. Got it?"

"You don't know that, Jax. You don't know shit now."

I move in close and cup her face, looking down at her. "I do."

"What are you doing?" she questions quietly.

"Wondering what it would feel like to kiss you knowing that it's you."

Her gaze lowers to my lips as if she might be wondering the same thing. "Don't, Jax." She shakes her head, but before she can back away, I hold her in place and slam my lips against hers.

My body instantly reacts to the taste and feel of her lips, my heart skipping a beat when she kisses me back.

Fuck, this feels so much better knowing it's her.

Our kiss becomes deeper, more urgent as I back her against the wall and grab her thighs, lifting her up my body.

She moans against my lips and digs her fingers into my arm when I move my hips up, pressing my hardened cock between her legs.

I want and need her to feel that she's mine and always has been.

"I want you, Lex," I growl against her lips, before roughly sucking the bottom one into my mouth. I feel like a fucking wild animal right now, unable to control my need to take her again.

She gasps and slams her head against the wall when I bite her neck and roughly thrust her up it with my erection.

I'm just about to reach between us to undo her jeans when she places her hands on my chest and pushes me until I set her back down on her feet.

"Dammit, Jax," she says, fighting to even out her breathing. "I'm too drunk to resist you right now. So please... just please, don't."

I squeeze my eyes shut and run my hands down my face, pissed at myself for kissing her after we've both been drinking. I'm not thinking clearly, because the only thing I want is her here with me.

My tolerance is pretty high, but I didn't stop to think about her, because I can't control myself when it comes to her. All I wanted was to kiss her as Jax and Lex. Not two strangers trying to get off.

"You can sleep in my bed." I turn to look at her just in time to see her grip the wall for support. "Whoa. Let's get you off your feet for the night."

She nods and puts her hands up to tell me she can do it on her own. "I'm fine. It's not something I don't handle myself all the time. I'll walk home. You don't need to take care of me like when we were kids."

"Yeah, well you're not by yourself right now and you're not leaving." Grunting, I pick her up and throw her over my shoulder, showing her where the hell she belongs tonight. "I'll take you to bed my damn self then."

"What the hell?" she yells at me as I toss her down on my bed and walk to the door.

"You're staying the night, Lex."

She looks like she wants to say something, but chooses to throw my pillow at me and grunt instead.

"Thanks, but you'll be needing this." I toss it back to her and walk out, shutting the door behind me.

Dammit, fighting with her makes me want to fuck her at the same time.

She may be different now, but the old Lex is in there, hiding from me, and I'm going to change that...

ALEXANDRA

TRUTH IS, I LIED ABOUT being drunk because it was the only thing I could think of at the time to get Jax's lips away from mine, before I could feel too much.

Feeling too much for Jax will only make it harder to protect him in the end, and with the way it felt to kiss his lips, knowing it was him this time, made me want to cling to the feeling for dear life and never let go.

It made me want to forget about all my problems as if they don't exist. My depression. My addiction. And most of all, the scars I carry deep within my soul.

I've carried them too long to know better than that. There is no escaping the bad shit I've been through and the permanent damage left behind from them.

As I lie here in Jax's bed, the urge to pop a handful of pills to pass out so I don't have to feel anything is just as strong as it was before Jax walked back into my life.

The damage has already been done and he'll never believe I can't be saved. I know him well enough to know that.

"Fucking, shit. I can't. I can't." I sit up and look around the dark room, wondering if he has any sleeping pills lying around.

I can't stay here without wanting to go to Jax, knowing that he's less than twenty feet away, wanting me just as bad as I want him.

Being careful to stay quiet, I reach into his bedside table and feel around for any bottles. I move a bunch of papers and condom wrappers around, but don't find what I'm looking for.

"Shit!" I grip my hair and lean my head against the headboard. I left my purse in the kitchen, and getting to it and the few pills I have inside means seeing Jax again. I can't do that right now.

I just can't.

I lay here for a while, maybe an hour, maybe two. I can't be too sure. I'm wide awake, unable to force myself to sleep and it's becoming more painful with each minute that passes.

I have two options: take the chance that Jax has already fallen asleep and go grab my purse or I continue to lay here with a million thoughts racing through my head.

I haven't heard any noise come from outside the room since Jax shut the door behind him. Maybe that means he fell asleep right away.

Taking my chances, I crawl out of his bed and slowly open the door and step out into the darkness of the living room.

I almost make it to the kitchen when I make the mistake of looking at the couch to see Jax sitting in the dark, his tattooed hands in his hair. He looks restless and on edge, the muscles in his back and arms flexed.

"Couldn't sleep?" he questions, his voice coming out huskily.

I swallow and shake my head when he looks up. "Not really."

He stands and comes at me, my breath rushing out when he

stops right in front of me and looks me over with heated eyes. "I'll get you some water."

I watch as he walks past me to the cupboard and grabs a cup down, before making his way to the fridge to fill it.

"Thanks," I whisper when he hands it to me. "I take it you couldn't sleep either?"

"I've got too much shit on my mind to worry about sleep." He gives me a quick glance, before grabbing himself some water and quickly downing it. "You know me... I've never been much for sleep."

"True. How could I forget?" A small smile takes over at the memory of Jax staying close by my window sometimes for hours after I'd fallen asleep. I still remember the first time I woke up in the middle of the night to peek outside and find him watching the house as if waiting for something to happen.

Nothing made me feel safer than knowing he was right outside my window.

"I can help you fall asleep if you'd like."

His offer has me squeezing the glass in my hand, remembering all the nights I fell asleep in his arms. As soon as he would pull me in close and my head hit his chest, I'd be out within seconds.

Those were the most peaceful sleeps I ever had.

But things have changed. Shit isn't as easy as it used to be. I was a scared little girl, hiding from the big bad monster, before the monster became me.

"I'm a big girl now, Jax. I don't think you holding me will put me to sleep like when we were kids." I grab my purse. "Goodnight."

He grips the edge of the sink and nods. "Goodnight."

I quickly disappear into his room and shut the door behind me, my breathing heavy, my heart racing.

After all these years, falling asleep in the comfort of Jax's arms still sounds as good as it used to.

It's that thought that has me digging through my purse and swallowing back the few pills left inside.

Setting the empty cup down on the bedside table, I crawl back into his bed, trying my best not to notice the scent of him covering the pillows and blanket.

Before long, I'll be passed out with no worries eating away at me. I won't feel shit, and with Jax being close by, that's what I need.

All I want to do is forget. Forget that he's back in my life, and most of all… forget that I need him just as much as I used to.

JAX

IT'S BARELY PAST SEVEN A.M. and I've already been awake for almost an hour, unable to force myself to sleep any longer.

Hell... I don't think I slept more than two hours due to Alexandra consuming my thoughts last night. I didn't realize how hard it was going to be to keep my ass on the couch and not jump into my bed with her.

"Shit. This is going to be a rough day."

Grabbing the remote, I turn the TV to one of Alexandra's favorite channels before making my way to the bathroom to shower and clear my head.

It's not working, because I'm standing here under the steaming hot water, unable to keep my damn cock down. All I can think about is how good it felt to be inside Lex, making her scream for me that night.

There're so many other things I could've done for her; other ways I could've pleased her unlike any other man has before, but I didn't because I didn't know it was her.

"Shit!" I slap the wall and bow my head, allowing the hot

water to run down my tense muscles, hoping to relax and get through this shower without storming out of here naked to show her all the things I didn't that night.

I need to stop picturing all the ways I could fuck her again and focus on the shit I can do to get her to open up to me and let me back in, instead. That's what's most important, but it doesn't mean fucking her again wouldn't help to get her where I want her.

But that shit ain't happening right now since she's sleeping, and I need to take care of my dick before I lay eyes on her again. If I walk into the bedroom with my dick hard and throbbing I can't promise it won't end up between her legs.

Grabbing my length, I run my hand over it and growl out, imagining it were her tight little pussy.

Images of her naked body on top of mine, her screaming above me, has me busting my load in the shower quicker than normal.

"Fuck. Fuck. Fuck."

I place my hands against the wall and focus on steadying my breathing for a few moments, before I finish showering and make my way to the laundry room to find some clean clothes.

After throwing on a pair of old jeans and a black t-shirt, I quietly push the bedroom door open and peek in at Alexandra to see if she's awake yet. The sight of her sound asleep in my bed has my chest aching with the need to crawl in beside her and hold her in my arms.

It's insane how quickly my thoughts of her can change from sexual to emotional, but that's what she does to me.

Steeling my jaw, I close the door and walk away before I change my mind and end up in bed with her. What I need to do is take this time that she's asleep and take care of someone else important to me.

I just hope like hell that I can get back before she wakes up and decides to take off without a trace. I don't intend to keep her a prisoner at my place, though, so if she does wake up and see that the TV is on for her, hopefully it will be enough to comfort her so she stays and waits for me.

Gathering my thoughts and preparing for what I have to go do, I slip on my leather jacket, before grabbing my backpack and the keys to my bike. I quietly make my way out the front door, locking it behind me.

Less than an hour later I'm sitting out front of my mother's place staring at the big brown house I pay rent for. It's nice and comfortable in a safe neighborhood; completely the opposite of where I live and where I grew up at. I didn't care about the cost when I found this place, I just wanted her to stay clean and away from temptation, but she ended up turning this place into a shithole with her constant partying.

I quickly run my hands over my face, before grabbing the strap of my backpack and letting myself into the house.

The disaster I see when walking inside is nothing outside the norm, but it still has anger coursing through me, hating that this is who she chooses to be.

My mother is still passed out on the couch where Blaine left her and the place is littered with dirty dishes, clothes, beer bottles, and whatever the hell else you can think of.

It's a pigsty and smells of spoiled food and beer.

I'm going to have to pull up this carpet and replace it with hardwood floors, because I'm tired as shit of scrubbing and shampooing them just for her to ruin them repeatedly.

I walk to the kitchen and throw my backpack on the counter, before going to check on my mother to make sure she's still breathing. Thankfully, it looks like Blaine made sure she was left on her side so she wouldn't choke on her own vomit again.

Crouching down in front of her, I place my hand to her forehead and look down at her. She's warm and I can hear her breathing, so I leave her be to sleep her night off.

After putting away the groceries, I spend the next hour or so cleaning up her mess and doing a quick load of laundry. As long as the clothes make it to the dryer she'll be good to go for a few days. That's part of the responsibility of taking care of her, because she sure as hell doesn't care if she has clean clothes or not.

Once I'm done, I take a seat in the chair beside the couch and sit here for a while, wishing like hell I'd been enough to save my mother from herself.

I've done everything over the years for her, including sending her to rehab, but her depression always gets the best of her. I used to think that spending more time with her would do the trick, and it did for a while, but eventually that wasn't even enough.

I turn away from my mom and reach for my phone when it vibrates in my pocket.

It's a message from Mark asking if I want to meet him for breakfast, so I grab a glass of water for my mother and set it down on the coffee table before giving her a kiss on the forehead and heading out.

It's still early, so I figure I can get a quick bite with Mark and bring Alexandra something for when she wakes up.

When I show up at the diner, Mark's squad car is already parked out front, so I hurry inside to find him in his usual booth.

"You look like hell, man," Mark says when I take the seat across from him. "Couldn't sleep?"

I nod and thank the waitress as she pours some coffee into a mug for me. "Nah. I didn't sleep for shit. I've had too much going on."

He reaches for a menu and slides it across to me. "I heard. Went by to see Avalon and Royal the other day and he filled me in. That's some crazy shit." He runs a hand through his dark blond hair and exhales. "It's been thirteen years since you've seen her?"

I close the menu and place my order when the waitress comes back, before answering Mark's question. "The last time I saw her she was a scared thirteen-year-old girl taking hits from a belt by her piece of shit father. I never saw her again after that night."

"Well, shit..." He looks pissed now as he looks at me from across the table. "I would've wanted to kill that son of a bitch and probably would've tried too."

"I did," I say on a growl. "I was too young and weak to do anything to stop him. He ended up breaking my arm and leaving me on the side of the road somewhere. I can't even remember how I found my way home that night."

"And how is she now?" Mark questions.

"I can't tell yet. She keeps pushing me away and running from me. I don't get it."

We're quiet for a few minutes as we eat, but I can tell Mark wants to question me further on the situation. He's handled a lot of child abuse cases in his time being a police officer and I've never seen him want to kill anyone more than when he receives one of those calls.

"Don't let her get away," he finally says. "No matter how far she tries to run, she needs you. Everyone needs someone and it sounds like she's dealt with a lot of bad shit."

I look up, my jaw tense as I take his words in.

"I never planned on giving up. I didn't back then and I won't now." I stand up and throw some money on the table to cover breakfast. "Thanks for the talk, man, and for taking care of things last night. I should get back before she wakes up."

"Not a problem." He nods and gathers his wallet and keys to stand. "I've got a long day ahead of me, but call me if you need anything. I mean it."

I give his shoulder a slap and reach for the bag of food when the waitress drops it off. "Thanks, brother."

I've got some figuring out to do when it comes to Alexandra and I'll fight tooth and nail for her. That hasn't changed.

The moment I pull up in the driveway, I notice my truck is no longer parked where I left it.

"What the fuck?" It only takes me a few seconds to realize she must've taken off in my truck to get home.

As angry as I am that she took off on me without saying goodbye, there's a part of me that is happy she took my truck. I'll take that as a sign she doesn't plan on hiding from me this time.

"Well shit..." I run my hand over my beard and look around as if there's a chance I'll see my truck parked somewhere else. But apparently, she's still gone.

After putting the food in the fridge, I put my energy into unpacking and organizing stuff the best I can without really giving a shit what anything looks like right now.

It's hard to function when the only thing I can think about is Alexandra and when I'll see her again. If it's up to her, it could be days or even weeks. I don't know what she's thinking right now and I don't know what she was thinking when she left this morning in my truck.

She's not easy to figure out like when we were kids and that scares the hell out of me. Back then, I always knew she'd come back to me the first chance she got.

Things have changed.

She has one day. One fucking day. And if she doesn't come to me, I'm hunting her down and giving her no other choice but to let me back in.

I'm not easy to get away from. Not when the only thing I want in this world is her, and she's about to learn that real soon...

ALEXANDRA

I'VE BEEN STANDING IN THE dark living room for the past hour, trying to decide if I should show up at Savage & Ink or not.

It was a long, rough day for me searching for a new job, and I spent most of it thinking about Jax and wondering if he's pissed that I took off when he was gone.

Jax left his house this morning believing I was asleep, but the truth is, the sound of Jax's moans coming from the shower woke me up.

All it took was hearing that deep, familiar growl of his release to know that he was getting off in there. That knowledge was enough to have my body heated with need.

It's hard enough looking at Jax without needing him inside me, but hearing his sounds of pleasure was too much to handle.

I quickly buried my face into the pillow, covering my ears before I lost what little self-control I had left and ended up in there with him, naked myself.

I had a feeling he'd be checking on me after his shower, so I closed my eyes and just laid there, wishing I was brave enough to talk to him… to see him, but I wasn't.

I'm not ready to share my past with him yet. I'm not ready to open up about all the fucked-up things I've been through without him, but I know being around Jax will eventually force me to open up and show him the new me.

I heard the front door close not long after that, followed by the roar of the engine from his motorcycle pulling away, so I knew he had left. I didn't know for how long, so I quickly got out of bed with plans to walk home.

That plan changed the moment I stepped into the living room to find the TV on my favorite channel, just like back when we were kids.

It brought me back to the past and that feeling of warmth surrounded me, making me feel safe again. I couldn't run this time, even though my head was telling me it's what's best for him.

And the thought of him thinking he'd never see me again killed a part of me inside. It was hard to breathe, imagining the look of disappointment on his face, so I did something to let him know I just needed space and I'd find him soon. I took something that was his like I used to do when we were little. It was our thing to prove I'd be back.

I don't know how smart of an idea it was, but it's too late to take it back.

Swallowing, I look out the window where Jax's truck is parked and my chest instantly aches to be near him.

At least this way it gives me a reason to see him again. Eventually, whether it's tonight, tomorrow, or next week, I'll have to bring it back to him.

The boy I met just months before my ninth birthday. The boy that stayed by my side and took care of me for almost five years without asking for anything in return. He never wanted anything from me other than for me to come to him when I needed an escape from my hell.

He's always been my escape, but the pain was present last night when all I needed was to be near him. My heart ached to be close to Jax so badly that it hurt. Real, physical pain in my chest. The only way to numb those feelings and keep me from giving in was to take something to knock myself out for the night. I needed a different kind of escape than normal.

Exhaling, I run my hands through my tangled hair, before pulling it back into a bun and reaching for my phone to check the time.

I'm reminded that I have two missed calls and three texts from James. They're all from late last night. Exhaling, I read them over.

JAMES

I'm at Midnight Joe's. What the hell happened here?

There's a tatted-up cop here giving me a hardcore stare right now. Are you inside or no?

Dammit, Alex. Thanks for the warning. I came to share some blow with you... some good shit from my new dealer and you're nowhere to be found. That cop could've arrested my ass for possession.

After reading the last message, I lean against the wall and squeeze my eyes shut. Fighting temptation has never been so hard, but then again, I never really had a reason to fight it before.

"Are you all right?" Tessa asks the moment she steps through the front door. "I heard the cops shut down the bar last night and that you were nowhere to be found. Holy shit, woman. I almost thought you were dead." She places her hand over her chest as if relieved to find me still breathing.

"I'm fine." It's not exactly the truth, but I guess physically I am. "Someone from my past just decided that me working at the bar was a shit idea and took it upon himself to kick everyone out. That's all."

"Oh, wow. Is it wrong to say he sounds hot?" Tessa shakes her head, smiling. "That man must really care about you to do something like that... and the fact that he has the power to do so."

"Yeah," I whisper, my mind wandering back to last night. The hurt look in his eyes left there by me is enough to haunt me forever.

"What's this guy's name? Maybe I know him."

"Jax," leaves my lips before I can stop it and when I bring my attention back to her, she's looking at me with wide eyes.

"The Jax. The one from Savage & Ink?"

I nod and the smile on her face widens.

"And I was right. He's totally hot, girl." She plops down on the couch and reaches over to turn on the lamp, giving the room a bit of light. "I've seen him rough up some guys before, so I'm not surprised that he was able to empty out the bar. He deals with a much rougher crowd at Savage & Ink. That's the kind of guy I'd want looking out for me. Lucky you. I'm totally jealous."

"Yeah," I whisper, looking toward the window at the sound of a loud vehicle pulling into the driveway.

"Looks like jackass is here." She rolls her eyes and stands up. "I'll be in my room. It was a long day today. But you get it. You can only deal with so many assholes in a day's time."

"I don't want him here for a while, Tessa," I say, stopping her before she can leave the room. "Can you tell him I'm not here and I won't be back for a few days?"

She nods. "Of course, babe. I'll be more than happy to tell that prick to fuck off. I'd enjoy it, actually."

"Thank you."

As soon as I open my bedroom door to slip inside, James knocks on the front door. I listen as Tessa lies and tells him that I'm staying with a friend for a few days.

"That's bullshit, Tessa." I hear James say. "She's ignoring my texts and I have someone here who wants to meet her. Let us in."

"She's not here, asshole. Do you not understand the words that are coming out of my mouth? You and your friend can go now. Buh bye."

"Why don't you move out of the way like a good girl and let us grown men inside."

The fact that James keeps pushing Tessa to let him and some strange man inside pisses me off, and before I know it, I'm making my way through the house toward the front door.

"I said..." Tessa's words trail off when she hears me coming up behind her. "Never mind, asshole. Here she is."

James smiles when he sees me and gets ready to step inside, but I block the door with my arm and give him a hard look. "Don't ever come over here and disrespect my roommate." My gaze lingers over to the middle-aged man beside him, before focusing back on him. "And don't ever bring strangers here without my consent. Now go."

"Whoa. Whoa. Whoa." He holds his arm out, stopping me from closing the door in his face. "Come on, babe. Don't be rude. Jasper came here to meet you. It's not my fault you keep ignoring my calls and texts. Shit. What was I supposed to do?"

I turn back to this Jasper guy who is watching me with a cool, calm expression, as if he's untouchable. It gives me the creeps and makes my skin crawl. "So, this is the feisty one you've told me so much about?" He takes a step forward, placing his hand on the door as if to let me know that it will be staying open. "I'm sure you've heard about me. No one and I mean no one uses my supply without me meeting them." He nods toward James. "And my friend here says you've been getting high off my shit."

"You won't have to worry about that anymore," I point out. "Now move, so I can close the door."

He shakes his head and laughs. "Are you sure about that, sweetness?"

"Come on, babe," James says from over his dealer's shoulder. "You and me both know you're not quitting anytime soon. Just get to know Jasper, so he's comfortable selling to us. Loosen up for once."

"Fuck you, James. I'm done with your shit and I'm done with you." I push the door to show them I'm done with this conversation. "Nice to meet you, Jasper, now get the hell off my porch."

A cocky smile crosses his face as he takes a step back and watches me until the door is blocking my view of him.

My heart races as I quickly lock the door and press my back against it, listening as they jump into James' car and drive off.

A guy hasn't made me this nervous since before I left my dad's house and got away from him and his friends. My entire body is shaking as I run my hands over my face.

There's something off about this Jasper guy and I want to strangle James for showing him where Tessa and I live. That asshole could come back at anytime, and what if he doesn't listen the next time I tell him to leave?

"Are you okay?" I'm so pissed off that I almost forgot Tessa was in the living room.

"I'm good," I say, my voice slightly shaking. "James should've known better than to bring his dealer here. I'm going to hurt him if I ever see him again."

"Oh, I'm sure you'll be seeing him again. That guy doesn't get the hint. He might be slightly obsessive over you, Alex. Be careful."

I nod as I take in her words.

"I'll be careful. I want you to do the same. Make sure the doors and windows are locked, always. I don't want James coming in uninvited anymore."

"Gotcha." She watches me curiously as I reach for Jax's keys. "Where are you going?"

"To the bar." I walk over and peek out the window to be sure James and his dealer aren't creeping around outside, before making my way to the door. "I have a truck to return. I borrowed it without asking when I took off in it this morning."

"I was wondering whose truck that was outside. I was so relieved to see you that I forgot to ask about it." She leans over the back of the couch to look at me. "You took that man's truck without asking?" She laughs and shakes her head. "No one else has the balls to do that. Yeah... I have a feeling he's going to want that expensive thing back. It's nice."

"I won't be gone long, but if James comes back over call me, so I can take care of him."

"Yeah... okay." She stands up and gives me a worried look. "Are you okay to drive? You seem a bit on edge."

"I'm fine. At least I will be when I get out of this house." I walk to the front door and open it. My anxiety is kicking in and if I don't distract myself I know what I'll turn to. I'm too on edge right from the unexpected visit not to need an escape. "I just need some fresh air. That's all."

At least I'm hoping that will do the trick. Because I don't think there's any way I can stay away from Jax right now. He's the only thing I've been able to think about, and not being with him has me wanting to use more than anything.

Rushing outside, I jump into Jax's truck and squeeze the

steering wheel. I hate that I'm such a mess. I hate that I have no control over myself.

I sit here for a while, struggling with what to do, before I pull out of the driveway. Truth is, I'm weak when it comes to Jax. I'm so weak, and it angers me that going to him will only put him through hell.

JAX

SAVAGE & INK CLOSED ALMOST an hour ago, and here I am, drink in hand, drowning myself in whiskey in hopes of taking my mind off Alexandra.

I thought I'd be okay going a day without her. I told myself I'd give her until tomorrow to come back, but clearly I can't handle that.

She's been the only thing on my mind since I came home to discover her gone this morning. The asshole in me wants to go after her and look for her, even though she clearly doesn't want to be around me right now.

The fact that she needs time away from me fucking hurts unlike anything else I've ever felt. When she disappeared back when we were kids, at least it was because she had no choice, but knowing that she does now and still chooses to stay away feels like someone ripping my heart from my chest.

Tilting back the glass of whiskey, I keep my eyes on the door as if she'll come in any moment and give me her usual sass. It's that damn sassy mouth of hers that made me want to keep her away from this place to begin with. Now, all I want is for her to come back.

Knowing that she possibly won't has the need to find her and ensure she's safe consuming me.

How am I supposed to stop wanting to protect the girl I promised to always look out for? Being there for her is a habit I can't shake. How the hell am I just supposed to sit back while she continues to run every chance she gets? I still don't even know why she's so damn determined to run.

"Fuck this shit."

I finish the last of my drink and slam the glass down in front of me, before running my hand down my beard. There's not enough whiskey in the world to make me forget her. I'm done pretending that there is. I've waited too long to have her back with me to just sit here like a dumbass, knowing she's somewhere out there.

Anger takes over from my thoughts of needing to get to her. I swipe my arm across the bar, sending everything in my path down to the ground at my feet.

She may be afraid to admit it, but she still needs me just as much as I need her, and I'm going to show her that.

Standing up, I reach for my leather jacket and slip it on, before walking over to the jukebox to unplug it. Once I'm surrounded by nothing but silence, I pound my fist into the side of the jukebox, letting more of my anger and frustration out. I feel like my emotions are swallowing me whole, and I'm unsure of how much more I can take before I suffocate.

For a few moments I gather my thoughts, before turning off the lights and stepping outside, locking up behind me. I immediately reach for a cigarette and light it, my hands still shaking from my emotions getting the best of me. I look straight ahead and see my truck parked in front of me, Alexandra leaning against the side.

My heart skips a beat at the sight of her standing there in a loose-fitting black shirt and a pair of white skinny jeans all ripped up.

What gets me even more is noticing the shirt she's wearing is mine. It's the one I sent her home in the night we fucked, and seeing her in it now has my mind going wild with memories of that night.

"Here's your truck. I figured you'd be worried about it and want it back." She pushes away from my truck and takes a step toward me. "I didn't want to leave the keys inside it in this shitty neighborhood."

She looks torn, as if she wants to stay but feels like she needs to run again, and the only thing I can think of is what I can do to stop her.

"I don't give a shit about my truck, Lex. It's the girl that took it that I was worried about." I take one last drag off my cigarette, before flicking it across the parking lot and making my way to Alexandra.

Once standing in front of her, I grab the back of her neck and move in close, speaking against her lips. "Get in," I demand. "There's somewhere I want to take you."

She shakes her head and takes a step back, as if my closeness is too much for her. "That's not a good idea, Jax. I should go. I shouldn't have taken your truck to begin with."

I barely give her a chance to turn away from me before I'm wrapping my arm around her waist, closing the distance between us. "I said get in, Lex. Now."

"Don't tell me what to do, Jax. That's the last thing I need." She places her hands on my chest and pushes me away, giving her enough space to walk away from me. "I'm going home. Don't follow me either."

"The fuck you are." Before she gets too far, I scoop her up and throw her over my shoulder. This woman is insane if she thinks I'm letting her walk away from me. "I'm taking you there whether you like it or not."

"Fuck off, Jax!" She pushes and slaps at my back when I open the truck door. "Put me down. Now."

Aggravated, I throw her into the truck and slam the door shut behind her. She goes to push the door open, but I slam it shut again. "Don't fight me on this, because I'll spend all night chasing you down."

"You're an asshole," she says, moments later, most likely realizing she's in a losing battle. "But I guess you already know that."

I point at the door. "Don't move."

She narrows her eyes, most likely wanting to kill me for demanding her to stay. I just hope like hell she listens this time, because it sure as hell didn't work when I told her the same thing inside the bar. She made it a mission to do the exact opposite.

Before she has the bright idea of sliding into the driver's seat and driving off, I hurry to the other side and jump in, reaching my hand out. "Keys."

Her eyes raise to meet mine and she hesitates for a brief moment before tossing the keys at me. "Where are you taking me?"

"You'll see when we get there." I pull out of the parking lot and head toward the one place I haven't been to in over twelve years.

For the first year she was gone I went there almost every night hoping she'd show up and prove she wasn't really gone. That she just moved into a new house in a different neighborhood and needed time to find her way back to me. I was a stupid kid hoping and wishing for the impossible.

"Job searching is exhausting, by the way," she says after a few minutes of driving. "I've been looking for a new one, since someone had to go and get me fired."

"Yeah, well I did everyone there a favor. Trust me," I say stiffly, gripping the wheel tighter as we get closer to the spot.

She has no fucking idea the things I'd do to someone that hurt her. She hasn't witnessed half of what I'm capable of when it comes to protecting her.

"How is that, Jax?" she asks angrily, not bothering to pay attention to where I'm taking her. "I was pretty damn good at serving drinks and I was doing just fine until you showed up and dragged me out of there."

"Is that right?" Once the old path comes into view, I turn down it and park, killing the engine. "You were just fine when some piece of shit groped you? What the hell, Lex? What if he would've hurt you for hitting him? You think one of the lowlifes that hang out there would've risked their safety to protect you?"

She looks surprised that I know about what happened with that fucker. "How did you—"

"Because I broke that motherfucker's nose for placing his hands on you. He was quick to brag about it. He's lucky I didn't do worse. Stop pretending you were okay being at that place."

I can feel her hate and anger as her icy eyes look me over from the passenger seat. It's been a long time since someone else has looked out for her, so I don't blame her for looking like she wants to reach across the truck and slap me across the face for thinking I have the right to after all this time.

"Fuck you," she spits. "I can take care of myself now, Jax. I went almost thirteen years without anyone there to look out for me. I don't need someone to start now. Not even you. I'm not that weak little girl you used to know and I never plan to be again. You have no idea what I've been through. The hell I survived without you, Jax. The pain..."

"Then tell me what you went through," I bark out, gripping the steering wheel to keep from punching it. "Let me fucking be there for you, Lex. Let me back in, so I can carry some of that pain for you. I want to be that for you. I used to be..."

"I'm not the same little girl that used to be able to make you smile, Jax. She's dead." Giving me a dirty look, she snatches her purse from between us and jumps out of the truck, slamming the door shut behind her.

I can hardly breathe right now from all the emotions I'm being punched in the gut with. It's taking the air straight from my lungs and she's not getting that I'll gladly give every last breath for her.

"This woman is going to be the death of me." I take my eyes away from her and get ready to yank the key out of the ignition to go after her, when I notice a little white pill laying on the passenger seat that must've fallen from her pocket.

My heart pounds against my rib cage as I pick it up to see what it is. I know this one. The realization that it's Oxy has my stomach twisting into knots at the memory of how these pills, along with others, controlled my mother for years. Her addiction was a sickness, and nothing I ever did was good enough to save her. Not for a long time at least.

Closing my hand around the pill, I jump out of the truck and rush to the other side, grabbing Alexandra's arm to pull her to me. I feel like I'm fucking dying picturing Lex the way I've seen my mother so many times over the years. "How long have you been popping pills? How long?"

Her eyes widen when I hold the pill out for her to see. She stares at it for a few seconds before yanking her arm from my grip and pushing on my chest. "It's none of your damn business. Now move, so I can leave."

Before she can escape, I grab her waist and back her against my truck, blocking her in with my hard body. "How fucking long? I'm not letting you leave until you tell me."

"Does it really matter?" Her eyes rise to meet mine, and I can see the shame in them right before she turns away. "No one has given a shit before. Not my asshole father. Not my mother who abandoned me, and definitely not anyone I've fucked over the years. Now move."

Her words hit me in the chest. It destroys me that she feels like no one has given a shit about her over the years. Both of her parents can rot in hell for all I care, and the same for the assholes she fucked. I hate them the most. But she should know there is one person.

"It matters to me," I answer honestly. "I'm not them. Don't hide from me anymore, Lex. Tell me the damn truth, because I'm not giving up until you do. You can fight me all night, love. Trust me, I don't tire easily."

"Just let me go." She struggles to get away, but I wrap my arm around her waist and hold her to me. "Dammit, let go! It's not your problem." She shoves at my chest, screaming out her frustration for me to move, but I refuse to, which only pisses her off more. "I said it's not your problem. What don't you understand about that? Move, Jax! Just move!"

"The fuck it isn't," I growl out, anger taking over that she won't talk to me and tell me the damn truth. I don't care if it hurts her feelings; she needs to know the shit I went through with my mother after she moved away. "Do you want to fucking die, Lex? Huh? Because that's what could happen."

I move in so close that she can't take a damn breath without breathing the same air as me. "Do you know how many times I had to have my mom's stomach pumped because it was full of pills? Do you know how many times I cried because I had to watch my mom die in front of me? Do you know how long a few seconds feels when you're waiting for that next breath that might never fucking come? I was just a boy then, and still didn't give up on my mom. I'm a man now. What makes you think I'll give up on you? Now, for the last time. Tell. Me."

Tears form in her eyes as she silently takes in my words. It's the first time I've seen her cry since I was nine and it breaks my heart in two, but I need her to feel the pain she's feeling right now to get the message through to her.

After a few moments she looks up and I wipe my thumbs over her cheeks, drying them. "I had no idea things got that bad after I left, Jax. I was hoping your mom got better. I wanted to picture a good life for you." She closes her eyes and exhales in defeat, dropping her hands from my chest. "I'm sorry. I don't want to hide from you, but I don't know what else to do. I'm scared."

I bend down and press my forehead to hers. "You don't have to be scared anymore," I whisper. "I'll destroy anything that ever threatens to hurt you again. Letting someone be there for you doesn't make you weak. Let me show you that. Let me help you. Let me in, Lex. Please."

I've never begged anyone for a thing in my life, but I'd drop to my knees right here in front of her if it helps get me the answers I need.

Many seconds pass before she opens her eyes and speaks again. "Ten years, off and on. I tried stopping once, back when I was twenty, but a week later I was back to looking for ways to escape."

Her answer has my heart feeling like it's being squeezed inside my chest. Ten years. She's been hurting bad enough to turn to a synthetic means of escape for ten years? That knowledge is enough to make me want to punch my fist into my truck over and over again until every bone in my hand is broken.

"Fuck!" I growl out, moving my hands up to cup her face, wanting and needing to take care of her. "I wish you would've found a way back to me. How often, Lex? Is it something you can control? I need to know these things."

She's quiet again for a few seconds, standing still as I rub my thumbs over her cheeks to comfort her and show her I'm here for her. "I take enough to make it through the day without wanting to die. But there's some days when that isn't enough. Those are the days I can't control how many I take."

She pauses and looks up to meet my gaze. The pain in them makes me physically ill. I want nothing more than to take that pain away and bury it deep into my fucking soul where she'll never be able to find and feel it again. "Sometimes I can't get out of bed for days and I just lay there, popping pill after pill, wishing with everything in me that I had the courage to end it all. That's why I didn't find you, Jax. That's why you don't need me in your life. I'll ruin you. I'll ruin you and I will only end up hating myself more than I already do. Hurting you is the worst thing I could ever do. Nothing scares me more."

Her confession hijacks the air in my lungs and makes it hard to fucking breathe. I hate that she's in so much pain and is afraid to let me in, but I hate it even more that she's been hurt so much by the world she feels the need to end things.

"You don't need to worry about ruining me, Lex, or hurting me. You could hurt me over and over again and I'll never leave you. I'll gladly accept the pain if it means having you back in my life." I move my hands around and gently wrap them into the back of her hair, moving in closer, before I speak again. "And you don't need pills to fucking get by. Not anymore."

"Then what?" she questions, her voice shaky and desperate. "What do I need to get by? Tell me, because I have had shit luck with figuring that out and I can't take it anymore. I can't."

I grip her hair tighter and lean in until my mouth is brushing hers. "Me. Let me prove that to you."

Her breathing picks up as her gaze locks on mine. She's listening, and that's all I need. She needs me to prove it to her just as much as I need to.

Unable to control myself, I crush my lips to hers, feeling the air rush out of my lungs at the impact. I kiss her hard and desperate, wanting to show her I'm not going anywhere, no matter how hard she tries to push me away. This is me showing her she doesn't need to live in pain anymore, and I hope like hell it's enough.

After a few seconds, her hands move up to wrap into my hair as she kisses me back, her kiss just as hard and desperate as mine.

"Jax," she says, breathless against my lips. "I don't want to hurt you..."

"Then don't." Keeping my lips on hers, I strip my leather jacket off and toss it aside, before undoing my jeans and then move to undo hers.

She quickly kicks her jeans off, holding onto me as I pick her up to wrap her legs around my waist. I moan and bite her bottom lip as she pulls my cock out and runs her hand over it. "I can't make that promise," she whispers.

"Then I'll make it for you." I've never wanted to show a woman she's mine more than I do this very second. With one slow thrust, I bury myself deep inside of her and stop to look into her eyes. "You're mine, Lex. Always fucking have been. I'll die over and over again to show you that if I have to."

She moans out and digs her nails into my shoulder as I begin moving, burying myself each time.

I need to be deep inside her, burying myself into her soul just as she has mine.

Growling out, I run my lips over her neck, before gently biting it as I continue to move inside her. Something has been missing since she left. Being inside her makes me feel complete and whole and there's nothing in this world I wouldn't give to feel this way every day for the rest of my life.

I'm not a gentle guy, but for her, I'd be anything she wants me to be, and right now she needs to see my gentle side. The one I haven't shown anyone since Lex disappeared all those years ago.

Trying my hardest to be tender, I softly tug her hair as I move my lips over the front of her neck and then make my way back up to her mouth, claiming it with mine.

This is the first time I've ever been gentle during sex. The savage in me wants to break free and claim her so hard and deep that she feels me inside her for days. I fight it with each move of my hips, because the truth is... I love Alexandra and have for as long as I can remember.

"Faster, Jax," she speaks across my lips, before kissing me hard and rough, pulling my hair. "I'm anything but fragile, so don't treat me like I am. I need you."

"Dammit, Lex." I pull away to look her in the eyes, studying the desperation in them. I love that she wants me just as much as I want her right now, but my need to take care of her overpowers everything else. "I made a fucking promise to you." She moans and throws her head back as I slowly bury myself inside her and stop. "Don't make me break it."

She gives me an angry look and yanks my hair harder, knowing what that does to me. "I can't take you being slow with me, Jax. Don't... please."

Her words trail off as I kiss her neck and begin moving my hips again. She may want me to be rough with her right now, but I won't do that. There are things I want to show her right now.

I need her to feel me—all of me—so she knows I meant every word I said when I told her she was mine. She's fucking mine, and I'm not letting her get away again.

"Holy shit, Jax." She moans against my mouth as I brush my lips over hers and slowly push in and out, taking her deep and slow.

I bite her bottom lip, before running my tongue over it, tasting her. I'll never get tired of her taste. Now that I've had it, I'm hooked. "I'm yours, Lex. You can do whatever you want with me, because I'm not going anywhere." I push inside of her as deep as I can and stop. "Do you feel that?"

"Yes." She nods and digs her nails into my arms when I begin moving again. "Keep going," she breathes, squeezing me with her legs. "I believe you. Please move..."

Keeping my eyes on hers, I move one hand around to wrap

into the back of her hair, wanting her to look me in the eyes when I make her come this time. "Good. Look at me, Lex."

A few more deep thrusts is all it takes before she moans out her release, her body shaking in my arms as she comes undone for me.

I lean my forehead against hers, catching her moans in my mouth as she slowly begins to come down from her high. "I'm going to show you I'm all you need. Open your eyes and look at me."

She slowly opens her eyes and wraps both her arms around my neck, watching me as I begin moving inside her again.

With the way she's looking at me, need and want in her eyes, all it takes is me moving inside her a few more times before I'm releasing myself inside her, filling her with my cum.

She's mine. No one will ever be inside of her again. My cum coating her insides is me showing her that. I lost her once. I won't lose her again.

Looking each other in the eyes, we both fight to catch our breath as I hold her against my truck with my hips, while running my thumb over her face. "Fuck, that felt so much different than last time."

She nods, running her hands through my sweaty hair. "So much different."

We stay like this for a while before she clears her throat. "Put me down, Jax."

Releasing a hard breath, I pull out of her and set her down to her feet, keeping her blocked in with my body. "Do you know where we're at?"

She swallows and looks around us, while reaching to put her pants back on. "Yes," she whispers. "Is it still here?"

I shrug my shoulders and adjust my jeans. "I don't know. It's been twelve years since I've been here. Wanna take a look?"

"I don't know." She shakes her head when I grab her hand to walk. "Maybe we shouldn't."

"I've been wondering about that damn tire swing for twelve years now. I'm not going back without you, Lex."

She pushes away from my truck. "Fine. We'll just take a quick look and leave."

Keeping her hand in mine, I hold it, guiding us through the woods toward where the old tire swing used to be. It takes a few minutes of walking around the area to realize that it must be gone.

It may be dark out here, but it's hard to miss the disappointment on Alexandra's face when she realizes the same thing. "Let's get out of here. I'm pretty tired."

She pulls her hand from mine and takes off through the trees, not stopping until we reach my truck and she jumps inside.

I take a few minutes to stand here and gather my thoughts, because truthfully, I'm just as disappointed as she is that it's gone after all these years.

We spent so much time here as kids; me making her forget about her crappy home life every chance that I could. Sometimes we stayed for hours, and even though my arms ached from pushing her, I never stopped.

I run my hands over my face, before making my way to my truck and jumping in. "I want you with me tonight. There's somewhere I need to take you in the morning." I turn to face her. "Are there any more pills in your purse? Please don't hide the truth from me. I can't help you if you do."

She nods her head and reaches into her purse, pulling out a small bag. She looks down at it as she speaks. "This is everything I have."

I lean over and grab the back of her head, pulling her close to me. "No more, Lex. You don't need these, and tonight is just the beginning of me showing you that."

She hesitates for a brief moment, before placing them in my hand when I hold it out, but I can tell from the look in her eyes how nervous it makes her to give up the last of her stash.

"Now, let's get you home."

I just need to make sure I'm enough for her. I'll fight every fucking day to be that, starting right now...

ALEXANDRA

IT'S BEEN YEARS SINCE I'VE cried. I've tried so damn hard to be strong, telling myself that crying made me weak, but the moment I heard what Jax had been through, I couldn't fight back the tears.

I hate with everything in me that Jax had to go through almost losing his mother multiple times to drug abuse. I had no idea it was bad enough to the point she almost died right in front of him. He was just a damn kid. He didn't deserve to have to grow up that fast, to have to take care of her. He didn't deserve the pain he had to endure because of her habits. It hurts to imagine what that must've been like for him. It scares the shit out of me to think about that happening to me. It also terrifies me to consider being without them, but knowing it would hurt him had me handing the pills over, because I'm weak when it comes to Jax.

I can't do it.

I tried.

I really did.

I tried staying away from him, knowing that it would hurt him to know the current me, but I couldn't do it. I could've dropped his truck off at his house and left before he noticed, but I didn't. I went to his work and waited for him to come outside.

I knew he wouldn't let me leave, and a part of me wanted to see how hard he'd fight for me to stay. I don't know why. Maybe I was afraid he wouldn't fight as hard this time and I needed him to prove me wrong, because I was too damn close to popping that whole bag of pills I had. I think deep down I want to know there is something or someone to stop me.

The ride back to Jax's place is silent, lost deep inside my head, replaying the way it felt when Jax took me slow and deep in the woods. The first time we had sex was fantastic, don't get me wrong, but having him inside me and knowing it was him this time, made me forget about everything bad in the world. For that moment in time when we were molded together, breathing the same air, I was a different person. One with a future where I could be happy.

I felt safer and more loved in that short amount of time than I have in my entire life. All I needed was Jax, and that's the reason I'm walking into his house this very moment.

I've spent so much time worried about ruining Jax, when in reality he might be the only thing able to save me from myself.

He'll either save me or I'll ruin him. I'm terrified to take that gamble, but it's clear Jax doesn't plan to let me go anytime soon, and I can't deny that makes me happier than I've been in years.

I'm not going to lie; my stomach is still twisting into knots from handing my stash over to Jax in the truck, leaving me feeling physically ill. For a second I thought I was going to throw up. I've needed pills to get by for so long now—even if just a few—the fact that I have none scares the shit out of me. Considering withdrawals is enough to set me on edge.

What if I need them? He knows of my bad habit, my need to

escape, and I know he'll do everything in his power to keep me from getting more.

What if I can't cope without them?

I went a week without them before and I felt like I was dying. One damn week.

How will I feel after two weeks or a month?

My thoughts are scrambled, running around in my head, when Jax grabs my hand and guides me through the dark house to his bedroom. Once inside, I'm assuming he'll leave me alone like last time, but instead, he strips his shirt off and takes a seat on the bed, looking up at me. "Want a pair of my briefs to sleep in?"

I shake my head and strip off my Converse and jeans. I'm standing here in nothing but Jax's t-shirt, and I wonder if it has the same affect on him as it does me. I must've slept in this thing almost every other night since running off with it.

He looks me over, before reaching for my hand and pulling me down into his lap, holding me against him. I couldn't get away even if I wanted to, and right now, I don't think I do. I want to stop fighting for once. Even if just for tonight. "Do you need pills to sleep at night?"

I swallow and nod. "It's the only way I can sleep. Otherwise, my mind wanders to a dark place I can't control. It's been that way for as long as I can remember."

He takes a deep breath and slowly exhales, before picking me up and placing me down onto the mattress. I watch in silence as he strips out of his jeans and crawls in the bed beside me. "Then I'm staying in here with you. Don't think I've forgotten over the years how easily you always fell asleep in my arms. Come here."

My heart speeds up when he wraps his arms around me and pulls me against him, taking charge. I didn't think I wanted a man to take charge with me, but truthfully, I've never minded when it came to Jax. Even when we were kids I liked it when he told me what to do, because I always knew it was his way of taking care of me.

We lay here in the dark for a while, neither of us speaking. I was starting to think he was asleep until he gently brushes his lips over my neck, before kissing it.

A small moan escapes my throat when he does it for a second time, his soft lips lingering this time. It's such a distraction that all I can think about is him. Nothing else. It has me wanting to ask about what he said earlier. "Where are you taking me in the morning?"

He moves his hand around the front of my neck, before gripping it and whispering into my ear. "I owe you a new job. One that you deserve and that you'll feel comfortable doing. I need to know you're safe. Royal's wife owns a salon and last I heard they need some help."

I lay here in silence for a few moments, unsure of what to say. The thought of working in a salon occurred to me before at one point, I even got my cosmetology license a year back but couldn't push myself to find a salon that would consider hiring a fuck up like me. It just seemed too good to be true.

No drunk assholes to fight off anymore.

I could definitely get used to that, but I try not to get too hopeful yet.

"I have my license but no experience in an actual salon," I point out. "What makes you think she'll hire me?"

He growls into my ear, before pulling me closer, as if to protect me, even though it's just the two of us. "Because you're mine and that makes you family. Any family of mine is family of Royal and Avalon, and we do what we can for each other. Always have and always will."

His words silence me again, and I find myself wrapping my arms around his as tightly as I can. It's like I can't get him close enough, even though there's no space between us.

Why do I like it so much when he says I'm his?

"Tell me what happened that night, Lex," he says against my ear, a few moments later. "What happened after I blacked out?"

I squeeze my eyes closed at the memory. I'm afraid saying the words out loud will hurt just as much as witnessing it all those years ago. I don't think I ever fully recovered from seeing him hurt.

"I need to know," he whispers when I don't respond. "Did he hurt you worse because of me?"

I shake my head. "No. He actually took it easy on me that night. It was like he took all of his anger out on you." Tears sting the back of my eyes, but I hold them back as I continue. "He hit you over and over again after you blacked out. I was so terrified he had killed you or was going to if he didn't stop. I jumped on him and screamed for him to stop. Begged him to. He knocked me across the room and then dragged you through the house. I don't know what he did to you after that. I just remember him coming back a long time later and forcing me to grab the few things I cared about. I cried for you the whole time, and even though I knew you were hurt I had hope that you would show back up and save me. I wanted you to take me away from him. It wasn't until we were in the car that I knew I'd probably never see you again."

His breathing picks up against my neck as he squeezes me to him. "I would've come back for you if I had the choice, Lex. I need you to know that."

"I believe you," I whisper. It's the truth. Jax is the only person in the whole damn world that I know wouldn't lie to me. "I don't want to talk about things in the past anymore tonight."

Bringing up the past has a wave of nausea assaulting my stomach. There's so much I haven't told him yet. "I need some sleep."

"Goodnight, Lex."

The feel of his lips against my neck when he kisses me

makes my stomach flutter. It calms me. A feeling I never once got from James when he did the same thing.

The fluttering in my stomach turns to knots when I think about that son of a bitch. As much as I want him out of my life, I know he'll show up again soon. He doesn't know how to stay away for long when it comes to me.

Jax cusses under his breath at the sound of the back door opening.

"Does someone else live here?" I attempt to sit up, but Jax pulls me back down to him.

"It's just Blaine. Trust me, you don't want to go out there right now."

A few seconds later, the sound of something crashing to the ground is followed by the loud moans of a woman.

"That fucker is going to replace whatever the hell that was in the morning."

I jump when something slams hard against the hallway wall. "Holy shit... Sounds like he fucks like you. I'm surprised the walls are still standing in this place."

I can't help but to laugh when Jax yells at Blaine to take it to the backyard before he kicks his ass.

All Jax's threat does is cause his friend to fuck louder and harder, making the damn wall sound like it's about to fall down.

"I'm going to kill him in the morning," Jax growls beside my ear.

"Does he have his own place?" I ask on a laugh. "Or does he just come here to annoy you with his sexcapades?"

"Yes to both," he breathes angrily. "The asshole has his own place, but he drives me to wanting to murder his ass at least twice a week. He's lucky to still be breathing."

The banging suddenly stops, followed by what sounds like a fist pounding into the wall. A few seconds later a female voice shouts at Blaine and calls him an asshole, followed by the sound of the back door slamming shut.

"Looks like he's pissed off at Madison."

"Was Madison the girl that just left?"

"No. Madison is the girl who has him all fucked in the head. I have no clue who he brought here tonight, but it wasn't her. It's a bit complicated."

"Clearly," I say on a yawn.

The house is quiet after that, so I'm guessing Blaine has passed out on the couch. Either that or he's sitting in silence somewhere, lost in thought. I know that feeling all too well.

"Now we can get some sleep."

I yawn again and lose myself in his big arms, the comfort of them making it hard to keep my eyes open. For a split second my mind wanders back to the things I haven't told Jax about my past, but the moment his breath hits my neck, I focus on that, and before I know it everything goes black and I fall asleep in Jax's arms just like I used to when we were kids.

ALEXANDRA

ELEVEN YEARS AGO... FIFTEEN YEARS OLD

I FEEL DEAD INSIDE AS I sit here staring at the door, hoping with everything in me that my father's friend doesn't stumble into my room drunk again. He's been doing it more often over the last few weeks and it makes me hate my body.

Every time he looks me over with greedy eyes I feel dirty. But that's nothing compared to the way it makes me feel when he touches me.

Being around my asshole father all these years, taking his physical and mental abuse, has already broken me enough. I didn't think things could get worse. I didn't think there was anything else he could do to make me feel more worthless than I already do, but I was wrong.

Every single day I wake up wishing I would die, because death has to be better than the shit I live with every moment of every day. I'm stuck here like a prisoner.

I'd take my father hitting me any day over him allowing his

friend to come into my room and touch me. His big, rough hands on me makes me feel physically ill.

It didn't start until my fifteenth birthday when George pointed out how grown I was becoming. He said I was beautiful, and he couldn't stop looking at me. I expected my father to yell at me and force me to stay out of sight when they were drinking, but instead, he told his friend he could touch my thigh if he wanted; almost like a dare.

I still remember holding my breath, my entire body shaking with fear as he reached out and ran his hand up the inside of my thigh.

He may not have touched my private area, but it sure as hell felt like he had.

I tried not to cry as he moved his hand along my thigh and moaned in pleasure. I tried so hard to hold it back, because my piece of shit father always punishes me for crying in front of George. He said it makes him look bad and that he isn't going to tolerate me doing that in front of his friend, especially when he allowed us to move in with him.

But I couldn't hold the tears back that night. I cried right in front of George, which pissed him off, and he told my father I embarrassed him, making him feel dirty in his own home.

My father slapped me across the face, before dragging me through the house by my hair and threw me face down onto my bedroom floor. But at least I was away from his friend, and for that, I was thankful.

My entire body stiffens when I hear the bedroom door across the hall creak open, and then it closes shortly after. I hate not being able to lock my door. My asshole father made sure the day we moved in that wasn't a possibility.

It's late, which is usually when George decides to make his way into my room. The thought has me pulling the blanket around me for safety, even though I know it won't do shit to keep him away from me.

With every noise I hear close by, I look at the door, expecting it to open, and every time that it doesn't, I breathe a little easier.

It's nights like these that really make me miss Jax. I still look outside my window late at night as if he'll be out there, and every time he's not there, my heart aches a little more for the boy I left behind.

I still remember the night he tried saving me. It's been two years, and I'll never forget the way he climbed into my bedroom with that baseball bat. He took it to my father knowing he was putting himself at risk to protect me.

My father was much bigger than Jax back then, and even though I knew he'd hurt me even more, I jumped on my father's back in an effort to get him to stop hitting Jax with the bat that night.

He threw me across the room and then dragged Jax out of the house and drove him away.

Memories of that night still haunt me to this day.

Now we're more than four hours away and I'm stuck in this shitty house with no friends and no one who cares whether I live or die.

As the minutes go by I keep looking over at my window, wishing that I could climb out and escape for a while like I used to before we moved, but the night we moved in, my father nailed the window shut to ensure I wouldn't be able to sneak out anymore.

Each day I feel more and more like a prisoner, and I'd do anything for an escape. A kind of an escape where I don't have to feel anymore.

My eyes become weaker and weaker with each minute that passes, and just as I'm about to give in and let myself fall asleep, the creaking of my door opening has me gripping at the blanket and cussing under my breath.

"You're so beautiful, girl." My insides twist into knots as

George steps into my room and closes the door behind him. "Just be a good girl and this won't take long."

I back away and kick his hand away when he reaches for my leg to pull me down to the end of the bed. "No! Don't touch me. Just leave me alone."

He grits his teeth in anger and reaches for my leg again, but I back up and curl my legs beneath me. "You want to play games, little girl?" He slaps the bed and reaches for his belt, slipping it through the loops. "Hey, Hank. Might want to get in here and teach this little bitch of yours a lesson before you wind up on the streets."

My body shakes with anger and fear as my father appears in the doorway looking displeased. "She won't be a problem anymore, George." I watch, unable to turn away as my father grabs the belt from his friend and looks me over with hate-filled eyes. "Get over here, girl!"

I close my eyes and try my best not to scream as he grabs me by the hair and pulls me up to my knees. I know I should cower as I hear the sound of him adjusting the belt in his hand, but instead I sit up straight, prepared to get it over with.

The leather hitting me across the left cheek has me whimpering and grabbing at the bed. It hurts so bad that all I want to do is scream and cry, but I know all that will do is make my punishment worse.

"Don't embarrass me again or I'll come back in here and whip you till you bleed. That face won't be so pretty anymore. Do you hear me, girl?" When I don't respond fast enough, he slaps me across the face and then grabs a fistful of my hair, pulling me closer to him. "Answer me!"

"Yes," I cry out. "I hear you."

"Good." He hands the belt back to George and walks away without another word.

I hate him so much for this. I hate him so much that he could die tonight and I wouldn't shed a tear. Not a single one.

It's because of him that I'm damaged. The only thing I feel is hate, anger, and fear, because he took me away from the one person who made me feel something else.

I don't want to look at George while he touches me, so I lay down and close my eyes, facing away from him.

I flinch, but don't say a word when I feel his hand move across my hip, before lowering to my thigh. If I pretend to lay here asleep and don't move it seems to make him go faster.

It's disgusting.

I swallow and try to keep my body from shaking as I listen to the sound of him unzipping his jeans. The moan that leaves his mouth a few seconds later lets me know that he's touching himself.

His touch on my leg is gentle, his hand slowly making its way back up my leg until he grabs my ass in his hand and squeezes it.

"Oh yeah," he groans, moving his hand over the shape of my ass, before yanking my pants down so he can see my panties. "What a tight little ass. I have to remember to thank your daddy later."

His hand moves down my ass and I cry into the bed when I feel his finger slide between my legs, touching me in a place that makes me want to puke.

I cry silently, squeezing the blanket in my hands as he rubs me through my panties, his movements picking up speed as he pleasures himself to touching me.

Seconds of him touching me feels like an eternity, before he finally groans out his pleasure as he comes. I squeeze my eyes shut and hold back my bile as the sounds of him finishing echo throughout the room, dirtying my comforter, before buckling back up and leaving my room without another word.

As soon as I'm alone, I cover my face and cry into my hands, letting it all out as quietly as I can.

I sit here for hours, staring at the bedroom window, unable

to stop the tears from falling. I feel dirty and used. His filthy touch lingers. It makes me hate myself more.

I would give anything to have Jax come through that window and take me away from this life, and it kills me to know he never will. But what hurts the most is that there's a possibility he's already forgotten about me.

That's what makes me wish with everything in me that I could disappear from this world.

Because without him I'm truly alone in this world, and I'm not sure how much longer I can live this way.

JAX

AN INSTANT ACHE HITS MY chest when I wake up to find my bed empty, the spot beside me cold as if she's been gone for a while. The first thought that occurs is that she's taken off on me again, the ache in my chest growing.

After Alexandra fell asleep last night, I stayed awake for hours, lost in thought as I held her in my arms. Years of memories went through my head of all the times I held her late at night, giving her a few hours of peaceful sleep that she never got while at home.

Just a couple of weeks ago I was unsure if I'd ever see her again, so the thought of being able to actually hold her seemed impossible. There was a constant weight on my chest whenever she was gone and I'll never forget that feeling. That made having her in my arms last night—after all these years—that much more bittersweet.

I don't think I managed to get more than two hours of sleep, and tonight will probably be hell, but it was worth it just to feel her in my arms again. That peace I always got from having her close to me, to feel valuable by taking care of her. It was always the best part of my day.

Sitting up, I grunt, while running my hands over my face. I throw the blanket off and stand up, the salty smell of pork hitting me. Then I hear it—the crackling of grease. I breathe deep, my mouth watering—bacon.

Relief washes over me, because I know damn well it's not Blaine in the kitchen cooking. There's no way he'll be up before noon unless I shove him off the couch.

I step out of the room, and the first thing I'm greeted with is Blaine's naked ass as he sleeps face first on the couch. Hasn't the asshole ever heard of underwear?

Cussing under my breath, I walk past him to the kitchen. That fucker really needs to learn some limits, and I'm not pleased that Alexandra had to witness him naked this morning.

"Sorry you had to wake up to Blaine's naked ass," I say, my voice still tired from the lack of sleep.

Alexandra turns away from the stove and shrugs as if it's no big deal. She's still wearing my t-shirt, which consumes me with possessiveness over her since Blaine is exposed just one room over. "It's not a bad sight; he has a nice ass, so I'm not complaining."

I growl under my breath, despising her comment, which only causes her to smirk, no doubt enjoying my annoyance. Instead of commenting on it, she goes back to cooking.

I guess she still likes working me up just as much as when she thought we were strangers. She wants to go back to playing that way... I have no problem showing her what her playfulness does to me.

Walking up behind her, I grip her hips and pull her hard against my body, causing her to release a small moan. "So you like Blaine's ass, huh?" I gently grab the front of her neck and move around to speak against her ear. "Do I need to take you right here in the kitchen to remind you how much you like mine?"

I feel her throat move as she swallows. "Are you threatening me, Jax?"

"What if I am?" I reach my free hand around to turn the stove off. "And it's not a threat. It's a promise."

She moans and digs her nails into my arm when I press my hard cock against her ass and bite her neck. If it weren't for the fact that I want to keep Alexandra to myself I'd lift my t-shirt she's wearing and slip inside of her right here. "Dammit, Jax," she breathes when I grind my hips into her. "Do you know how hard it is to resist you?"

"Yes. You still want to play this game right now?" I question against the spot on her neck that I just bit. "If we are, then prepare yourself for Blaine to wake up and witness that you're mine."

She spins around in my arms and grabs my dick, giving it a hard squeeze as she bites her bottom lip. "What makes you think I wouldn't like Blaine watching?"

Oh, she's pushing it now.

I growl out my frustration and take a step back. I was wrong when I said she'd never win at this game. When it comes to her and anything involving another man...

"How did you sleep?" I ask, changing the subject before I lose my shit and kill Blaine in his sleep. Because for once the fucker would be innocent.

"Pretty well, actually." She grabs a fork and transfers the rest of the bacon onto a plate, before setting the food down on the table. "Sit and eat."

"Yes, ma'am." I smile and pull out a chair for her, before taking a seat and reaching for a piece of bacon. "I talked to Royal last night and told him we'd be at the salon by eleven. I'll take you home after we eat so you can shower and change before we go."

I expect her to give me a hard time about wanting to go to her place, figuring she still wants to be shady about where she lives, but instead, she nods and reaches for some bacon. "I woke up early this morning to watch some video tutorials on YouTube. The least I can do if I'm expecting them to hire me is refresh my memory. It's been years since I've gotten practice."

I smile, my gaze going to her fiery red hair. "Well if you did your own hair then I'm damn confident you can do the job just fine, but I'm sure the girls will appreciate that you took the time to watch tutorials. It shows you're serious about the job."

She's silent for a few moments as we eat, and as hard as I try to keep my hands to myself, I can't. Everything inside of me is aching to touch her again. Making eye contact with her, I grab the leg of her chair and scoot it toward me. It's hard to miss the way her breathing picks up when I grab her waist and yank her into my lap so she's straddling me.

"What are you doing, Jax? Are you trying to put on a show for Blaine?"

"Hell no." I wrap one arm around her waist and grip the back of her neck with my free hand, pulling her close until our mouths are brushing. "Thanking my woman for breakfast the best way I can with jackass sleeping just fifteen feet away, naked."

"Who says I'm your woman, Jax?" She's trying hard to resist me, but I can tell with the small breath that escapes her lips when I pull her harder against me, she wants to give in and stop fighting me. She's afraid, and I need to break that damn wall down.

"No one has to say it." I run my tongue over her bottom lip, before sucking it into my mouth and releasing it. "You've been mine since the day I found you behind your garage."

"Hell fucking yes." Blaine's tired voice comes from the doorway, causing us to both look his way. "I woke up just in time for breakfast and a show." He winks and grabs a piece of bacon. "Go on. My cock doesn't mind."

The dumbass is lucky he decided to put his jeans on before making an appearance. I'm not much of a fan of his at the moment. Especially now that I know Alexandra finds him attractive. Or at least his ass.

"Nice to see you own some goddamn clothes," I growl out as he pulls out a chair and joins us at the table. I'm tempted to kick it over, but I keep my cool, eyeing him up and down as he looks at Alexandra in my lap.

"My head is just fine by the way," Blaine mutters. "You have pretty good aim."

"Yeah, well I've had a lot of practice."

She gets ready to move from my lap, but I grab her ass with both hands and hold in her place before she can. "Stay. Blaine can eat in the living room."

She narrows her eyes at me and pinches my nipple so hard that I cuss and hit the table. "Fucking shit, Lex!"

"I have a mess to clean so we can get to the salon." She pushes her way out of my lap and tosses the last piece of bacon to Blaine when he opens his mouth and tilts his head back.

He manages to catch the end of the piece with his mouth and the rest of it crumbles to the table as he speaks. "The salon?" His nostrils flare and I have a feeling his little show last night had to do with Madison.

"Yeah. Lex is getting a job there."

"Good. I'll go with then." He stands up and walks to the fridge, yanking it open to grab a water, before slamming it shut so hard that it shakes.

"Are you going to take your anger out on my fridge or tell me what you're so worked up about?"

"What? A motherfucker can't do both?" He stops to watch Alexandra as she leaves the kitchen to most likely get dressed.

"She went on a date last night. A fucking date. Can you believe that shit?"

A small smile curves at the corner of my lips as I watch him mutilate the bottle in his hand, while drinking it. "Yeah, I can asshole."

He stops drinking to give me a hard look. "Are you serious? Have you seen me, motherfucker? Why would she need to go on a date when all she has to do is call me?"

"Because maybe she wants more than a fuck, which is all you're willing to give her, dumbass." I stand up and push my chair in, my gaze focused on Blaine as he gets lost in thought. "Meet us at the salon at eleven if you're going. Lock up on the way out and don't make an ass of yourself there either."

He nods but doesn't say anything, so I walk away to throw some clean clothes on if we're going to make it to Alexandra's in enough time for her to shower and get ready.

After grabbing my keys, I walk to the bathroom in search of Alexandra to find her standing in front of the mirror, gripping the sink as if she's battling something in her head.

I don't hesitate before coming up behind her and wrapping my arms around her to show her that I'm here for her. "You don't need that shit, Lex. I'm here and I'll do anything you ask me to. What do you need from me?"

She shakes her head and squeezes her eyes closed when I kiss her neck and hold her tighter. "I'm fine. I'm good." She releases a deep breath and forces a smile. "I just needed a minute to get my head straight."

"Let's get you home and cleaned up then."

We make it to the salon with five minutes to spare and I can tell from the way Alexandra keeps running her hands over her jeans that she's nervous.

Wanting to calm all those nerves down, I reach across my truck and grab her chin, pulling her in for a kiss. "There's nothing to be nervous about. You're with me, Lex. Fuck everything else."

She closes her eyes and grabs my hand that's still on her chin. "What if they don't like me? Most women don't. Usually, that doesn't bother me, but..."

I grab her face with both hands and kiss her again, causing her to moan and grab my hair. "Most women are intimidated by strong women, and you're by far the strongest woman I know. But these women—Avalon and Madison—are strong too. That's why I know without a doubt they'll love you."

She takes a deep breath and slowly exhales, before opening her eyes and grabbing my beard to pull me in for another kiss. The moment her tongue swipes across my lips my cock hardens, and I have to fight the urge to fuck her right here in my truck for good luck.

"Thank you, Jax. Here goes nothing," she says, breaking the kiss.

My heart beats wild in my chest as she releases my beard and steps out of my truck. It's the first time she's kissed me since finding out who I was, and I can't deny that it has me happier than shit. Makes me feel like I'm getting somewhere with her. With us.

My heart still racing, I jump out of my truck and catch up with her as she reaches the door, opening it for her to walk inside.

Avalon looks our way and smiles the moment the bell above the door dings, letting the ladies know someone has opened the door. Her eyes go from me to Alexandra, her smile widening as she takes her in. "Please tell me you colored your own hair. It's gorgeous."

Madison stops cutting her customer's hair and looks our way to see what Avalon is talking about. She raises a brow in approval and goes back to cutting. "That hair has me crushing on her, Jax. Better keep her close."

"I did." Alexandra smiles and looks around the salon, taking everything in. I can tell from the way her shoulders relax she feels a bit more comfortable and is warming up to the idea of working here. "I'm confident I can do the job."

"Jax assured me that you can and there's no one I trust more than him and a few other people. Today we'll just show you around and we'll get everything else sorted out later." Avalon walks over and grabs Alexandra's hand as if they're already friends. "Let me show you where everything is." She turns and gives me a quick kiss on the cheek. "Lex is ours for the next few hours. We'll be sure to take good care of her. Maybe you can hang with Royal at the bar for a bit."

I smile and watch the girls fall into easy conversation as Avalon walks her around the room. "Text me when you're done and I'll be back."

The girls are so busy getting along that they ignore my ass as if I'm not even here. I laugh to myself as I step outside and head for my truck. It looks like I'm going to need to learn to share her with the girls and that has me relieved. Alexandra needs some new people—better influences—in her life and there's no one I trust more than my family.

I almost forgot that Blaine was meeting us here until he pulls up beside my truck on his motorcycle and quickly hops off, making his way to me. "You might want to stop by your mom's before heading wherever the hell you're going."

"Why?" I nervously run a hand through my hair, unsure of what to expect.

"I saw a familiar vehicle outside her house when I drove by on the way here. One that you won't be the least bit happy about."

"Fucking shit." Anger courses through me as I jump into my truck and drive off in a hurry. I know exactly what vehicle he's speaking of and that thought has me gripping the wheel and driving a lot faster than I should to get there before that fucker takes off.

It's been years since he's been around and I was hoping that meant my mother was done with him for good, but I guess that was just wishful thinking.

I pull up outside my mother's house, adrenaline pumping through my veins when I see Jasper and some asshole I don't know, standing on the porch smoking.

Jasper flicks his cigarette across the yard and grins as he watches me jump out of the truck and head toward the porch. "Little Jax sure did grow up."

"What the fuck are you doing here?" I growl out, stopping inches from his face.

"You're Jax?" the guy I don't recognize questions, looking me over as if to size me up. "Well, hell." He tosses his cigarette aside and clenches his jaw, as if he doesn't like what he sees.

But he isn't my damn concern, so I concentrate on the piece of shit in front of me. He's aged quite a bit since the last time I saw him, and I know he's checking out the ways I have changed as well. I'm a lot bigger and tatted up than when he last set eyes on me six years ago.

"Ran into your beautiful mom at the bar last night. We had a few drinks and caught up. I've wondered off and on what she's been up to over the years." He grins and pulls out another cigarette. "I'm glad we got a chance to catch up."

"You son of a bitch." I grab him by the shirt and slam him against the door, getting in his face. "Don't let me catch you here again."

He laughs and takes a drag off his smoke, slowly exhaling in my face. "Or what, Jax? Are you going to stop me? We both know that didn't work all the times you tried in the past. But moving her into a new home and changing her number. That worked. But we're reconnected now."

"Fuck you," I growl in his face. "Get off her property and

don't let me catch you here again. A lot has changed since the last time you dealt with me. Don't make me show you how."

He laughs and pushes me away so he can walk. "James and I were just leaving anyway. We have someone my buddy here wants to visit."

James looks me over one more time, taking me in from head to toe as he takes a drag off his cigarette, before flicking it my way and walking off in a hurry. If I didn't know any better I'd say the asshole was desperate to get somewhere.

I'm so pissed that I can barely catch my breath as I let myself inside the house to have a little talk with my mother. I hear the shower water running, so I pace around the living room for a bit before finally taking a seat on the couch to wait for her.

She steps out a few minutes later, wrapped in a towel, her eyes widening when she spots me sitting on the couch. "Holy shit, Jaxon!" She places her hand to her chest. "You scared the living shit out of me. I wasn't expecting you."

"What was he doing here?" I stand up, my jaw clenched as I look her in the eyes. "Do you know what you've done by letting that asshole know where you live?"

She waves her arm as if to brush it off, like it's no big deal. "Nothing happened. We just had a few drinks and talked. I'm not even hungover. You don't need to worry about Jasper. He knows I'm not using anymore."

"Don't you get it?" I stop and punch the door, before turning back to face her. "He's a dealer. The biggest dealer around. He doesn't just want to talk and hang out. He wants to use you again and that shit ain't happening. I won't let it."

"Don't start, Jaxon," she says, her voice now laced with anger. "Goddammit, I'm a grown woman. I don't need you telling me what my friend wants or who I'm allowed to have at my house. I've known him since before you were born. He understands I've been clean for six years and didn't push anything on me."

I push away from the door and walk over to stand in front of her. "If you're a grown woman then why have I been taking care of you since Dad took off?"

"Fuck you, Jaxon!" She pushes my chest and gets in my face. "You can leave now. I'm not in the mood for your shit. I was feeling good for once, until you showed up."

I stand in place as she pushes me again. "I'm not leaving until you promise me you won't let that piece of shit inside the next time he shows up."

"I don't have to make that promise."

"Oh, yes the fuck you do, or I'll make sure myself that Mark or Blaine is stationed at your damn door every night." I keep eye contact, wanting her to see the seriousness of my words.

"Fine," she breathes, giving up. "I'll tell him not to come around anymore. Are you happy?"

I nod and give her a quick kiss on the forehead, before looking down at her. "For now. We'll see how long that lasts."

"Don't worry, Jaxon. I've got it under control." She walks away and reaches for the TV remote. "Now go on home so I can get dressed and catch up on my shows. It's been a while since I've been up this early and I plan to enjoy it with no more distractions. Got it?"

"I'll be back to check on you later." I run my hands over my face in frustration, before heading out the door and jumping into my truck.

I sit here for a while to be sure he doesn't come back, before I head to the salon. I park, pull down the tailgate of my truck, and light a joint to get my thoughts in check and calm down before I end up hunting that son of a bitch down and killing him.

I'm finally starting to get things together for Alexandra and my mother has to go and fuck my head up by letting that piece of shit from the past back into her life.

Damn, these women know how to keep me on my toes. But no matter how hard they make things for me, there's not a damn thing in this world that will make me give up on them. Either of them.

ALEXANDRA

EVEN THOUGH AVALON AND MADISON have been doing a great job to make me feel welcome here, I couldn't help the disappointment I felt when Jax left earlier. I thought I'd be okay spending the day without him, but the moment he walked out the door, my chest tightened and the air became thicker.

I could barely make out what Avalon was saying to me for the first five minutes after he left, because all I could think about was how much I missed him and wanted him to come back.

I wanted that safety and comfort that he brings.

I know it sounds crazy. I've never been the type of person to miss anyone except for when it comes to Jax. He's always been the one person I miss the second he walks away and he still has that effect on me.

After spending the night in his arms, I want him more than ever, but there's that part of me that is still terrified of letting him back in completely, in fear of hurting him.

But the truth is, I'm not thinking about escaping right

now or ways I can get my hands on drugs. I don't need something to numb my mind to make it through the day. I'm thinking about being in Jax's strong arms, snuggled up against him, and for the first time in a while I feel somewhat normal.

It makes me wonder if I can have a life like this. A life where I can breathe easily without the horror of my past weighing me down.

I don't have that answer, but I'm hoping with time that I do. All I can do is take it one day at a time.

"Oh, wow." Avalon grins and walks around Madison, checking out the aqua-blue-ombre job I did on her hair. I just got done blow-drying it. I have to admit that it does look pretty impressive. "This looks amazing, Lex. I owe Jax for bringing you to us. You're exactly what we need and you're going to fit in perfectly."

Checking out the pretty colors, I spin Madison's chair around so she can see how it turned out. She's been sitting there impatiently and honestly, it has me on edge to see what she thinks.

"Holy shit!" Madison squeals and runs her hands through her new hair in excitement. "Please never leave me, sweets. I can't believe I'm saying this, but I'm in love with a woman. Wonder if Jax would mind if I keep you."

Her excitement has me smiling, and I have to admit that I feel pretty damn good about myself for the first time in a long time. I feel like I've accomplished something and even though I'm missing Jax like crazy, I'm enjoying being here with the girls.

Conversation has been easy since the moment I stepped into the salon and I can see myself working here and actually being happy. I was never happy at previous jobs and all that did was make me want to get out of my head more.

My heart swells at the idea of having a new start.

"I'm sure Jax wouldn't mind," I joke, tossing my gloves into the small trash. "I'm not easy to handle."

"Oh, he definitely would mind," Madison says, still looking in the mirror. "That's why he's been sitting out in the parking lot for the last two hours watching you."

Butterflies fill my stomach when I look toward the window to see Jax sitting on the tailgate of his truck, his arms crossed over his chest.

He smiles at me and that little gesture sends my heart into overdrive and warms my body.

I was so busy making sure I didn't mess up on Madison's hair that I didn't even notice his truck pull into the parking lot.

He came back and waited for me?

I try to smother my smile as I turn away to look at Avalon, but it's impossible to hide what I'm feeling at the moment.

"Doesn't look like Jax wants to share you with anyone," Avalon adds with a smile. "We should let you go for today and tomorrow can be your first official day. I'll put out word on social media that we have a colorist and will be taking appointments starting tomorrow. Are you ready for that?" she asks with hope.

I nod and turn my gaze back to Jax, watching as he jumps down to his feet and lights up a cigarette. Even the way he does that gets me excited. Is there anything that man does that isn't completely hot? I'm not used to this feeling with him. Back when we were around each other before we were just kids. "Yeah. I think I'm ready."

"Perfect." Avalon laughs and pulls me in for a hug. "You're a lifesaver, babe. I'm so excited to have you join the Savage family. Don't forget to bring everything you need tomorrow so we can get you in the system as an official employee."

Keeping my eyes on Jax as he takes a drag off his cigarette and slowly blows the smoke out, I smile and nod, feeling bad that I can't give Avalon my full attention. "Thank you."

"See you tomorrow, sweets." Madison jumps from the chair and gives me a quick hug and a kiss on the lips, surprising me. "I love you."

"Madi," Avalon says on a laugh. "Don't scare her off before she even starts. You're letting your crazy show too damn soon."

"What?" Madison shrugs and winks at me. "I do. I love her. She's amazing and Jax can kiss my ass if he doesn't want to share, because I'm making him."

"It takes a lot to scare me off, trust me. I'm excited to start tomorrow." I'm in the middle of cleaning up my mess when the bell above the door dings, letting us know Jax has joined us inside.

I turn around and the sight of Jax standing just inches from me heats me to my core. Those eyes. And the way he uses them is like magic. I'm instantly under his spell, ready to fall right back into his arms.

"Fuck, call me crazy, but I missed the hell out of you." He smirks and grabs my hips, pulling me to him. "I was wondering when you'd realize I was here."

Before I can speak, he slides his hand around and grabs the back of my head pulling me in for a kiss that stops my heart mid-beat.

I spent years wondering what kind of man Jax had become and what it would feel like to have his hands and mouth on me. It feels way too good to keep fighting it. I want him touching me. I want to touch him.

"I think I owe you," I whisper when he breaks the kiss.

"For what," he smiles and speaks against my lips, "being an amazing kisser?" His smile widens as Madison and Avalon start whistling. "Haven't you girls ever heard of privacy?"

"Not when it's in my shop," Avalon says playfully. "Where do you expect us to look?"

"I don't know..." He kisses me one more time before backing away and grabbing my hand. "The wall."

"And miss such a rare display of affection from Jax Kade?" Madison says, plopping down onto the chair at her station again. "I don't think so. I might've taken a picture for proof."

"What time do you want me here tomorrow?" I ask, trying to keep my composure from hearing it's rare for Jax to show affection to a woman. I don't want anyone to see how happy that truly makes me.

"Ten works. Would you be okay with working until five?"

I smile at Avalon, loving the idea of a ten to five job. "Works for me."

The bell dings again and two girls walk inside, immediately walking over to admire Madison's hair. I overhear her telling them I'm starting tomorrow and joy fills me when I see their excitement.

"Let's get you out of here before the girls decide to keep you," Jax whispers in my ear, before guiding me to the door. "Later, ladies," Jax calls before hurrying me outside.

"Have you really been here for two hours?" I question once we get to his truck.

He shrugs, before pulling me against him and running his hand through my hair. "Maybe longer. I liked watching you work and didn't want to leave."

Smiling, I grab his beard and pull him to me. "You really are the same Jax I remember, aren't you?"

"When it comes to you, yes," he says across my lips. "I'll always be that Jax for you."

I swallow, emotions overwhelming me as I look into his sincere eyes. "You're so beautiful, Jax. You always have been. I don't deserve you."

"That's a fucking lie, Lex." He moves his hand down to grab mine, lacing our fingers together. "You're the only one who deserves me. We were meant for each other. I've always known that. That's why it's been so damn hard to breathe without you all these years."

I can hardly catch my breath as I look up at him. I love Jax so damn much that it hurts. It physically hurts, and it scares the shit out of me that his heart is in my hands.

But at the moment I need to kiss him. To taste him.

So I do.

Before he can say anything else to steal my breath away, I grab his neck and kiss him long and hard, showing him without words how much I need him.

His tongue flicks out, swiping across my lips so I open for him, allowing him to claim me. His taste is intoxicating, making me dizzy off his mouth.

I'm so lost in kissing him that I don't even realize I'm attempting to strip him until he laughs against my lips. "Are you going to jump me right here in the parking lot? Not saying I'd mind."

I shake my head and laugh. "Are the girls watching?"

He smiles and nods. "All four. But, ya know what? Fuck it." Lifting a brow, he backs me against the truck, blocking me in with his body. "Better than having Blaine watch us."

"Are you sure about that?" I love to rile him up.

He growls and opens the truck door. "Get in."

I cross my arms and stand firm. "Or what? Are you going to throw me inside again?"

"No." He presses his hips into me, causing me to moan as his hard cock digs into my skin. "I'm going to fuck you right here in the parking lot and give everyone a show."

Jax has no idea how much I love this side of him. The rough, savage side that took me home that night and fucked me hard against his door. I want him just the way he is.

"Fine." I push him away and hop into the truck, watching with a smirk as he hurries to other side to jump in himself.

He barely sits down and shuts his door before he's starting the truck and peeling out of the parking lot in a hurry to get me alone.

The bulge in his jeans has me reaching over and undoing his pants, just as in a hurry to get to him as he is to me.

He bites his bottom lip and grips the steering wheel when I pull his thick, hard dick out and begin stroking it with both hands. "Keep this up and we won't make it back to my place."

I unbuckle my seatbelt and move across the seat to get closer to him. He looks down at me, a small growl leaving his lips when I wrap mine around his cock.

"Holy fuck." He palms my head, gentle at first, but wraps his fist in my hair and tugs when I pick up speed, taking him deep into my mouth. Which isn't far because of his size. "Lex..."

I work my way back up to the head, swirling my tongue around it, getting a taste of his pre-cum. His salty taste has me moaning around his dick, before taking it back in as deep as it will fit, wanting all of him.

"I'm about to pull over right here if you keep using your damn mouth that way."

I'm curious to see how serious he is, so I suck harder, using my tongue in ways I never even knew I could. But when it comes to pleasing and teasing Jax I'm willing to learn new things.

"Fucking shit!" I hear the leather on the steering wheel stretch as he fists it tighter with the hand that's not wrapped in my hair. "Get in my lap."

His demand has heat flooding through my body and my pussy pulsing with need. The fact that he can't even wait ten minutes to get me alone has my heart pounding with excitement.

He pulls into an alley and parks, growling over at me as he kills the engine. "I need you on my dick, riding me. Now, Lex."

Breathing heavily, I keep my eyes locked on his as I strip off my jeans and straddle his lap, pulling my panties to the side.

The second his cock lines up with my entrance, he grabs my

hair and pulls me down, burying himself deep inside me, stretching me to his size.

I moan into the air as he groans into my neck, holding me still for a moment.

"Holy fuck, baby. I can't be gentle this time."

"Don't," I demand, grabbing his hair to yank his head back. "I don't want the old Jax right now—the one you think you still need to be for me. I want you. Right here, right now, just as you are. Savage and wild," I breathe.

His jaw steels and he examines my face, as if trying to decide if I meant what I said.

"Fuck me, Jax."

Moments later, his hold on my hair tightens and he pulls me down to meet his warm mouth. "Dig your nails into my flesh if it hurts. Rip me apart, because I won't be able to stop once I start."

I smirk, flicking my tongue out to run it up his lips, making my way around to whisper in his ear. "I never want you to."

He growls into the air and grabs my hips with both hands. "Fuck. You're not going to be able to walk into the house after this."

His fingers dig into my hips as he lifts me up, before slamming into me so hard I feel like he's splitting me in two.

I scream out and grab onto the leather seat, fighting to catch my breath. "Don't stop," I whisper.

"Fuck!" he screams into the air. "Hold on, babe."

I do as he says, digging my fingers into the leather as he fucks me deep and hard, owning my pussy in a way no other man has before or no other man ever will.

No one can fuck me like Jax.

No one can make me feel the way Jax can.

Jaxon Kade is the only man for me, and I know without a doubt, now that I have him back, I'll never let him go without a fight.

I will fight for him. For this. For us.

He pushes into me one last time, causing me to grab his shoulder and dig my nails in as I scream out his name through my orgasm.

Seconds later, he's filling me with his cum and we're both exhausted, fighting to catch our breath.

"Are you okay?" he whispers, moving his hands up to cup my face. "Did I hurt you?"

I nod. "Just a little," I admit. "But in a good way. So, so good."

He smiles in relief and rests his forehead to mine. "I'm calling in tonight. Blaine can handle the bar by himself. I'm not letting you out of my sight. I can't. Not yet."

I smile and lean in to kiss him. "Good," I say against his mouth. "Because I don't want you to."

With the way I'm feeling right now, right here in this moment, I'm not willing to let him out of my sight either.

I want to spend the night with him. No fighting or running away. Tonight, I want to be his.

JAX

I'M COVERED IN SWEAT AND haven't been able to catch my breath for the last hour. I was wrong to think she couldn't handle my roughness, because she's been taking me like a champ all night—biting, choking, and fucking just as hard as I do.

We barely made it into the house before she jumped on me, nearly knocking me into the wall, eager for me to take her again. Since then, we've hardly left my bed except to grab another bottle of whiskey to satisfy our thirsts.

I lost count of how many times we've had sex already, but shit, I'm not complaining. For her, I'd go all through the night. I wouldn't care how bad my muscles ached from holding myself above her. I can't get enough of her in my bed.

"We should eat." I brush my lips over hers before speaking again. "It's close to midnight. I'll make us some dinner."

I get ready to roll off of her to get out of bed, but she grabs the back of my head, stopping me. "Not yet, Jax." She shakes her head and reaches between us to grab my cock that hasn't gone down all damn night. "One more time. Just one more..."

She wraps her legs around my thighs and pulls me to her, causing me to groan into her neck when my sensitive cock enters her again.

I've never had a woman want me so much and I've never wanted a woman as much as I want her.

"Are you trying to kill me, baby?" I move my hips, pushing her up the mattress with each thrust, catching her moans with my mouth.

"Shhh..." She places her finger in my mouth and smiles when I bite it. "Don't talk. Just move those sexy hips." I move slow, keeping a steady rhythm, burying myself deep each time. "Yessss... Oh God... Yes."

I smile against her mouth, before biting her bottom lip and then slowly licking it. "I'm going to come inside you again. You like me filling you with my cum?"

She throws her head back and lets out a silent moan as her pussy clenches tightly around my cock. "Yes. Holy shit," she breathes, slapping my sweaty chest. "It's extremely sensitive now."

I laugh and still my hips. "It's only about your tenth orgasm of the night. Have you had enough?"

She raises a brow and gives me a mischievous look. "Have you?" I let her push me over so she can climb on top of me and sink back onto my hard cock.

"Shit, Lex!" I grip her hair and pull when she begins moving.

She grabs my neck with both hands and squeezes while she rides me hard and fast, and within minutes, I'm coming inside her again.

"Shit." I roll us over until I'm towering over her, getting a perfect view of her sexy-as-fuck body. I grab the base of my dick and slowly pull out, watching my cum drip out of her with every tightening of her pussy. I can't help but feel pride as I grab my shirt and clean her off, again. "No more excuses. I'm grabbing us something to eat."

She looks up at me with her eyelids heavy as she watches me slip into my boxer briefs. "Don't take too long," she says quietly.

My stomach sinks when I notice the uncertainty in her eyes —the fear of what will happen if I leave her alone too long. I know she's afraid she'll need an escape the moment I walk away. "I'll never leave you for too long," I reassure her. "We're in this together, Lex. I promise you."

She nods, but then stiffens when her phone vibrates. It's about the fifth time it's gone off tonight, and every time it does she gets this frozen look on her face like she wants to hide.

"Who keeps calling you?" I ask, my gut telling me I'm not going to like any answer she gives me. I can feel my muscles flexing while my entire body comes alive with adrenaline, ready to hurt someone if it comes down to it. "I don't want any secrets between us."

"It's no one I can't handle." She crawls out of bed and grabs her phone, silencing it. "I told him to fuck off the other day, so it'll probably take him a few days to get it through his thick skull that I was serious."

My stomach twists into knots at the thought of her being involved with another man. "Someone you were fucking?" I barely get the words out without punching my fist through a wall.

She swallows, keeping her eyes downcast on the mattress. "He's no one important to me. Just a guy I was sleeping with before I moved here. He's... attached to me is all. We fucked and got high together. That's all James was to me and he knew that from the beginning, but he still chose to follow me to town."

Rage spreads through me and it takes me gripping the

dresser to keep from tearing this whole room apart. I know I have no right to be angry. It was before me. And it's not like I expected her to still be a virgin after all this time. Until her, I've never cared about who the girls I'm involved with fucks before me, but Lex has always been different. Always. "He keeps calling and texting still? Even though you ended it?"

"He's never been good at staying away from me, but he'll eventually forget I exist and move on to someone else desperate enough to take him."

"I doubt that," I grind out. "Did he supply you with drugs?"

She runs a shaky hand through her hair, looking up to catch my gaze. "He started to after a while. It's probably the only reason I kept him around for as long as I did as shitty as it sounds, but James made me feel nothing. And the more drugs he brought around, the more out of my head I was able to get. I got used to living... surviving that way."

I can't stand here any longer and listen to her talk about this piece of shit James guy, without wanting to find him and rip him apart limb by fucking limb, so I give Alexandra a kiss on the forehead and make my way to the kitchen to calm down.

I slam the fridge and cupboard doors shut, not really knowing what I'm looking for. All I know is that I need a distraction, because I hate the way I'm feeling right now.

Hearing about this James guy makes me wonder just how many assholes gave her the impression over the years that she wasn't worth saving; that all she was valued for was a high. It had to be every son of a bitch she's ever been involved with for her to believe she's ruined.

It started with her piece of shit father and continued throughout her life with every guy she's come across. How am I the only person who has ever cared enough to protect her?

She doesn't deserve the shitty hand she was dealt.

I'm not sure how long I've been in here, but after a while I finally give up, grab the leftover pizza from the other night, and head back to the bedroom.

Alexandra is sitting in the same spot she was in when I left her and she looks up at me with eyes that practically break my heart in two. "There are a few things I need to tell you, Jax. Things about my father and the past. After I do, I won't be able to eat and I don't think you'll want to either."

Anxiety hits me and I run my hand over my face.

I'm not sure I'll ever be ready to hear what I could've saved her from all those years ago but never got the chance to.

But I also need to know.

I toss the pizza box down on the bed and get down on my knees in front of Alexandra, cupping her face with my hands. "Are you sure you're ready for this?"

She nods and grips the blanket as if she needs something to hold onto for this. I grab her hands and place them on my shoulders. "Hold onto me, babe. I don't care if you have to slice me open with your nails to get the words out. Don't let go."

"I never thought the day would come that I'd speak these words to you, Jax. You have no idea how many years I looked out my bedroom window, waiting for you to show up... but you never did. I knew it was impossible. I knew you'd never find me, but hope that you'd come in and save me was the only thing that kept me going for a long time." Her nails dig into my flesh when she continues.

"For most of the years it was the same abuse I was used to from my father. He got drunk, got mad, and would hit me. But..." She stops to swallow and my heart speeds up, nervous to hear what she's going to say next. "My body developed... my breasts came in... my curves..."

My nostrils flare out in anger at the thoughts running through my head. There's nothing in this world that could stop me from finding her father and killing him if this story goes where I think it's going.

"His friend let us live with him for free when we had nowhere to go. It was his place, and so was everything in it. And when I turned fifteen that included me too." Her hands tremble and I grip them and hold them against my lips, fighting with everything in me to hold back the tears stinging my eyes.

"Tell me, Lex. Tell me everything." My heart is beating so fast and loud I can hear it thundering in my ears. I can't handle this. I can't hear the words without exploding. "I need you to fucking tell me."

"At first, he just touched me above my underwear," she continues, "and my father would beat me with his belt if I wasn't a good girl by letting his friend do what he wanted. A few times he hit me across the face with it. It hurt so badly, but I wouldn't allow him the pleasure of seeing my tears. I held my ground, no matter how bad it got. Then one night..." She begins to tremble and shiver even more against my heated skin.

I pull her down into me and press my forehead to hers. Everything inside me wants to stop her from going any further. Stop her from saying aloud the very torture that ruined her all those years ago and still torments her now. But I need to hear it all. I have to know how bad I'm going to destroy this motherfucker. "Say it. Tell me what happened."

"He raped me." She forces the words out, tears wetting her face. "He fucking raped me while my father listened to me screaming for help and did nothing. My own dad didn't care what happened to me, and that's when I knew I was ruined. He let it happen more than once, Jax. He let it happen."

I can't breathe. I'm fucking suffocating. It's like I've just been punched in the gut a hundred times and I can't find air. I want to destroy everything in this room, but I hold her close instead, because comforting her comes first.

Her needs will always come first with me. They always have.

"I'm going to kill him, Lex." I press kisses all over her face and head, keeping her as close to me as possible. "I'm going to find him and I'm going to tear him apart with my bare fucking hands."

"It's over, Jax." She grabs my face and forces me to look into her eyes. "I only told you so we wouldn't have any secrets. I haven't seen him in almost ten years. All I want to do is forget about him and find a way to move on."

"That's what I'm going to make sure of, Lex. Now tell me where he lives."

"I don't know if he's still there."

"I'll find out. Just give me the address and I'll take care of the rest."

"Can we talk about this later? I'm tired. I think I just want to sleep now."

I wrap my hands into the back of her hair and kiss her long and hard, before pulling her further into bed with me and pulling her against me.

Hours after she has fallen asleep, I lie here wide awake, staring up at the ceiling, and thinking of all the ways I can hurt her father and make him feel just as helpless as he made her feel.

That motherfucker is going to wish for death to take him once I'm through with him.

AFTER DROPPING ALEXANDRA OFF AT the salon this morning, I called Royal and asked him to send Big Brute and Frankie my way for the road trip I'm on today. I found her father's address. A simple search revealed where the filth sits in squander. Even though Alexandra didn't hand the address over, she admitted the piece of shit's name that raped her. It's the name I needed all these years to find her but didn't have.

Big Brute and Frankie are the two most ruthless, sick

bastards I've ever met. Even I know better than to fuck with them, but for the job I want done, they're the only two that will work.

When I told Blaine and Royal my plans to find Alexandra's father today, they both offered to go on the road with me. But they can't do what I have in mind.

They may be crazy and willing to do anything to help me out, but even they have limits. They're not willing to get this dirty and I'm not about to tell them the details of what my intentions are. I need this to start quick and I don't have time to explain myself and have them try to talk me down.

I pull my truck in front of a small, rundown house and kill the engine. My blood pumps with need to tear the whole place down, starting with the fuckers inside.

Brute and Frankie pull up seconds behind me and climb off their bikes, waiting for direction from me. The old station wagon he had over thirteen years ago catches my eye. I know the asshole is here.

Closing my eyes, I grab my old bat and squeeze it in my hands; the feel of the grip a reminder of how Alexandra looked the night I walked in on him beating her. It's the fuel I need to get this job done. I've waited too damn long to use this bat on him again and this time shit is going to end differently.

My mind continues to flash with memories of everything that happened all those years ago. When I went back to Alexandra's house days later, the only thing I found besides some random things left behind was my bat. I've been holding onto it ever since... waiting for the right time.

Climbing out of my truck, I motion for Brute and Frankie to stay put as I make my way around to the back of the house. I want my time alone with these fuckers first.

I need it.

Just before I turn the corner on the backside of the house,

my body freezes when I see a boarded up window with old wood covering it... nails sticking out everywhere. Hot rage burns through my chest, because I know deep down this was Alexandra's room.

All those times she climbed out of her window to be with me back before they moved and then he made her a prisoner in this house.

I pick up speed, only stopping at the back door long enough to kick the half-broken thing open.

As soon as I step into the kitchen, I hear two male voices as they scramble to their feet and hurry to see who just intruded on their nasty fucking property.

The moment Alexandra's father comes into view I crack my neck and spin my bat around in my hand. He may be older and gray now, but there's no mistaking the crooked nose and bushy eyebrows from my childhood.

"Who the fuck are you?" He takes a step forward, but stops when he notices the bat in my hand. "We don't have anything worth stealing. Go ahead, asshole. Take a look around."

I flex my jaw, watching, as the piece of shit looks me over, sizing me up. He looks much smaller than I remember him as a kid, but back then I was barely five-three and weighed under a hundred pounds soaking wet.

I'm a beast now compared to this rat.

"Take what you want." My attention turns to the second person that just stepped into the room. He's tall and thin and looks to be around the same age as Alexandra's father. He's oily and disgusting, dressed in only a pair of old stained jeans. My blood boils at the sight of him, knowing what he did to Alexandra.

I can't decide who I want to annihilate first—the piece of shit who started her pain and suffering or the one who took her innocence from her when she was nothing but a scared kid.

"Jax," I finally say, taking a step closer, my muscles flexing as I look him over and allow the bat to smack against my palm. "Remember me, Mr. Adams?"

His eyes go wide when it finally registers what I'm here for. And it sure as hell isn't anything they have in this shitty house. He knows that now and the fear in his eyes is unmistakable.

He swallows and stumbles backward, his eyes focused on the blood-stained bat in my hand. "That was a long time ago. I've changed since then. I haven't touched her in over ten years. I swear."

I tilt my head and walk toward him. "That's because you don't know where she is." I back him against the wall and get in his face, so when I speak he'll see the savage in my eyes and just how fucked he truly is. "Now be a good boy and this will only hurt… a lot."

Before either of them can comprehend what's going on, I grip the bat on both ends and shove it against his neck, choking him against the wall, lifting him off the ground with ease. I leave him there to struggle and fight for air, before I turn to his friend and warn him when he makes a move to run. "Don't fucking move."

"Screw this! I'm out of here."

Despite my order, the piece of shit tosses his beer and makes a run for it, so I let her fucked-up excuse of a father fall to the ground. He begins gasping for a few of his final breaths as a free man before I take a swing at the other fucker and knock him out cold.

As soon as he hits the ground, I turn my attention back to Hank. I take my time, making sure I have a good grip before I swing out, hearing the bone in his arm snap when I make contact.

"Oh shit! Oh shit!" He grabs his arm and falls against the sink. "You son of a bitch. When will you learn that she's not worth a damn? She's damaged goods, Jax. You don't need to do this."

"You fucking piece of shit!" His words have me seeing red and the next thing I know, I've lost it. Anger and rage take over everything inside me and I snap. I can't stop myself from each and every hit, even when he stops fighting me. Memories of each blow I felt of the same bat hitting my body consume me as I continue. I don't stop until he's almost lifeless and covered in blood.

He makes an attempt to crawl away on his hands and feet, so I stand above him, shoving my boot into his throat and the tip of the bat against his forehead. I want him to see how long it is. I want him to see how fucking filthy it is. I want this image to burn into his fucked-up brain.

"Who's not worth a shit now?" I press my foot harder, crushing his throat until his face turns red. Killing him would be kind compared to what I have planned.

Removing my boot from his throat, I grab him by the hair and pull him up to his knees to get a good look at him. He looks up at me, his eyes swollen and barely open. His mouth moves as if he's trying to speak, but I can't comprehend a damn word through the blood he keeps choking on.

"Look how fucking pathetic you are. Your wife left you, because you couldn't provide her with what she needed and you took it out on a innocent child that didn't deserve your wrath. Your goddamn daughter! You broke her over and over again, and now I'm about to break you before I make sure you're ripped in fucking half."

Growling out, I slam my fist into his face two times before throwing him down to the ground.

Then I turn my attention back to the piece of dog shit that raped Alexandra. He's just now coming to, so I bend down and grip him by the throat, swinging out with my fist repeatedly, my ring digging into his flesh. I don't stop until the fucker is gasping for air.

By the time I'm through with him, his face is such a bloody mess it's unrecognizable.

I stand up, my head spinning as I look down at the two of them mangled and covered in blood. Their punishment isn't over yet. Not until they experience what Alexandra did. That's where Big Brute and Frankie come in.

Grabbing my bat, I step outside and motion for the guys.

The two big motherfuckers appear within a few seconds, both eager to do their part in this.

I hand my bat to Frankie and grip his shoulder. "Rape them bloody with this."

They both grin and step inside.

I light up a cigarette and lean back against the house, wanting to hear their screams echo through my ears. I take another look at her bedroom window, thinking about her crying for me every night. My body aches as I imagine all the nightmares she must've lived through.

Her father stood by and listened to her scream while his friend raped her and I won't leave here satisfied until I'm certain they know what it feels like.

They'll never walk right again after tonight. I made sure of that. I've decided a quick death would be too easy for what they've done. Brute and Frankie are fucked-up and don't mind providing a torture that will burn into the minds of the most deserving victims. That's why they're here.

Seconds later, I hear the first gut-wrenching scream, followed by another one, and I know the guys are about to handle shit in a way that I never could. I don't need to hear it all to know how it's going to go, so I toss my cigarette on the ground and walk to my truck.

This might not erase what was done to Alexandra, but

hopefully she can feel just a small bit of relief to know that those fuckers are finally getting what they deserve.

I'll make sure the guys give both of them a daily reminder of what they've done until they take their last breath. And I'll make sure the bat is there every fucking time.

ALEXANDRA

DROPPING TO MY KNEES, I grip the toilet bowl and empty my stomach for the second time since walking through the salon door.

It's been three days since I popped my last pill and the lack of drugs in my system has had me sweaty and nauseous all day, leaving me feeling like complete shit. My body aches, my hands are shaky, and it's taking every ounce of strength I have not to find a supplier and escape this shitty feeling, since I know how easy it'd be to make it go away. I've been so good at hiding my fix-all and numbing myself for the last ten years that it's my first instinct.

I wish I could scream right now.

I slept fine last night and even felt somewhat okay when Jax dropped me off this morning, but as the minutes ticked and the hours went by, the symptoms worsened from dull but noticeable to kick-ass mode.

It doesn't help that Jax took off this morning set on going after the one person I hate the most in this world. I saw it in his eyes when he kissed me goodbye. There was nothing I could say or do that would stop him from his mission.

Except maybe this.

If only this would've hit me sooner... then I know he would've stayed. He wouldn't have left my side, even though it would've been painful for him. I know this is something he feels he needs to do.

I've been doing my best to make it through the day without him, but it's hard to think straight. It doesn't help that he hasn't responded to my texts all day and it's nearly five now.

I hate not knowing whether or not he's okay. He means more to me than anything in this world and I don't know what I would do if anything were to ever happen to him. Especially if it was because of me.

My father is a drunk piece of shit and so is George, but put the two of them together and who knows what they're capable of.

The thought has me clenching my stomach in pain.

"Are you okay, sweets?" Madison steps into the bathroom and places her hand on my back. "You don't look so hot; all day really. I'm not sure how you got through your appointments and still did such a bang-ass job. I'd be in bed crying like a baby if I was sick, forcing Ava to take care of me."

I release the toilet and stand up to wash my hands and face. "It's been tough, but I've survived worse." I force a smile and pull my sweaty hair out of my face. "I feel a bit better now. I'll be out in a minute to help clean up."

"No need to, sweets. Blaine is here for you. He said Jax asked him to pick you up." She gives me a sad look in the mirror. "Go home and get some rest. Jax will take care of you when he gets home."

The moment she steps out of the bathroom and leaves me alone, my stomach sinks at the thought of when that might be.

I just hope Blaine knows more than I do and can fill me in, because I can't take not knowing anymore.

I take a few more minutes to gather myself until I look somewhat presentable before I step out of the bathroom and thank Avalon for giving me the opportunity to work for her.

Other than feeling physically and mentally sick, I enjoyed being here today with the girls and I can't imagine going back to working at a bar after seeing what it's like to work here.

Blaine walks out from the back room, looking uptight, Madison following right behind him. "You good to go?"

I look down at my phone and swallow, before shoving it onto my jacket pocket. "Yeah."

"Don't worry about Jax. The last thing he's concerned with right now is his phone. He can't talk when he's in savage mode."

"Have you heard from him?" He shakes his head and looks down at me. "Not since he text me this morning at the ass crack of dawn to tell me I was giving you a ride to his house from the salon today."

"Who's watching the bar?" I question as he guides me outside to his bike. I hate that everyone has to make sacrifices because of me. I never want to be that person, but when Jax sets his mind to something there's no stopping him. He's always been that way.

"Mark." He hands me his helmet and climbs on his Harley. "He'll be good for a bit. Climb on."

I feel weird, standing here about to get on the back of some other man's bike, but the fact that Jax sent Blaine to pick me up has me climbing on the back and grabbing onto his leather jacket.

"Don't be afraid to wrap your arms around me, babe. You don't have to tell Jax my body feels better than his. He already knows and he's learned to live with it."

I roll my eyes and move my arms to wrap around his waist. "Just drive."

I don't have to see his face to know that he's smirking as he drives off. At least he seems to be in a better mood now than he was a few seconds ago.

When we get to Jax's house, Blaine unlocks the door and motions for me to go in, before following behind me.

"I need a drink," Blaine immediately says the moment his eyes land on the bottle of Jack in the kitchen.

"Pour me one too. A tall one." I need a drink just as much or even more than he does right now, because I'm moments away from losing my shit. "Quick."

We both take a seat at the table and he pours two glasses, scooting one in front of me. His jaw tenses as he looks down at his glass before emptying it in one shot.

"Female problems?" I lift a brow and tilt my glass back, watching as he refills his.

"You can say that, amongst other shit."

"Are you and Madison... a thing?"

He freezes mid-drink and turns his gaze on me. "She doesn't talk about this Dean fucker at work? Guess that shit didn't work out."

I shake my head and take another drink. "She hasn't mentioned him at all..." I pause, looking toward the door as if Jax will come in any second. "But she did mention how much of a pain in the ass you are. She seems to be really pissed at you for some reason. She even snapped a few combs in half today and said she wished the combs were your stupid neck."

When I turn back to face him, he's smirking down at his glass as if he's happy she's pissed at him. "She's having Blaine withdrawals. All women want to kill me once we stop fucking."

I let out a small laugh, despite the fact that I'm feeling like complete garbage. Blaine may be crazy from what I've heard, but he's good for a laugh when needed.

It's helping to distract me from what I really wish I had

right now, but I made a promise to Jax and I don't plan on breaking it.

We sit here in silence for a while, us both seeming to need the peace and quiet to think while waiting on Jax to arrive.

It's close to six-thirty now, and the more I stare at the front door waiting for it to open, the more anxious I become.

"Did Jax go alone?" I finally ask, bringing the glass to my lips with shaky hands. "Is there someone else we can call to see if he's okay?" I'm desperate at this point.

"He didn't go alone, but no, we can't call these two. They'll be busy for a while."

My heart speeds up at the sound of Jax's truck pulling into the driveway. I jump to my feet, anxious to see him and know that everything is okay.

"About time," Blaine mutters, standing up. "He must've been driving like a pussy on the way back."

Moments later, the front door opens and Jax walks inside, his hands covered in dried blood. He doesn't have a scratch on him, so I immediately know he's okay. Relief hits me, making it easy to breathe for the first time today.

Trailing my eyes along every inch of him, they finally go back up to his face. "Shit, Jax. You had me worried like crazy."

He releases a breath before coming at me, wrapping his hands in my hair as he looks down at me. "All you need to know is that they're both suffering and alive... for now."

A weight has been lifted from my chest and a slew of emotions hit me, making it hard to keep my composure. A few tears fall down my face and Jax wipes them away, before kissing me. "Don't cry, Lex. They got what they deserved. I should've killed them both there on the spot for hurting you."

I shake my head and wrap my arms around his neck. "I'm not crying for those assholes, Jax. I hate them both. They can rot in Hell for all I care. I'm just overwhelmed. I spent the entire day terrified that something happened to you. The thought of you getting hurt or arrested over me had my stomach in knots all day and my chest felt heavy. Hearing that you hurt them and seeing that you're okay is a relief. I can breathe for the first time today. I don't like you being that far away from me, Jax. Don't ever fucking leave me again."

He pulls me in closer and kisses me again, his kiss deeper and more powerful this time. "There's nothing in this world that can make me leave you, Lex. I'd die first. That's a promise and you know I keep them."

"Shit. I gotta go. As much as I'd like to stay and watch this lovefest, Mark needs backup at the bar."

Jax turns his attention to Blaine for the first time since walking through the door. "Thanks for staying with Lex. I owe you."

"I needed to get away from the chaos of that place for a bit tonight anyway. It's all good, brother. I'm just glad you're good."

Jax nods and brings his attention back to me as Blaine rushes to the door to take off.

"Do I need to kill Blaine?"

I shake my head and smile through my pain, loving the way he's so protective over me when it comes to other men. "Not unless you want to kill him for saying he has a better body than you."

"That fucker." He smiles down at me, before stripping off his jacket, revealing his firm chest in the tightfitting shirt he has on. "I think we both know that shit isn't true."

"Or is it?"

He looks as if he's about to smile, but his face falls when he takes a good look at me for the first time since walking through the door. "Shit. You're covered in sweat, Lex."

He doesn't give me a chance to react before picking me up and carrying me to the bathroom.

"You need a cold shower to cool off."

He sets me back on my feet and starts the shower, before

slowly stripping my clothes off and guiding me into the brisk water.

I'm not sure I can handle the chill until Jax strips his clothes off and steps into the water with me. Every hard dip of muscle calls to me, making me want to jump him for a distraction. I don't care how much pain I'm in right now, when he's here it subsides. Jax is the only thing that can distract me and make me feel better.

Grabbing the bar of soap, he quickly cleans his hands off before grabbing my face and pulling me close to him, so that we're both standing under the water. It's almost unbearable, yet Jax doesn't make a move to leave.

"You don't have to do this with me, Jax."

"I don't have to, but I want to." He rubs his thumb over my cheek, before leaning in to kiss me. "I'll do this with you as many times as it takes."

I wrap my arms around his neck and he picks me up, my legs instantly wrapping around his waist. The moment he enters me, I throw my head back and moan, getting lost for a short time. Nothing else exists other than him.

Every step is going to be hell and a long, bumpy road to recovery, but having Jax here with me, right now, makes me believe I can get through it this time.

Jax is the only drug that I need, and knowing him, he won't give up until my body believes it just as much as my heart does.

JAX

THE LAST FIVE DAYS HAVE been rough for Alexandra, and nothing kills me more than having to watch her suffer through withdrawal symptoms.

I promised her I'd stay by her side through it all and I have. Neither of us has left my house in days and I'll stay here for weeks if that's how long it takes. I'm not leaving her to go through this alone.

Thankfully, the guys have all been helpful and understanding that I took the week off to take care of Alexandra. They didn't ask questions or even give me shit about having to take on so many shifts at the bar, but instead, offered to help in any way they could.

Mark helped me get my hands on some anti-nausea medication and sleep supplements, which have relaxed her a bit. She hasn't eaten much, but I've been making her drink plenty of fluids to keep her hydrated.

Looking down at her in my bed, I run my hands through my hair and slowly exhale. She's been sleeping most of the day, but I want to be at her side in case she were to wake up and need me.

Every time she stirs, my heartbeat speeds up, anxiety kicking in for her to wake up and tell me how she's feeling. I need to hear that she's okay.

"Jax," she whispers, sitting up. "How long have you been sitting there?"

I look down at my phone to check the time. "Close to five hours." I stand up and reach for the glass of water as she adjusts her position. "Drink this."

She grabs it from me and takes a sip, before looking up at me. "You don't have to sit there and watch me every second that I'm sleeping. I know you won't leave me, Jax. You've proven that many times already."

After she sets the glass down, I grab her face and kiss her, before crawling into bed beside her. "Are you ready to eat yet?"

She shakes her head and leans into my chest. "I think I need a little more time. I'm finally not feeling nauseous for the first time in days. I don't want to push it since I just woke up."

I wrap my arms around her and kiss the top of her head, before grabbing the remote and flipping the TV to her favorite channel. At least the one she used to favor when we were kids.

She smiles against my chest and lays a kiss in the center of it. "I don't know what I'd do without you, Jax."

"You'll never have to find out again," I whisper. "Just relax and watch TV."

"That's the best idea I've heard in a while." And that's what we do for the rest of the night. Lie in bed watching TV while I hold her. Every time she laughs it makes me laugh as well, because just like when we were kids, her laugh makes me happy.

It also gives me hope that she's feeling better and I couldn't ask for anything more right now.

ALEXANDRA

IT'S THE FIRST TIME IN eight days that Jax or myself has left his house. Getting over the withdrawal symptoms has not been easy; in fact, it's been one of the hardest things in my life other than losing Jax all those years ago.

The first few days I was so depressed that all I wanted to do was sleep. Being awake was a reminder of what I was putting Jax through and I couldn't handle it. I made a promise to myself when I moved back to stay away from Jax for that very reason.

He's been through enough, and the idea of putting him through taking care of me hurt like hell. I was terrified I'd break down and fight Jax for an escape. I didn't think I'd be strong enough to walk away from the one thing that's been keeping me together for so long, but he pushed me and fought along with me, not willing to give up on me.

Now, the only thing I can do is stay strong enough to stay clean for him. For us. Because I don't think I'll ever be able to survive without him again. Not after finally getting him back.

It's been over a week since Jax took the four-hour drive to pay my father and George a visit. It took me until the next day to actually comprehend what Jax had done for me the night before.

The only thing I wanted to think about when he walked through that door was that he was safe and back home where he belonged. Nothing else mattered.

But once I actually took the time to think about those two assholes suffering because of Jax, I realized part of the relief I felt was from them finally getting what they deserve after all these years.

It doesn't take back all the bad things my father put me through, but it feels good to know that him and his asshole friend understand the feeling of being as helpless and weak as they made me feel.

I didn't ask Jax too many details, but judging by his bloodied fists when he walked into the house that night, I'd say they both got a pretty good beating and Jax got his point across.

We haven't talked about what happened since, and I don't plan on asking and making Jax have to think about it anymore. It's done. I'm ready for us both to move on and forget my father ever existed. He forgot about me easy enough.

The last week has been rough, but things are finally beginning to look up and I want to keep moving forward as smoothly as possible. No more looking back.

"It's looking good, babe." Jax looks up from the tattoo he's been working on, his amber eyes locking with my green ones. I can see the concern in them before he speaks again. "Are you okay? Do you need a break?"

"I'm fine. Keep going, Jax. I need this right now." I close my eyes and relax as much as I can, even though I lied, because it hurts like hell at this point. But this tattoo means a lot to me. I changed my mind and decided to get something different than what I originally came in to get. Something that means something to me.

It's a black and gray tattoo of a little girl on a tire swing with a boy pushing her. I told him to do his best to capture the Apple Blossom tree and the night sky as he remembers it from when we were kids. He stayed up all night drawing it and we've been here at Savage & Ink for almost five hours now.

I can't tell how much he's done, but I've never been more anxious for a tattoo in my life. There's nothing I want marked permanently on my body more than the memory of the only happy part of my childhood.

It expresses that Jax has been there for me through my toughest times and never once gave up on me.

"How are you feeling besides the pain from the tattoo?" He pauses and looks up at me again, waiting for an answer. I know exactly what he's asking and I want him to know that he can stop worrying about me.

"Better," I answer honestly. "I feel as close to normal as I have in years. The craving will always be there, in the back of my mind, but I haven't had any urges to look for a handful of pills and go crazy, so you can relax. I promise."

He sets the tattoo machine down and grabs my face, pulling me in so close that his beard tickles me. "Fuck, Lex. You have no idea how happy that makes me. I know this shit isn't easy. I went through it with my mother, but I need you to tell me whenever you feel like you're seconds away from caving, so I can be there for you. Promise me this."

I swallow and close my eyes when he pulls me in for a kiss, giving my bottom lip a slight tug as he pulls away. His mouth is perfect at making me forget everything else when it's on mine, and he knows this, so he makes sure to use it on me as often as possible. I'm not complaining. "I promise," I whisper against his lips. "I'll let you know."

This man.

His touch.

His kiss.

His closeness.

They're the only things that have kept me strong through all of this. In the past, nothing was good enough to keep me straight. I would've already been looking for a way to escape, but even with the numerous phone calls and texts that James has been sending for the past week, I haven't broken yet.

"Let's get this tattoo finished so I can get you home and in my bed."

I nod and make myself comfortable again as he goes back to work. "Can we swing by Tessa's on the way? I need to grab some more clothes if I'm staying at your place longer."

"We're grabbing all of your clothes, Lex. Tell Tessa I'll pay her the rent for the next two months. That should give her enough time to find a new roommate. It's our place."

Butterflies flutter in my stomach at the thought of moving in with Jax, and I can't stop the smile that takes over. I spent so much time worrying he wouldn't want me after discovering the true me that it feels extremely freeing to know I was wrong.

"Jax, are you sure you—"

"It's the only thing I've wanted for as long as I've known you, Lex. Yes. You're moving in with me and if you try fighting me on it you're going to lose."

I'm not fighting him on this, because the truth is, after spending the last week in his bed and in his arms, I can't imagine going back to my bed at Tessa's. It never felt like home there; no place ever has, aside from where Jax is.

I can't find the right words to say, so I say the first thing that comes to mind. "I'll let Tessa know."

He grabs the tattoo machine again and I reach beside me for my phone to text Tessa and distract myself from the pain.

I have a few missed texts and my stomach sinks when I read the one from James.

JAMES

This is bullshit, but I'm not giving up, Alex. Sooner or later you're going to beg me to come over with a buffet of pills. The urge will never go away. You're an addict. Just admit that to yourself and answer my fucking texts. I know you're reading them. Jax will never accept you the way I do. You're damaged goods. That will never change.

I squeeze my phone in my hand, wanting nothing more than for it to be James' neck. He's trying to get to me and weaken me, but I won't let that happen, because I know he's wrong about Jax.

"Fucking asshole," I mutter.

"Another text from James?" He doesn't look away from the tattoo, but his jaw steels when I nod. "That fucker is sadly mistaken if he thinks I won't hunt him down and break his neck. I've kept it together for the past week, because there was no way in hell I was leaving your side, but he won't get so lucky this week."

"I need to text Tessa and see if he's been giving her a hard time. If he has then I'll kick his ass myself."

My other two messages are from Madison checking on me, but I ignore those for now and pull up Tessa's name.

ALEXANDRA

Has James been coming around the house since I've been gone?

Tessa is most likely at work, so it takes a bit to get a response.

TESSA

Yeah and he's about to get kicked in the balls the next time him and that dealer of his shows up. I've already told them you haven't been around, but they keep coming back.

They stood outside the house for almost three hours last night. It was creepy as shit. I almost texted you, but I didn't know how you were feeling. Are you okay?

My stomach sinks when I read over her messages to see that James and Jasper have been creeping around the house. Jasper gave me a bad vibe that night we met and it's a little strange he keeps coming around with James.

"Everything good?" Jax sets the tattoo machine down and cleans off my side.

"I don't know. Tessa says James and his dealer have been hanging around the house. I don't feel comfortable with her being there alone, Jax. Maybe I should—"

"You're not staying there, Lex. Hell no. Not happening. I'll send Blaine to keep an eye out. He needs a distraction right now since him and Madison are no longer talking. The asshole is moody as hell."

I watch as he does a few finishing touches, before cleaning it off one last time.

"All done. Shit, Lex. I'm so happy you wanted this on your body. You have no idea how many times I've thought about those nights with you at the tire swing."

I push the thoughts of James and Jasper out of my mind and do my best to focus on this moment, before it's ruined.

"I've thought about them too." I grab the back of his neck and pull him close, needing his touch. This whole situation with James has me worked up. "The memories helped me through some hard times and I'll never forget them. You made sure of that. I still remember laughing like nothing else in the world existed except the two of us and that tire swing."

My heart skips a beat from the way he's looking at me, and that look alone is almost enough to make me blurt out what I've been feeling since the day he found me. But the thought of saying the words out loud and not hearing them back scares me enough to stop myself.

"That's how I wanted to make you feel. That's how you deserved to feel." He gives me a quick kiss on the lips, before grabbing my hand and helping me to my feet. "Take a look in the mirror and tell me what you think."

The moment I get a glimpse at the ink on my side, my breath catches in my throat. Jax captured us perfectly and it's hard not to get overwhelmed with emotions right now.

"Do you like it?" He moves in behind me and pulls my hair over my shoulder. "Is it what you pictured?"

I shake my head. "No. It's so much better, Jax. It's absolutely breathtaking."

"I hope it was worth the six hours of pain." He kisses my neck, before slowly moving his mouth around to kiss my chin. "Because I hate hurting you."

"It was more than worth it. Thank you, Jax." I turn around to face him and wrap my hands into the bottom of his hair. "I can't thank you enough for everything you've done for me. I've loved you since we were kids. I've never loved anyone else and I never will. I want you to know that."

With his eyes locked on mine, he bows his head and cups my face with both hands. My heart races as I wait for him to say something. Anything. "Do you mean that?"

I swallow, trying to my best not to pass out. I'm so damn nervous right now that my head feels like it's spinning. "Yes. I mean it."

His jaw flexes as he looks me over, taking in my expression.

"I've loved you since the day I found you behind your garage and I fell in love with you the day you walked back into my life with your sassy attitude. It always has and only ever will be you, Lex, regardless of how much time passes. That's the fucking truth."

Gripping my face with both hands, he leans down to my height and desperately presses his lips against mine, while moving his hands up to grip at my hair, as if he needs any and every part of me. When he kisses me this way it leaves me breathless, every single time, and now is no exception.

When we finally break the kiss, I look into the mirror to see Blaine leaning against the door watching us. He winks at me and I can't help but to smile at the cute asshole.

"Do you ever knock, asshole?" Jax asks, trying to hide his smile.

"Not in all the years we've known each other, brother." He flashes us a grin, but it's not his usual cocky one. "Good thing I didn't, because I got to witness your confession of love. How fucking sweet and sappy."

"Fuck you," Jax says, watching as Blaine walks over to check out my tattoo. "Is Mark still here?"

He nods, leaning in to get a better look at my ink. "Holy shit, asshole. You're better than I expected."

"Ask Mark if he can stay and close up. I need you to stay with someone tonight and possibly tomorrow until I can take care of something."

Blaine stands up straight and cracks his neck. "Do I need to get into ass-kicking mode? It's been a while and I'm itching to fuck someone up."

"Someone from my past won't stop harassing my roommate Tessa. I don't feel comfortable with her being there alone. It would mean a lot if you could stay with her in case he comes back again."

Blaine runs a hand through his hair and nods. "I don't feel

like sleeping at my house right now anyway. I'll be your watchdog."

"Appreciate it, brother." Jax grips his shoulder. "Go talk to Mark and then meet us outside."

Less than ten minutes later, we're headed to Tessa's house with Blaine following us on his motorcycle.

It's half past one, so Tessa won't be home for a while, but I sent her a text to let her know Blaine will be sleeping on the couch. I get a response as we're pulling up in the driveway; her thanking me in all caps.

Blaine and Jax stay in the living room discussing some things as I grab a bag and shove all the clothes I care about into it. The rest I'll leave for Tessa to decide if she wants or not. I don't have much else to take, since I came here with practically nothing, so it doesn't take long for me to finish.

"I'm ready."

The guys look my way and Jax immediately walks over to grab my clothes from me. "Tessa is good with a stranger sleeping on her couch?"

I smile and turn my attention to Blaine. "I'm guessing from the thank you she sent me she knows of Blaine."

Blaine grins and takes a seat on the arm of the couch.

Cocky fucker.

"Then she's aware there'll be a psychotic asshole alone in the house with her. Glad we don't have to explain that shit to her."

"A hot psychotic asshole," Blaine adds. "I haven't had any complaints yet."

"Keep telling yourself that." Jax shakes his head and places his free hand on the small of my back. "Let's go home and get some rest. Blaine will call if anything goes down."

We open the door to step outside and my heart drops to my stomach when James' shitty car pulls up in front of the house.

"Get inside," Jax says, his voice firm. "Tell Blaine I can handle this by myself."

I don't fight Jax on this, because the truth is, I can't stand to look at James right now. All I want is to get him out of my life. Seeing him will only remind me of all those nights we got high together. I'm not ready for that.

I step into the house and Blaine is already making his way to the door, so I place my hand on his chest and push him back inside. "Jax said he'll handle it by himself."

Blaine stiffens and cracks his knuckles, as if he's ready for a fight to go down. He listens for a few seconds before, "fuck it," flies out of his mouth and he walks outside.

I watch from the window, looking out at James' car, waiting for him and Jasper to step outside, but they don't. After a few minutes they drive off.

With my heart pounding, I hurry outside to see Jax and Blaine smoking a joint, staring at the street.

"Jasper," Jax says after a few seconds. "That's James' dealer. I should've known."

I swallow. "You've dealt with him before?"

He nods and hands the joint back to Blaine. "He was my mom's dealer. Him and some prick were at my mom's house a while ago. I'm going to assume that's why the fucker sized me up when hearing my name."

"You've met?" Nerves take over thinking about the two of them meeting face to face.

"Yeah, but I had no clue he knew you. I just got a feeling he didn't like the looks of me. Now I see why."

"Fuck it," Blaine says, passing the joint back to Jax. "We'll take them on. I don't have shit else to do."

"I'll handle it." Jax tosses the joint and runs his hands over his face. "You take care of things if they come back and give Tessa a hard time."

"Gotcha."

After saying bye to Blaine, we head back to Jax's, both of us tense from learning about Jasper and James.

Jax doesn't say much the rest of the night. He checks my tattoo one more time and then pulls me into bed with him, keeping me as close as possible. I can tell he's fighting hard to keep it together and I hate that he feels he has to keep his guard up now.

It takes me a while to fall asleep, because I can't stop wondering if James and Jasper will come back again.

If they do. I have a feeling it'll get messy.

JAX

I WAKE UP TO ALEXANDRA'S hand running down my chest and abs, stopping on my hard cock. The moment she realizes I'm awake, she rolls over and straddles me, slowly sinking onto my erection.

"Fucking hell, baby." I reach up and wrap my fists into her hair, growling out my pleasure as she rides me. "You feel so fucking good."

"How good?" she whispers against my ear. "Tell me, Jax."

"Good enough that I'm going to come in less than a minute if you keep grinding your hips like that." I grab the back of her neck and hold her still, unable to handle her moving right now. "And we both know I refuse to come before you do first."

Wrapping my arm around her waist, I maneuver her so that she's face first into the mattress with my hard body hovering above her. "Dammit, Jax. I just wanted this one time."

I smirk and grab her wrists, pinning them above her head as I slide between her slick thighs and bury myself deep. Fuck, she feels too good from this angle, but I also know this position makes her orgasm fast every single time.

She moans into the mattress and wiggles to free her wrists when I move my hips. "I know how much you love taking my cock from this position, Lex." I shove into her and stop, leaning in to speak against her ear. "I wonder how quickly I can make you come this time." I pull out and push back in, moving in a slow rhythm, wanting her to feel every inch of me inside her. "Your tight pussy loves taking me."

"Jax. Oh fuck, Jax... Yesss..." She moans and bites the mattress as I continue to fuck her how she likes it. "I'm about to..."

I bury myself inside her one last time, feeling her pussy clench tight around my dick as she comes for me.

I give her a few seconds to recover before I pull my cock from her sensitive pussy and lay back down beside her, knowing that's where she'll want me now.

Climbing on top of me, she grips my throat and growls at me. "You're an asshole."

I smile and grip her ass hard. "So I've heard. Show me how much."

Keeping her gaze locked on mine, she begins riding me fast and hard, her roughness making me come within minutes.

"You keep waking me up to sex every damn morning, I'm going to get too used to it and expect it for years to come. You get that, right?"

She smiles down at me and releases my throat. "That's what I'm counting on." I roll us over and she laughs as I place kisses all over her face and neck. "Your beard. It tickles, Jax. Stop!"

"That's what I'm counting on," I say against her neck, teasing her back as she wiggles beneath me.

"Okay! Okay!" She pushes me away and looks up at me, smiling big. Her smile is so beautiful that it stops my heart. "Stop torturing me, so I can cook us breakfast."

I allow her to push me off of her, so she can crawl out of bed. I watch with a satisfied grin as she grabs my worn shirt and slips it on. "Are you sure you don't want me to help?"

She shakes her head, while throwing her hair into a ponytail. "You've taken care of me for nearly two weeks, Jax. You better not move a damn muscle."

"What'll happen if I do?" I lift a brow as she throws me a dirty look.

"You don't want to find out. Now stay, and you better still be naked when I return."

"I'll do anything you ask of me, Lex." I grab her arm and pull her in for a kiss, tempted to take her again, but she escapes with a laugh before I get too far.

"I'll be back."

Less than twenty minutes later, Alexandra returns with a plateful of eggs, sausage, and toast and crawls back into bed beside me, so we can share off the same plate.

It feels good to just relax and have a normal morning with Lex. This is something I want for us every day. I was just joking about it being the sex I could get used to.

It's this.

Us.

Moments like this are what I want to get used to.

I've lost count of how many times over the years I've pictured a life like this for us. One where we'd be together every day and she'd be mine. Those girls before her were just something to pass the time till I could find her again.

Now I have her. There's nothing in this world that could make me give this up. Even if we had to go through the same shit we've dealt with over the last two weeks again, I'd do it for her. I'd do it with her over and over again until she realizes I'm the only thing she needs to get by.

Lex is my world. She has been since the age of nine. Even though we've barely left each other's side for almost two weeks now, the idea of dropping her off at the salon soon and not seeing her until I get off work tonight has my chest feeling heavy.

It's going to be a long night, and hopefully, I make it through without feeling the need to fuck someone up...

I'VE SPENT MOST OF THE night here at Savage & Ink thinking about Jasper and James, wondering if those motherfucking pieces of shit plan to make a reappearance in Alexandra's life.

I didn't go into too many details with her about my history with Jasper, because I didn't want to worry her, but there's no one out there that wants to get to me more than that asshole.

He's been waiting for a good enough reason to come at me for years since he walked away from my mother. Once I was grown he had no choice. I was big enough to take him. But to him, I stole from him.

I know how much of a piece of shit he is, and when he doesn't get what he wants, which seems to be someone important to me using, he plays dirty. First Mom and now Alexandra. He knows she's special to me. He'll use that as his way to get to me after all these years.

He'll use her. And right now she's too vulnerable.

That thought has me squeezing the bottle I'm holding. It pisses me the hell off that he could be out there somewhere, just waiting for a chance to get her alone, so he can get to her. It doesn't help that I'm clueless to where he lives, because he never stays in one place too long. He likes to make sure none of his enemies can get to him if it comes down to it.

I need to have Mark on getting me a location, so I can get to him before he decides to make an unexpected appearance when I'm not there to help her.

"Hey, man. How is Lex?" I look up to see Mark pull out the stool directly in front of me and take a seat. He's dressed in his uniform, so I'm guessing he's here to talk and not get wasted.

"Just the man I want to see." I grab a glass and pour in a little whiskey, before topping the rest off with Coke. He may not be able to get drunk right now, but that doesn't mean he can't relax and enjoy just enough to chill. "She's doing really good. Madison is with her at my place. She started back up at the salon today and has a full schedule set up for next week. It's been a long two weeks, but she has a new normal now."

He nods and grabs the glass, taking a small drink before speaking. "Well, if she has Madi to keep her company, then you know she's entertained at least. It'll be good to keep her busy for a while. Solitude is a recipe for failure with an addict. I'm not saying she'll be tempted to use again, but it's hard to tell. Just keep an eye on her."

"Yeah. If she is we'll deal with it together." I pour myself a glass and lean over the bar, taking a quick look around. It's quiet tonight, so I sent Blaine to Tessa's over an hour ago. But at this place you never know when shit's going to break loose. "She's strong though. I know it. A lot stronger than my mother ever was or will be, because she believes she has a reason to get better. My mother never thought she did. Not after my father walked out on her."

"Good thing Lex will never have to worry about you walking out." He cocks a brow at me. "Right?"

I run a hand over my beard, before tilting the rest of my drink back. "Not a fucking chance. She couldn't get rid of me if she tried, and trust me, she did."

Mark laughs and takes another drink. "You said you wanted to see me?"

"Yeah. I need you to find out where someone is staying. I need to know ASAP."

He sets his glass down and reaches for his phone to see

who's calling when it rings. "Shit. I need to head out. Give me a name and I'll do my best to get you an address."

"Jasper Moore," I say stiffly.

"That piece of shit motherfucker?"

I grab his glass and toss it into the sink. "Alexandra refused his drugs."

That's all I have to say for Mark to understand why I need to get to Jasper.

His jaw flexes as he fixes the top button of his uniform. "I'll get someone on it tonight. You'll hear from me soon."

"All right, man. Take it easy."

He drops some money down on the bar and turns around to leave. He almost makes it to the door when Ted—a regular—stops him to give him shit about being a cop.

Ted only gets about three insults in before Mark cracks his neck and headbutts him in the forehead, sending him down to his ass. I smile as Mark looks down at him and tells him to fuck off before walking away.

I swear he gets more savage the more time he spends with us.

My phone vibrates in my pocket and I quickly reach for it in case it's Alexandra, but I grunt when I see that it's only Blaine.

BLAINE

Tessa decided to stay at a friend's house tonight. Said they were going to have a girls' night and get drunk on wine or some shit. I'm having a few drinks with your hot-as-fuck mom. She's still good. Jasper hasn't been around.

JAX

Just keep your dick in your pants this time, asshole.

BLAINE

She's already grabbed it once. I can't promise it won't come out to play again.

I ignore the asshole's message, because that's the last image I need in my mind. I witnessed that shit once, and the image of Blaine's ass flexing between my mother's thighs haunted me for weeks. I couldn't look at the asshole without wanting to kill him for a long time after that.

But I guess he's made up for it over the years by helping me keep an eye on her, and I'm thankful for that. I haven't really been able to make it to her house since I've been helping Alexandra recover, so he's been there every other day almost for the past two weeks.

Exhaling, I shove my phone back into my pocket and take note of which bottles need to be restocked. I need something to make these last two hours go faster before I go crazy.

It feels like it's been forever when two finally rolls around. I was tempted to ask Alexandra to meet me here a while ago, so I didn't have to go another second without seeing her, but the last thing I wanted was her out on the streets alone. Especially this late at night, not knowing if Jasper and James are hanging around waiting to get her alone.

Alexandra hasn't heard shit from James since Blaine and I had a stare down with him and Jasper, but that doesn't mean they're gone.

After flipping off the lights, I lock up and make my way across the parking lot to my motorcycle. I straddle it and take off, eager to get home. I haven't heard back from Alexandra in a while, so she's most likely sleeping, and all I want to do is crawl into bed with her and hold her close.

Being away from her this long feels like torture.

I pull out of the parking lot and turn on the side road I take when I'm in a hurry to get home. I'm so focused on all the shit going on in my head that I don't even notice when a car comes out of nowhere until it hits me hard enough to send me flying across the road and into the grass.

Pain spreads through my arms and legs from the road rash, but I barely have time to notice how much the shit hurts before a foot connects hard with my stomach, knocking my breath out.

"Fuck..." I'm in the middle of trying to catch my breath when that same boot connects with my jaw, sending me back down to the ground.

"Fucking Jax Kade. You have no idea how many times I've had to hear my girl say that name. Stay away from her. She's mine. Do you hear me?"

Multiple hands grab me from behind, two people holding my arms, while someone grabs my hair, forcing me to look up at James. He's standing there with a grin on his face as if he thinks he's won. The fucker is sadly mistaken, because I'll never back down when it comes to Alexandra.

"Fuck you." I spit blood at him and laugh, making my way to my knees. It's the closest to my feet I can get and I need him to see I'm serious. "I'm going to kill you, James. Remember that."

"I'd love to see you try." He turns to face another body that appears from the darkness. "Teach him a lesson."

I growl out and attempt to break free, but I'm pulled backward so hard that my head slams against the road.

Once I'm flat on my back where they want me, someone kicks me in the side and spits in my face. "Not so tough now, are you, asshole?"

I don't have a chance to recover from the kick before I'm grabbed from behind again and yanked into position. Some fucker holds me in place while multiple pussies take turns using my face as a punching bag.

Everything after that is a blur and I can't keep track of how many of them there are, because the swings keep coming until blood is dripping down my face and I'm close to blacking out.

I couldn't care less what they do to me. It's the fear of them going after Alexandra that has me fighting to stay conscious.

"That's enough. I think he gets the message." James grabs my hair and forces me to look up at him once again. "If not, I'll be back, and next time your punishment will be worse. Now stay away from Alexandra, asshole. I've been fucking her for the last year and giving her what she wants and needs. You can never help her the way I have. She's an addict, Jax. Soon enough she'll need me to make her forget again."

"I'm going to kill you," I spit out.

James laughs before bending down to get face to face with me. "I'm one of Jasper's guys now. We'll see how far you get."

He walks away and jumps into the car that hit me, and seconds later, the two men holding me release me with a shove. I remain on my hands and knees, trying to keep steady as I watch four guys climb into the same vehicle as James before he drives off in a hurry.

I growl out in anger and grab my stomach, fighting to get back to my feet. There's no doubt that I'll be hurting for a while after this beating, but this motherfucker is crazy if he thinks it'll keep me away from Alexandra.

It takes me a few minutes to recover enough to walk the ten feet to my bike, but it looks to be in good enough shape for me to drive it home.

Yanking off my leather jacket, I take my shirt off and use it to clean the blood that's dripping down my face enough so that it won't be a distraction on the road. Then I shove my shirt into my back pocket, slip my jacket back on, and climb onto my bike.

The moment I hit the road, the only thing on my mind is getting home to Alexandra to make sure this dumb fuck hasn't figured out where I live.

I may be busted up and hurting, but I'll kill every motherfucker in my path if I pull up at the house to find they've hurt her.

Less than five minutes later, I'm parking my motorcycle in the yard and jumping off to run to the door. It's locked, which has relief settling in, until realization hits me that my truck is no longer parked in the driveway.

"Fucking shit!" I punch the door in rage and rush into the house for my pistol, a feeling occurring that I may need it tonight after all.

If she's where I think she is, then there's a good chance she could already be hurt and I'll be putting a bullet in someone's skull...

ALEXANDRA

ONE HOUR AGO...

MADISON WENT HOME A WHILE ago, and since then, I've been sitting here, restless, and unable to stay still for longer than five minutes at a time.

Until today, Jax hasn't been away from me for longer than a few hours at a time and I hate that he's not here right now and won't be for close to another hour.

Every time a text comes through from him, I have the urge to take off and go see him. This day seriously couldn't go by any slower.

"Screw it." Making a rash decision, I snatch up the keys to Jax's truck and lock up on my way out. Jax doesn't want me out alone right now with everything that's been happening, but I need some fresh air before I go crazy waiting on him.

I miss his touch. His smell. His taste. I miss everything about him. And even though Madison kept me company for most of the night, I couldn't stop thinking about how much I miss him when we aren't together.

There are a few things I forgot to grab from Tessa's the last time I was there, so I'll swing by, grab those things and surprise him at work. He may be upset at first, but I can't just sit here anymore. With no one to talk to it's making me crazy.

The streets are quiet with it being so late. The drive to Tessa's seems to go by pretty quickly. Judging by the empty driveway when I pull up, I can only assume she must be working tonight and Blaine is out doing whatever it is he does since he doesn't have to watch her for the time being.

I climb out of Jax's truck and quickly let myself inside, wanting to get in and out of here as fast as I possibly can, so I can get to the bar.

I'm in my old room, gathering my makeup and jewelry, along with a few random belongings when I hear the front door open and close.

"Tessa." I swallow nervously, waiting to hear my old roommate's voice. "Is that you?"

When I don't get a response, my heartbeat speeds up at the possibility that James decided to show up. I wouldn't put it past his crazy ass. I wasn't thinking. It was really stupid to come here alone.

He's the last person I want to deal with right now, so I grab my purse and head into the living room to tell him to fuck off so I can leave.

"James. You need to—"

My words cut off when I step into the room to see Jasper leaning against the door, his arms crossed over his chest. He smiles and locks the door, before pushing away from it. "James is a little busy tonight, so I thought I'd swing by and check on you instead."

On instinct, I reach into my boot and pull out the knife I used to keep hidden under my mattress. It may not be much, but I want to make sure Jasper sees I have some sort of defense. “I don’t need James checking up on me. I don’t want shit to do with him or you. Leave before I call Jax.”

He lets out a cocky laugh and takes a step closer, as if to let me know that my little knife doesn’t scare him. “Jax will be a little busy when he gets off work. That’s another reason I decided to keep you company.”

My heart drops. “What is that supposed to mean?” I hold my hand with the knife up and take a step forward. I’m not afraid to use this thing when it comes to protecting Jax. “Fucking tell me. Now!”

“James and some of my guys were a little bored tonight and thought it might be fun to play with Jax. I figured playing with you would be more fun and would piss Jax off more.”

My eyes lower to his hand when he reaches into his pocket and pulls out a bag of pills. My heartrate spikes at the sight of them and I stumble back into the wall, losing my composure. “Take your shit and go. Now!”

“Why?” He opens the bag and empties the pills into his hand, coming at me and knocking the knife out of mine, before blocking me against the wall with his huge frame. “My shit not good enough for Jax’s girl? Just like it wasn’t good enough for his mother? We’ll see about that.”

Keeping me in place with his body, he grabs my face with his free hand, his nails digging into my flesh. I fight against him, struggling to get free against his strength. “Get off of me, you bastard!” I push and scratch at him, but he shoves his hand into my face, forcing what pills he can into my mouth, the rest of them falling to the floor.

I cry and scream, doing what I can to spit them out, but he grabs my face with both hands and forces my mouth shut.

“Swallow like a good girl.” I refuse to obey him. Getting aggravated with me fighting still, he tosses me down to the ground and straddles me, before slapping me hard across the face. "Swallow, bitch!"

Tears roll down my face as I shake my head side to side, the nasty taste from the pills coating my tongue.

"Those not good enough for a cunt like you?" He slaps me again and releases my face long enough to reach into his shirt pocket to grab something. I take the few seconds of freedom to turn my head and spit out as much as I can, but some have already dissolved in my mouth.

The bitter taste has me almost choking on my puke, but he turns me over enough that I'm able to spit out the acid burning my throat.

"Jax is going to kill you." I look up at him and spit in his face, my saliva mixed with the chunks I wasn't able to get out.

"Stupid bitch!" He wipes his face off and reaches for the plastic bag he dropped on the ground beside us, before gripping my face again to yell in it. "You want to play! Huh? Do you?"

I kick and push at him, trying to shove him down to the ground, but he places his full weight on me while opening the bag of cocaine and shoving it into my face, doing his best to make me inhale by taking away my ability to breathe in clean air. "How's my shit now, bitch? Tell me!"

I blow out the best I can, while coughing on the powder I've inhaled, the back of my nose and throat going numb within seconds. "Fuck you." I cry out, unable to stop the tears from coming now. "I hope he kills you. I hope he puts a bullet right into your skull. 'Cause he will."

Fear registers in his eyes for a split second, before he punches me across the face and stands to yank me up by my hair. With all of his strength he slams my face into the wall, not once, but twice before he throws me across the room.

The blood from my face stains the floor below me, most

likely from my nose being broken, but I can't feel my face, due to numbness.

Next thing I know he's on top of me from behind, ripping my jeans down my legs.

I grip the carpet and cry, my body becoming too weak to fight back, and all I can think is that I might never see Jax again.

That scares me more than the thought of death, and there's a chance I might not make it out of here alive tonight. For whatever reason he's determined to hurt me and I have no idea why. I was involved with James not him, although I have a pretty good idea this is a message for Jax.

I lay here frozen, tears wetting my face as Jasper rips my panties to the side and forces my legs apart, giving him access to shove his fingers into my pussy.

With a few forceful acts I'm taken back. Just like when I was fifteen, I feel dead inside, as I lie here helpless, being used like the piece of trash my father raised me to be.

He rips my head back by my hair and shoves his fingers deeper inside, before leaning over me to whisper in my ear. "You're fucking lifeless, you worthless whore. I'll be back when you have some fight in you. I can't wait to tear the fuck out of this pussy of yours while you scream."

I'm in and out of consciousness after that. I don't know how many times his fingers enter me or how long I take his hits before I finally blackout.

JAX

MY CHEST FEELS HEAVY AS I straddle my motorcycle and head toward Tessa's house, hoping like hell Alexandra is safe and that Jasper didn't send those motherfuckers after me as a diversion to get to her.

I know Jasper well enough to know that fucker always has an agenda. He didn't send his men with James for his benefit. He just made James believe that when he most likely had plans of his own. He's a selfish fuck.

Every thought makes me dizzy as I rush through stop signs, barely taking the time to look for vehicles. Nothing else matters to me at the moment except getting to her. If anything has happened to her, or if she was threatened in the slightest, I'll kill Jasper and there will be nothing that can stop me.

It feels a hell of a lot longer than it should when I pull my bike up in front of Tessa's to see my truck parked in the driveway. A part of me is relieved to get to Alexandra, while the other part is terrified I'll walk into something that will fucking break me.

Climbing off my bike, I crack my neck, preparing for shit to go down, before I rush to the door and push it open.

The living room is dark, the only light in the house coming from the hallway where Alexandra's old room is.

"Lex!" I take off toward the room, not waiting for a response from her, but my heart sinks when I find the room empty. "Goddammit. I'll put a bullet in this fucker's head, I swear." I grip the doorframe and squeeze it, before turning around, heading back to the living room.

It's too dark to see shit, so I make my way over to the couch to turn on the floor lamp, pausing for a split second when I hear something crunch under my boot. Whatever it is there seems to be a lot, because there's some more crunches beneath my feet as I continue my way to the lamp.

As soon as light fills the room, I look down at the ground, my stomach twisting into knots when I see pills scattered on the floor and what looks to be residue of cocaine. "Fucking shit!"

I flex my jaw, prepared to lose my shit as I look away from the mess on the floor to find Alexandra slumped against the back wall, her red hair covering her face. It takes me right back to the first time I laid eyes on her when she was just eight, except then she was curled up with her knees to her chest, a wave of white-blonde hair surrounding her.

"Lex..." I barely get her name out, because the air gets sucked straight from my lungs when I get close enough to see blood staining her gray shirt.

I immediately fall to my knees in front of her, everything around me spinning as I reach for her face and lift it. "Fuck! Fuck! Look at me, Lex. Look at me." My gaze scans her face, everything inside of me close to exploding when I see it's swollen and bloodied. She's not responding to me which has more panic setting in.

It takes me a few seconds to remember the pills on the floor, which has me pulling her into my arms and shoving my fingers down her throat.

Tears fall down my face as I desperately try to force the pills out of her system. The scary part is that I don't know how long she's been like this. She feels lifeless in my arms. "Let it out, Lex. Fucking let it out! Please, just listen to me! Let it out, dammit!"

I shove my fingers further into her throat and turn her over to her side as puke begins running down my hand. "Wake up! Fucking wake up," I plead with her to wake up, but even after puking some of the pills out, she doesn't come to.

The door swings open, and on instinct I reach for my pistol and aim it toward the door, ready to put a bullet in someone.

"Whoa! It's me. It's me." Blaine throws his arms up. "What the fuck happened to your—? He stops, his eyes widening once they lower from my face to see Alexandra in my arms. "Holy fuck!" His eyes raise to meet my wet ones and he loses it, breaking the closest thing to him before he rushes over and grabs my shoulder. "Get her up now! Are the keys in the truck?"

"I don't fucking know! I don't..." I run my hand over my wet face and Blaine rushes out the door, most likely to see if the keys are outside.

My mind is on autopilot as I pick Alexandra up and carry her toward the door.

"The keys are out here!" Blaine screams, running over to open the passenger door when he sees us step outside.

I place Alexandra into the truck before I climb in and pull her into my lap, burying my face into her neck. The door slams closed behind us and within seconds Blaine is backing out of the driveway and we're headed to the hospital.

Blaine is talking, screaming shit, but I don't understand a word that leaves his mouth, because the only thing I'm focused on is her.

I can't lose her.

I can't.

I won't survive without her again. Not after knowing what it feels like to have her back.

Everything happens so fast. We made it in record time, pulling up out front of the emergency room. I'm so distraught that I barely remember carrying her inside and screaming for someone to help us.

I remember fighting to go back with her and then standing here frozen, my face wet with tears as they take her away from me.

I HAVEN'T SLEPT IN OVER twenty-four hours and neither has Blaine. He's been at my side the entire time, keeping me calm the best he can as Alexandra comes in and out of it.

She had enough drugs in her system that she should've died. If I hadn't gotten to her when I did, and if Blaine hadn't shown up and rushed us to the emergency room, then she would've.

There's nothing I want more than to get to Jasper. He fucked-up in the worst way possible, and now he's going to pay the ultimate price. But I can't and won't leave Alexandra's side.

Every time I look at her beautiful face and see the cuts and bruises Jasper left behind, I can't breathe. I'm surprised I've survived the last twenty-four hours from my lack of oxygen.

"We'll get that piece of shit back." Blaine stands up from the chair he's been sitting in and begins pacing the hospital room. He's been doing this off and on since we arrived.

"I know," is all I can manage at the moment. All my fucking energy was drained the moment I saw her helpless on the ground.

"I should've stayed there." Blaine runs a tattooed hand

through his hair, his nerves as shot as mine. "If I had been there this shit never would've happened."

"You had no reason to," I say for the fifth time. "Tessa wasn't there. This is not on you."

He stops pacing and looks at the door when it opens. Everyone has been in and out to check on her whenever they can. I'm not sure who it is this time and I don't want to look away from Alexandra to see.

"Hey." Mark's voice is quiet as he steps into the room. "Any updates?" he asks Blaine.

Blaine called Mark right after we got to the hospital and explained to him that we don't want to give up Jasper's name, because this is something we have to handle ourselves.

He nodded, knowing exactly what that meant. He may be a cop, but he's a loyal-as-fuck one. He knows when to keep shit on the down-low.

"She's still drugged up and will be in pain for a while, but she'll be okay..."

I phaseout their conversation and crawl back into bed with Alexandra, pulling her into my arms.

Over the next ten hours she wakes up every so often and cries into my arms. It kills me over and over again, and I don't give a shit who's in the room with us. I cry with her and hold her to my chest, letting her know I'll never let anyone hurt her again.

THE CREW IS IN THE cafeteria getting something to eat, but eating isn't something I can do right now, and with all the bad thoughts running through my head I haven't been able to stand still.

It's torture, because seeing Alexandra this way tears my fucking insides out, yet the thought of leaving her here in this bed, so I don't have to look at her beaten to hell hurts just as much.

"Jax." Alexandra's scratchy voice has me turning away from the wall and rushing over to her side. "I need to tell you what happened. Keeping it from you hurts and I don't want to keep anything from you ever again."

I run my hand over her head and kiss her forehead, feeling torn up inside as tears well up in her eyes. "Fuck, baby. I hate seeing you cry." It's the worst thing in the world and I've seen it too much over the last few days since she woke up in this bed.

My heart races when she looks up into my eyes and I know right then that it's going to take a lot of strength not to destroy everything in this hospital room when I hear the shit that asshole put her through.

Sitting on the bed, I cup her face in my hands and place my forehead against hers, letting her know I'm here to comfort her through this, whatever it is. "Are you sure you're ready?"

She shakes her head and places her hands over mine. "I don't know, but I need to tell you, Jax. It's eating me up inside." She swallows nervously, her hands shaking on top of mine. "He punched me and threw me around as if I was garbage. But that's nothing I'm not used to. I could've handled that just fine, Jax. But..."

I run my thumbs over her wet cheeks when she pauses. "Dammit, I'm going to kill him. I hate with everything in me that this happened." My heart slams against my rib cage as I wait for her to continue, because I know that's not the worst part.

"He said his drugs weren't good enough for me just like they weren't good enough for your mother. He forced a handful of pills into my mouth to prove a point. He kept hitting me and throwing me around, not caring that it was hurting me. I thought he was going to rape me, Jax. He yanked my pants down and shoved his fingers inside of me and said he'd be back for me. I felt disgusting and dirty. I blacked out after that, so I don't know what else he did to me. I don't know..."

She begins shaking and tears fall heavier down her face as I hold her against me, rage coursing through me. After a few minutes, I can't hold my anger in any longer, so I walk away from her, knocking shit over as I make my way to the wall and punch it over and over again.

Someone opens the door and yells out for help, but I keep swinging out, unable to gain control.

I don't stop until Royal runs into the room and struggles to hold my arms back. "Save it for that dead motherfucker," he growls beside my ear. "Let that hate you feel build up inside you and then use that explosion to destroy him."

I push Royal back and walk away, needing some room to breathe. How the fuck am I supposed to keep everything in when I can picture that motherfucker on top of her, violating her? I can't.

I grip my hair with both hands and kneel down in front of the wall to take a few breaths in hopes it will calm me down and help me think, but it doesn't.

The only thing on my mind is getting to Jasper and killing him. He deserves a slow, painful death, but every second he's on this earth is a second too long.

He has to die now. He's done too much damage over the years and what he just did to Alexandra—he signed his death warrant.

JAX

SEVENTEEN YEARS AGO... NINE YEARS OLD

IT'S BEEN TWO DAYS SINCE my mother last came out of her bedroom. She's been in there crying and sleeping and yells at me whenever I open the door to ask why.

She doesn't do anything anymore now that my dad is gone. I can't even remember the last time she went to the store to buy us food. I've gotten used to feeding myself lately, but every time I go back into the kitchen to look for something to eat, there's less than before.

We have cereal, but no milk. Bread, but no lunch meat or peanut butter and jelly. An open box of macaroni and cheese, but for some reason the cheese packet is missing.

I haven't eaten anything all day besides some stale crackers that have been sitting on the table for weeks and it's already past my bedtime.

Turning off the TV, I go back into the kitchen again and look through the fridge, my stomach growling as I search to find something that hasn't gone bad yet. Every bowl I open stinks and makes me feel sick to my stomach, so I close the fridge and pull out the box of Lucky Charms I found in the cupboard earlier today.

My stomach growls louder when I set the box on the table, and it makes me wish we had some milk, so I can eat something good for once.

The store isn't very far from here. I could walk there by myself, but I don't have any money of my own and my dad didn't leave my mom with much when he took off.

Having a smart idea, I run into the living room and lift the cushions on the couch to search for change. My dad used to always yell at me and make me give any coins I found to him, but he's not here anymore to take them from me, so I pocket all of the quarters and dimes I can find, before quietly walking to my mother's room to see if she's awake.

I doubt she'll care if I'm gone, but I want to tell her I'm leaving so she won't worry about me like she used to.

When I push the door open, my mother is sleeping with a medicine bottle clutched in her hand. I don't know what the pills are for, but she seems to be taking them a lot lately.

Since I can't tell her where I'm going, I decide I'll run as fast as I can so I'll make it back before she wakes up.

Grabbing my jacket, I hurry outside and take off running through the grass, cutting through the backyard and across the yards of other houses.

It's faster this way, instead of walking all the way down the street and going around. That always takes forever.

Once I get two blocks over, I stop to let a car drive by, before I run across the street and then slow down when I reach the grass.

I'm cutting through another yard and get ready to run again, but stop when I hear what sounds like a little girl crying.

I don't know where it's coming from, so I stay quiet and try my best not to make any noise. I listen to find out where it's coming from.

"Hello?" No one answers me, but I start walking toward the sound of the little girl's cries until I find her curled up on the ground with her knees pressed to her chest.

White-blonde hair covers her face, so I can't see what she looks like or why she's crying.

"Are you okay?" I bend down in front of her and grab her arm. She flinches as if she's afraid of me, so I let go and move away a little. "I won't hurt you. Please tell me what's wrong."

"Do you promise?"

"I promise."

It feels like a long time before she finally looks up. When she does, her small green eyes search my face. I hardly notice it at first, but there's a bruise on her left cheek and a little blood on her lip.

Tears are streaming down her tiny face and she's shaking. She's so little. I don't know how anyone could hurt someone so small. Even upset she's pretty. I bet she's real pretty when she smiles.

The helpless look in her eyes hits me in the chest and I feel my cheeks become wet as I reach out to touch her arm. "Who hurt you? Will you tell me?"

She shakes her head and reaches up to wipe at her face, before she hides it in her arms. "I can't."

"Why not?"

"Because I'll get in trouble," she whispers.

"What if I promise not to tell anyone? Will you tell me then?"

She stops crying and looks up at me. "You really won't tell no one?"

I move closer to her and grab the bottom of my shirt to dry her face off a bit. My mom used to do it when I was upset and she didn't have a tissue. "Not if you don't want me to. I wouldn't want to get you in trouble."

"My daddy. He's been angry with me since my mom ran away. I miss her and he gets mad when I cry for her. He says me crying isn't going to bring her back, because we're worthless to her and she doesn't love us."

Her words make me angry, but also make me forget about being hungry. I just want to sit here with her and make her feel better. "Don't listen to your dad. He sounds like a big jerk." I sit down beside her and grab her hand, so she'll look at me. "What's your name?"

"Alexandra." She squeezes my hand and scoots closer to me, as if I make her feel safe. I like that feeling. "What's yours?"

"Jaxon."

After I tell her my name she rests her head on my shoulder and we sit here in silence for a while. I'm not for sure how long, but it feels like an hour or more.

My heart fills with happiness that she trusts me. She needs me. No one else seems to need me. My mom won't let me help her. She's letting me help her. I'm never going to leave her side.

"Can I call you Lex?" I whisper.

I hear her sniffle before she wipes an arm over her face. "If I can call you Jax."

"You can call me anything you want, Lex."

Because after tonight, I'm not going anywhere. She's my Lex and I'm her Jax...

JAX

ADRENALINE COURSES THROUGH ME AS I pull up at the shitty rundown motel just out of town that Mark discovered James has been staying at.

It's just past midnight, so I'm hoping this motherfucker has decided to stay in tonight, because I'm running extremely low on patience.

I toss my helmet and climb off my motorcycle when Blaine pulls up behind me, right in front of the room number James is supposedly staying in. If he is here, the asshole has another thing coming if he thinks about running.

He knows we're here. He heard our bikes pull up, there's no doubt about that.

Climbing off his bike, Blaine pulls out a cigarette and his fancy-ass Zippo he loves so much. Looking at the motel door, he places his smoke between his lips and lights it, taking a long drag, before slowly blowing smoke out. "I'll give you a head start. Just don't have too much fun without me, brother."

I take a deep breath and slowly exhale, because if I don't

then I'll end up killing this dick before I get my answer. That's something I refuse to let happen.

Mentally preparing for the shitshow that's about to go down, I walk over to the door and check the handle. When I discover it's locked, I pull the bandana from my back pocket and wrap it around my fist, before punching it through the cheap window.

I faintly hear James' footsteps before a door slams. I'm assuming the dick thinks hiding in the bathroom will save him. A humorless laugh leaves me as I kick the rest of the glass out enough for me to climb in.

"Go back inside your room." I hear Blaine growl to someone behind me.

But I couldn't care less who's watching. Mark has assured us he'll be the first one on the scene if anyone calls the cops, but with as shitty as this place is, I doubt anyone wants to deal with the cops. All that lingers around here is hookers, homeless people, and addicts. It's a good place to run drugs out of, which is probably why James chose to stay here to begin with.

After climbing through the window, I flex my jaw in annoyance when I notice the bags of drugs covering the bed. The sorry fucker must be preparing to make a run. It makes me sick that Alexandra was ever involved with this piece of shit.

Growling out, I kick the bathroom door open and come at James who is standing on top of the toilet, trying to fit out the tiny-ass window above it.

I grab him by the back of the shirt and throw him down to the ground, before placing my boot to his throat. "Tell me where the fuck I can find Jasper. Now."

He shakes his head and grabs my boot, attempting to push it away from his throat. "He never told me where..."

I push my boot harder, gargling sounds already commencing, while leaning over him to turn on the cold water and fill the tub.

His arms are flailing below me, panic setting in from the lack of oxygen, so I step on his right arm with my free foot and bend down to look him in the eyes. "Because of you that motherfucker almost took my girl's life. Alexandra has been in the goddamn hospital, because of what he did." I remove my boot from his throat and punch him across the face, forcing his head to the other side, before yanking him up to toss him into the tub. "Now tell me and maybe I'll put you in the hospital versus the ground!"

His eyes widen right before I press down on his face, holding him under the shallow water.

I remember every bruise, every area of blood, and every injured place on her body. My anger builds. The reminder of what happened to Alexandra has me holding him under water a little too long, before yanking him up by his hair and slamming my fist into his face. The cycle continues—I ask him where Jasper is, he doesn't know, and each time I hold him down longer than before.

I've lost count of how many cigarettes I've smoked to calm my nerves between each time, trying to stop myself from just killing him.

I didn't want to leave Alexandra while she's still recovering, but it's time to stop stalling. I can't wait until she's out of the hospital and risk Jasper coming after her when I'm not around. This needs to end. Now.

That motherfucker needs to be dealt with before.

Mark hasn't been able to get me a location on Jasper yet, since the asshole must have a different legal name, but he was able to find this place.

My grip around James' throat tightens as I hold his head above the bathwater, giving him a few moments to catch his breath.

The prick can hardly remember his name at this point from the lack of oxygen to his brain, but I don't give a fuck. Either that or he's not talking still. Too bad his loyalty doesn't lie with someone that would return it. One way or another, he has answers that I need and I'm not leaving here without them.

"Where is he?" I ask again, my voice gruff as I lean in close to his bloodied and swollen face. "This is your last chance."

He coughs and digs at my hands when I give his throat a firm squeeze and lift him higher out of the water.

"I don't..." he coughs, "...know."

"You're lying! Do you think I'm stupid? Tell me, or I'll rip your fucking throat out." Anger courses through me, making me see red when I don't get the answer I need. "Fuck this."

Growling out, I shove him back into the water, watching with dead eyes, all the fucks in the world gone as he gasps for air and slaps at the porcelain surrounding him.

It's hard to see him through the bloodstained water, yet I keep my gaze on him, not wanting to miss a second of his suffering.

With my hand still around James' throat, I step into the water and kneel above his body, so I can get a better grip. Looking him dead in the eyes, I reach into my boot and pull out my knife, placing it to his cheek.

"Tell me where the fuck he is before I start cutting you into pieces, starting with your tongue. Now!" I scream in his face, before releasing his throat with a shove.

I keep my body above his, not giving him a chance to escape even if he had it left in him, which he doesn't.

We've been at this for over twenty minutes now.

"I don't know..." he gasps out, gripping at the bathtub. "I swear! I fucking swear! Please, don't. Please..."

Letting out some pent-up anger, I slam my fist into his face, knocking him out cold this time.

I still need him alive, so I grab him by the shirt and pull him above the water, before walking across the room to grab another cigarette from the sink.

"Fuck!" I smash the box in my hand, before tossing the empty package at the wall. This is not a good time to run out of smokes. They're about the only thing keeping me from killing this asshole.

Yelling out, I grip my hair, before reaching for the closest thing to me and breaking it against the wall. I don't stop until everything in this small bathroom is broken and out of place.

When I stop to catch my breath, I look into the mirror, staring long and hard at the monster I've become for her. She is the only girl I'd kill for. Always has been.

I slam my fist into the glass repeatedly, not stopping until my skin is hanging from my knuckles.

Blood covers everything.

My fist.

The sink.

The floor.

It looks like a horror scene in here. And I know more blood will spill until I get what I need, because I won't stop until I'm standing above Jasper's lifeless body and he's paid for hurting the one person I love most in this shitty world.

"Need me to get crazy in here?" Blaine appears in the doorway, staring at James in the bathtub, while he cracks his neck. He's been anxious to draw blood since he saw me on the ground with Alexandra in my arms. "I'm ready to get bloody."

"Fuck it. Give me a cigarette."

Blaine grins and hands me a smoke, not wasting any time before he slaps James across the face to wake him up. "Let's play, bitch."

James' eyes widen as he watches Blaine pull the knife from his pocket. He screams out in pain as Blaine shoves it into his bicep and twists.

"Fuck! Fuck! I already told you I don't know where he is!" Tears stream down his face as Blaine puts a little pressure on the knife. "Check my phone! Check my phone!"

"Where is it?" Blaine pulls the knife from his arm and smiles as blood gushes out. "I said where is—"

"Next to the TV! It's next to the TV. Jasper was supposed to text me tonight when he needs me. I swear that's all I know. He gives me a new place to meet him every time. I swear."

Tired of his pathetic voice, I knock him out again, before draining the tub and leaving him there. I toss my cigarette in the water and rush to find his phone.

There aren't any missed texts from Jasper, so I shove his phone into my jacket pocket. "I hope you're ready for a long night. If not, then I can handle it on my own."

"Let's get out of here and wait for that fucking text, because I'm not going anywhere until that fucker takes his last breath. This has been a long time coming."

I nod and we both head outside to our bikes.

Jasper is going to be in for a huge surprise when James isn't the one showing up tonight. He doesn't know this, but tonight he has an appointment with the devil...

JAX

IT'S BEEN CLOSE TO TWO hours since we left James at the motel, barely breathing, and a text from Jasper hasn't come through yet.

I'm anxious, because I'm ready to get back to the hospital to be with my woman. I'm close to losing my shit and taking it out on Blaine since he's here with me and won't stop talking about how Madison broke shit off. First, he pushed me to tell him what happened with James and those fuckers jumping me and now this shit.

That's the last thing I care about right now. Everything he says keeps going in one ear and out the other.

I'm focused right now, all of my attention aimed at James' phone, waiting for the message we desperately need to come through.

"...she knew from the beginning that I'm fucked-up in the head. It's not my fault she chose to jump on my dick and expected me to change. I can't."

"Would you shut the hell up?" I squeeze James' phone in

my hand, trying my best not to break it against the wall of Blaine's living room. "I'm starting to think this asshole isn't texting tonight."

"He'll text and we'll get to him. Just hold your fucking dick and be patient. It'll happen. Even if I have to drive around all night to find him." Blaine stops by the window and looks outside for the hundredth time since we got here. "I don't have shit else to do."

The phone vibrates in my hand, causing my heart to skip a damn beat. It's from a number with no name, so I open it and read it.

My stomach twists into knots as I read the location for a second time. It's the same spot in the woods Alexandra and I used to go to when we were kids. The spot with the tire swing that is now gone.

"Let's go." Blaine barely has a chance to grab his jacket before I'm out the door and jumping into James' shitbox of a car, about to drive off.

"Damn. I couldn't leave without my gun and jacket." He slams the door shut and gives me a hard look. "I'm more intimidating in this badass leather."

"Shut the hell up, Blaine." I grip the steering wheel and flex my jaw, mentally preparing to come face to face with Jasper.

I've thought of all the slow, painful deaths, deciding which I'd like to deliver to him, but the more time I had to think, waiting to get to him tonight, the more I keep imagining a quick death, ready to rid the world of this scum.

This should have been done long ago. He's taken up too much time of my life already. He took my childhood from me, forced me to provide for myself, because he kept my mother high and barely functioning. Then he had the balls to come after the woman I love, trying to take her from me too.

My insides burn with rage and by the time we make it down

the long path and park in front of Jasper's truck, I'm on the verge of exploding.

He's sitting on the tailgate, chilling, as if he's the king of the world. The fucker doesn't even look up from his phone to see who has pulled up. All that does is piss me off more.

Jasper seems to be alone, so I shoot Blaine a look that tells him to stay put, before I step out of the car and close the door behind me.

I can barely catch my breath and my heartbeat skyrockets as I walk down the path to where his truck is parked. The unsuspecting bastard is still paying too much attention to his phone to look up and see that it's me approaching and not James.

"This son of a bitch wants to fuck with me," he growls, while punching a text into his phone. "Got the money?"

He finally looks up from his phone, shock visible on his face when his eyes lock with mine. He fumbles to reach behind him for what I'm assuming is a weapon, but I grab him by the throat and throw him down to the ground before he can reach it. "Nothing can save you now," I growl down at him, before placing my knee on his chest and aiming my gun at his forehead.

"Jax, you don't have to do this." He swallows nervously, keeping his eyes on mine. "Come on, man. I've known you since you were a kid. Put that away and we can talk this out like grown men."

"Shut the fuck up!" I scream in his face and push the barrel of the gun harder into his forehead, digging it in. "Don't fucking talk! Your words won't save you." I hit him across the face with the pistol, before cocking the hammer back and tilting my head.

His eyes widen and his breathing picks up when he hears Blaine's car door shut. "Who's with you? Who the fuck—"

I hit him across the face again to shut him up, before

turning to Blaine once he's standing beside me. "Check his truck for his stash."

Jasper growls as if his merchandise is more important than his life. But he doesn't dare say shit as Blaine walks over to start his search. He comes back moments later and holds up a brick of cocaine. With a grin, he pulls out his knife and slices the top of it open, chunks of the white powder spilling from the knife blade slicing through it.

"No! No! No!" Jasper shakes his head and starts struggling under my weight when Blaine comes at him with it. Blaine shoves the cocaine in Jasper's face, smothering him with his own supply.

I watch, numb as fuck as he struggles to breathe, while Blaine shoves the cocaine into his eyes, nose, and mouth.

Everything inside of me is screaming to take him out. To shoot him right now and end his life, so I put my hand up, letting Blaine know that I'm ready.

He nods and takes a step back.

"You're not worth my fucking time. I'm done wasting it on you." I place the gun back to his forehead and look him in the eyes. What I can see of them at least, since they're covered with residue of white. Just as he gets ready to say something, I pull the trigger, blood splattering all over the white as I blow his brains out.

I sit here for a while, covered in his blood as I stare down at his lifeless body. A part of me doesn't believe he's gone, even though I'm the one that pulled the trigger.

"He's gone, man." Blaine grips my shoulder. "Mark is on the way to handle shit. We need to get out of here in case someone called the cops."

I swallow and slowly stand up, my hands shaking as Blaine takes the gun from me. There are so many things I should've said to that piece of shit before ending him, but once I came face to face with him, the only thing I could do was think how relieved I'd be to finally live in a world he wasn't in. I wanted to be the one to take his life and ensure that he'll never fuck with anyone I love again.

Blaine drives us back to his house and I barely remember getting cleaned up and changing into some of his clean clothes before we head to the hospital.

It's past three in the morning, yet when we walk through the door to Alexandra's hospital room, she's wide-awake, as if she's been waiting for us to come back.

The moment her gaze lands on mine, I nod, and she covers her mouth with her hand, understanding what went down.

I spare her the details, because honestly, I don't want to relive them. The sight of blood flowing onto the ground beneath his head will stick with me for a while.

She doesn't say anything, she just sits up and holds her hand out, letting me know that she wants me in bed with her. So I climb in beside her and pull her against my chest, holding onto her as if my life depends on. She holds me just as tight and it lets me know that we're going to get through this fucked-up night together. I never want to let her out of my sight again. Not for a while at least.

"I'm going to sit here for a while. Hope you guys don't mind." Blaine takes a seat in one of the chairs and runs his hands over his face.

No one talks.

I don't think any of us knows what to say right now. All I know is that I can breathe again for the first time in days, knowing that motherfucker will never be able to hurt Alexandra again. I'd do it over and over again if it meant she's safe and happy.

She's my world, and without her I can't fucking breathe. I won't risk anyone hurting her or taking her from me again...

ALEXANDRA

IT'S BEEN ALMOST TWO WEEKS since I was released from the hospital, and other than the yellow remains of the bruises left behind from Jasper, everything has gone back to normal for us.

The small bit of normal we were able to experience before everything turned into shit, at least. It's been a long, hard road to get things to where they are today. Seventeen years with me to be exact, and Jax never gave up on me once any of the times he's been in my life. He's proven to me multiple times and in many ways that he never plans to.

Every day we're together my love grows deeper for him and my trust for him strengthens.

A smile takes over when the salon door opens to Jax and Mark walking inside. Today was my first day back here and Jax has made it his mission to stop in every other hour.

"Oh, it's you again?" I tease as he moves in behind me and wraps his arms around me. An instant feeling of warmth and happiness surrounds me as he pulls me in close.

"Damn straight it is." He smiles against my neck, before kissing it. "Think the girls will let you go early? I miss you like fucking crazy."

"I already told you no the last five times you asked. You can't have Lex." Madison steps out of the back room, her face turning red when she notices Mark sitting in her chair. "You're in the wrong chair, handsome. Ava's is right there." She points at the chair next to hers. "And she's on break right now."

Mark smiles, before running a hand through his messy hair. "I thought I'd change things up this week. Mind giving me a cut?"

Madison seems nervous as she runs her hands over the front of her jeans. I hadn't noticed it before, but it's pretty clear now that she has a crush on Avalon's uncle. From what I can tell, Mark isn't much older than her, maybe four to five years, and it's hard to deny that he is a damn good-looking guy.

A bit different from Blaine, in the more clean-cut with tattoos sort of way, but as far as I've heard they're no longer sleeping together, because Madison is tired of him being incapable of opening up and committing.

"This should be interesting," Jax whispers in my ear. "Let's go next door and grab some lunch while they talk."

"We'll be next door. Want anything?" I add in passing.

Madison waves me off as if she's in a hurry to get rid of us.

The moment we step out of the salon, Jax backs me against the building and kisses me hard and deep, wrapping his hands into my hair and groaning as if he's been waiting forever to get me alone.

When he breaks the kiss, I smile against his lips and wrap my arms around his waist, getting used to the way it feels to be able to touch him whenever I want. "Keep kissing me like that and I'm going to have to quit my job, so we can be together twenty-four-seven."

He moves his hands down to grip my ass. "The only thing

I'd hate about that is seeing all the assholes eyeing you over at the bar. Besides, Ava and Madison would probably rip my balls off or kill me if I took you away from them. Especially the crazy one inside."

I laugh and slap his chest when he nods toward the salon. "So, are you going to take me to lunch now? Whatever the hell it is that I'm smelling has my mouth watering."

"Only if I get to have you for dessert after..." He moves his mouth up to brush over my ear. "I've been dying to make you come all day."

His dirty words heat me to my core and I almost forget we're in public until Ava clears her throat beside us. "Am I going to have to kick your ass, Jax?" She smiles and pushes Jax's arm. "If Royal can't take me away during the work day to fuck me like he wants to then I can't let you take my colorist. Business has tripled since she joined us. Feed her and bring her right back."

I laugh into Jax's firm chest as he picks me up and pretends to carry me to his truck.

"Twenty minutes, Jax!" Ava gives Jax a small smile and a wink before she disappears into the salon.

Jax looks down at me in his arms, before placing me back on my feet. "Well, shit. Twenty minutes isn't enough for what I want to do to you, so I guess I better do what I'm told."

"That's probably best, because you're going to need your balls later." I grab his beard and pull him in for a kiss, taking my time to enjoy the feel of his soft lips on mine, before I ask him what I've been trying to hold back. "Are you sure you're okay, Jax?"

"I don't regret what I did if that's what you're asking." He flexes his jaw and looks down at me. "I won't hesitate to take another man's life when it comes to you, Lex. Do you hear me?" His hands move up to cup my face. "There's nothing more important to me in this world than you. Do you understand that?"

I nod, my heart beating faster from his confession. "We better hurry and eat."

He kisses me again, before guiding me to the door of the little burger spot next door.

I know there's nothing Jax wouldn't do for me and there's nothing in this world I wouldn't do for him in return.

He's my Jax and I'm his Lex. Have been since I was eight and there's nothing in this world that could change that...

AX

IT'S BEEN A QUIET NIGHT here at Savage & Ink. Not that I'm complaining, because I've been contemplating closing the bar down early. I want to get home and finish what Alexandra and I started before Blaine's dumb ass called me in early, so he could go home and sleep his hangover off from last night.

He's been spending a lot of time getting demolished over the past week and I haven't seen him this way since his sister died. It has myself, Royal, and Mark keeping a closer eye on him just to make sure he doesn't drink himself into an early grave.

Blaine may be the biggest pain in the ass I know, but he's also part of our family. I hope he gets his shit together soon or finds a woman able to do it for him, because we all know he needs one to help level him.

I was hoping that woman would be Madison, but he went and fucked that shit up, just as expected. In all the years I've known him, he's been an idiot when it comes to women.

"...some bullshit, I tell ya." Ted lifts his bottle and shakes it. "Another one, man." I grab him a new beer and toss his empty one into the trash. He's still salty as shit about being assaulted by Mark, so he's been grumbling about the "pig" since he walked through the door.

I haven't listened to a damn word that has left his drunken mouth other than him asking for more beer.

I look down at my phone when it vibrates across the bar. My annoyance is temporarily replaced with happiness when I see who it is.

ALEXANDRA

Miss me yet?

JAXON

Fuck yes, baby. This night is dragging.

ALEXANDRA

I miss you too. Which is why I'm almost there... too bad you're not alone.

This woman knows I'll give her anything she wants, which is why these pricks are about to find their way out the door much sooner than they expected.

I press down on my painful erection and toss my phone down in front of me. I haven't had sex with my woman in almost two weeks and my body is craving to devour every inch of her.

"Time to leave. You have thirty seconds to finish your drinks and be out the door, before I drag you out one by one. The time starts right fucking now."

I get a few grunts from around the room, but this is an easy crowd tonight. Every last person in here knows not to question me, or any of the other guys when we give them an order.

That's why everyone complies, and in less than thirty

seconds I'm standing here alone, watching the door, and sipping on a glass of Jack.

A few minutes later, the front door opens and Alexandra steps inside, wearing the sexiest goddamn dress I have ever seen. I tilt my glass back and watch as she locks the door behind her.

She takes a moment to observe the empty room, before taking a few steps, stopping beside the jukebox. "I told you people are intimidated by you. That's so damn sexy."

"Is that right?" I stand up and walk toward her, stopping once our bodies meet. I slide my hand into the back of her hair and gently tug it, so that she's looking up at me. "Does that turn you on?"

I watch the curve of her throat as she swallows. "Yes."

"Good," I whisper against her throat. "You look so incredibly sexy that I'm about to bust my load just from looking at you. I'd rather be inside you when I do."

A small smile tugs at my lips when I notice goose bumps form across her smooth, tanned skin. I love how my words alone are enough to work her up. With a growl, I grip her thighs and lift her up, allowing her legs to wrap around my waist.

She moans into my neck when my hard cock presses against her pussy. "I couldn't wait for you to get home, Jax. I've been dying to have you inside me since Blaine interrupted us earlier." Her mouth moves along my neck, making its way up to my ear, where she whispers, "Fuck me."

Her request sets me off, causing me to desperately reach between us to pull my throbbing dick out and enter her, slow and deep. She's so wet that one thrust is almost enough to make me come, but I bite my bottom lip and still for a moment.

"Fuck, baby. It's been too long." I move my hands around to grip her ass, spreading her cheeks apart as I begin moving in and out of her.

Each time I enter her, her moans become louder and more satisfied and I know from the sounds she's making that she's just as close to coming as I am.

"Not yet, Lex." I back her against the jukebox and move my hand up to grip the back of her neck. "Hold on with me, baby."

She shakes her head and digs her nails into my arm. "I can't, Jax. Not if you keep moving."

I smile against her mouth, because I feel the same way. We haven't enjoyed each other's body in so long that not coming right away is close to impossible.

With a small groan I push inside of her and stop, before moving my lips up to meet hers. I capture her mouth with mine and kiss her, showing her that she's mine and mine alone. I want her to know that no other man will ever touch her again as long as I'm alive.

"Move, Jax." She grips my biceps and begins riding me, coming down deep and hard each time.

"Fucking shit, Lex," I groan.

We're both breathing heavily, seconds away from losing control as I walk us over to the bar and set her down. As soon as she feels the surface beneath her ass, she leans back and grips onto anything she can get her hands on. "Harder, Jax. Keep going."

Using all of my strength, I pound into her, taking her deep each time, not stopping until she screams out her release and squeezes me with her thighs.

She smiles below me and reaches beside us for the bottle of whiskey I was drinking from before she showed up. My cock twitches inside her at the memory of what happened the last time whiskey was present during sex.

Leaning up, she brings the bottle to my lips and sloppily pours it back, some of it going into my mouth while the rest drips down my neck.

She grips my shirt and pulls me to her, making it easier for her to run her tongue along my neck, licking the liquor from my body.

"Take your shirt off, Jax."

I do as she says, fighting to catch my breath when she pours the whiskey down my chest and slowly licks it off, looking up at me.

I'm so turned on that I grip the back of her neck with both hands and fuck her slow and deep, groaning out moments later as I fill her with my cum.

"Damn..." I smile and pull her to me, so I can kiss her. "I don't want to go that long without being inside you again."

She smiles against my lips, running her fingertips over my sweaty, wet chest. "It won't happen again."

"Good," I whisper, running my thumb over her cheek bone. "Let me clean up and get you home."

After I clean up our mess, we head home and take a quick shower, before spending the rest of the night out back, lying on the grass with her in my arms.

It's moments like these that mean the most to me. Just the two of us, together, like when we were kids.

I knew from the first time I held her against me that it was a feeling I wanted for the rest of my life. I may have only been nine at the time, but I had never been so certain of anything in my life, and that hasn't changed.

If thirteen years of being apart wasn't enough to erase her from my thoughts, there's nothing or no amount of time in this world that can...

ALEXANDRA

SIX MONTHS LATER...

I CLOSE MY EYES FOR a moment and enjoy the feeling of the light breeze hitting my face. It's been scorching hot for the last few days and today is the first day it's been possible to step outside without breaking into an instant sweat.

Contentment fills me as the voices of our family surround me. The family I've grown to love and admire over the months. I've never felt so at home in my entire life, and I never once imagined having a single person to call family, let alone a group of people who mean so much to me.

As much as I want to erase what happened with Jasper six months ago from my mind, the fact that Jax took a man's life to protect our future solidified there was nothing that could keep us apart again.

Jax loves me and treats me like I'm not only his girlfriend, but his everything. Not a day goes by that he doesn't remind me

I'm his world. Others may look at Jax and see a savage, but I look at him and see life, and how he gave mine back to me.

"You look really happy." I open my eyes to see Ava smiling at me. I didn't even know she was watching me.

"I am," I say honestly, pushing away from the picnic table. "Happier than I've been my entire life. And the news we recently got made me the happiest girl in the world."

Ava's smile widens and I can see in her eyes that she's truly happy for us too. It makes me all giddy inside when I think of all the things we can do as a family.

I get ready to say just that when Jax slips in behind me and wraps his arms around me. He gives me a soft kiss on the neck, before rubbing his hands over my belly. "I still can't believe that in less than thirty-six weeks I'm going to be a fucking dad."

"Language!" Ava pinches Jax's arm and rolls her eyes for about the hundredth time since the cookout started. "If one of you grown men need to be told one more time to watch your mouth, I'm going to throw you out on your butts before it's even time to eat."

I can't help the huge smile that takes over at hearing Jax say he's going to be a father. I don't think I'll ever get tired of hearing those words come from his mouth. "You're going to have to work on that dirty mouth before our little one comes. I'm going to need to work on not cussing so much too. We're both bad, Jax."

"Why does it matter?" Blaine steps through the sliding door and closes it behind him. "I've been cussing since I was three and I turned out just fine."

"God help us," Royal mutters from the grill. "You're far from fine, so everyone watch their mouths around Kylie. The last thing I need is for her to take after one of you assholes." He grins, because he knows he's just as bad.

"Really?" Ava shakes her head and tries not to smile when Royal grabs her hip and pulls her to him. "You cussing every time you tell someone else not to isn't helping any. We've been having this discussion for almost two years now."

"Kylie knows better. I've had plenty of discussions with her." Royal walks over to the pool where Kylie is playing with her dolls and bends down to her size. "Tell Mommy what you are not to do, angel?"

Kylie laughs and jumps up and down, as if what she's about to say is funny. "Don't repeat anything my uncles say. Especially Uncle Blaine."

"There you go," Royal says with a satisfied smile, before picking Kylie up and kissing her on the side of the head. "She listens to Daddy."

"Really?" Blaine throws his arms up, as if he's offended that everyone thinks he's the worst of all of them. "Don't be mad because I'm the coolest uncle she has. She'll learn on her own once she's old enough."

"Think we should let our child call him uncle?" Jax asks beside my ear, before wrapping his hands in my hair and pulling back, so he can kiss me on the mouth.

"Hell yes! Who wouldn't want me as an uncle?" Blaine grabs a hot dog, shoves it into his mouth, and then jumps into the pool fully clothed.

"Is it bad that I still want to choke him?" Madison lifts her sunglasses and pushes them on top of her head, watching as Blaine swims back up to the top and gives us all the middle finger. "He's such a pain in the ass. A sexy one, which makes me want to choke him more."

I laugh and follow Madison over to the food table to fix a plate. Even though her and Blaine haven't spoken much in months, you can tell they still get under each other's skin. But there's someone else that she seems to be more attracted to and he's walking through the back door now, looking extremely hot in his uniform.

Mark rushes over to Kylie and picks her up, swinging her

around while she laughs. It's hard to miss the smile on Madison's face as she watches him play with his niece.

"Yeah. Blaine is quite choke worthy," I joke, not knowing what to say now that she's checking Uncle Mark out. "You can stare as hard as you want, but it's not going to make that uniform magically fall off."

"Oh, trust me, I've learned that over the years. Hasn't stopped me from wishing though." She smiles and begins making a plate. "He's the hottest damn uncle I've ever seen."

"He has handcuffs too," Jax teases, snatching up a burger, before joining the guys by the pool again.

"Oh, hell. I need to cool off." Madison leaves the plate she was making and walks over to jump into the pool.

I'm about to walk over and join Ava and the guys when Tessa walks through the sliding door. We've kept in contact over the months, but we haven't seen much of each other since she's been busy at Midnight's. I thought it would be nice to invite her to Ava and Royal's cookout since it's her day off.

"Oh my goodness. I'm so happy for you." Tessa rushes over and throws her arms around me, rocking back and forth. Her dark hair surrounds us, flowing in the wind as she congratulates me. "You two are going to make a beautiful baby. I'm so excited for you both."

"Thank you, Tessa. I'm glad you made it," I say once she breaks the hug. "I was afraid you'd get called into work again."

"I told Joe he could kiss my ass. The new bartender he hired is horrible and I'm sick of going in to pick up her slack. That shit wasn't happening today. I miss you too much. I had forgotten how lonely it is living alone."

"No luck on finding a roommate still, huh?"

She shakes her head, before turning to face the guys. They're taking turns tossing Kylie around the pool. Everyone breaks into laughter when Jax tosses her to Blaine and he accidentally gets kicked in the forehead, but still manages to catch her.

Blaine has finally stripped out of his shirt and jeans and I can't help but to notice Tessa checking him out. As far as I know nothing happened when he was keeping an eye on her, but that doesn't mean it won't happen. Blaine is a manwhore, after all.

After everyone is done eating, I'm in the middle of helping Ava and the girls clean up when Jax picks me up and starts carrying me away.

"We've gotta go, ladies. I have a surprise for my girl and want her to see it before it gets too dark."

Everyone yells their goodbyes, laughing as I slap and scream at Jax to put me down when he begins tickling my neck with his beard, walking around front at the same time.

"Stop!" I scream right before he sets me down next to his truck. "That tickles and itches, Jax."

"Yeah," he says against my ear. "But you love my beard. Especially when it's between your legs."

"I do," I admit, my body heating at the memory of last night when he held me against the wall on his shoulders. "I especially like it there."

He smiles and rubs his thumbs over my cheeks, his eyes turning meaningful now. "There's something for you at the house. I've been dying to show it to you all day. Let's go."

"Okay." I climb into the truck when he opens the door for me. "What is it?" I ask once he joins me inside.

"I love the shit out of you, baby, but I'm not telling. You'll see when we get home." He bites my bottom lip, before reaching for my seatbelt. "Now buckle up."

Curiosity has me on the edge of my seat the entire drive back home, which only seems to make the drive seem longer.

When we pull into the driveway, he quickly kills the engine and jumps out in a hurry, leaving the keys inside. He rushes over and opens the door for me and picks me up, shutting it behind me.

I smile and wrap my arms around his neck when he begins walking. I expect him to go to the front door, but instead he walks around the side of the house.

"It's back here?"

"You'll see."

The moment we reach the back of the house and the tire swing comes into view, I'm overwhelmed with happiness. I can't seem to stop smiling as he sets me down to my feet and I walk over to touch it.

I can picture Jax pushing our child on the swing just like he used to push me when we were kids. He was always so careful not to hurt me or go too high unless I asked him to.

Jax couldn't be more perfect for me and I know with everything in me that he's going to be the best father to our unborn baby.

I've never been happier for what lies ahead or even looked forward to having a future before, but Jax showed me at two different times in my life that he was always what fate had in store for me.

He is and always was my future…

JAX

I GRIN FROM EAR TO ear as I watch Alexandra walk over to the tire swing secured to a thick branch on an Apple Blossom tree in full bloom and touch it. The smile in her eyes tells me everything I need to know.

I thought about tracking down the old one I used to push her on as kids, but the more I thought about it, the more I realized finding that one after all these years would be unrealistic, so I bought a new tire to hang.

I want a fresh start for me and my family. I want this house to feel like a home to Alexandra. A place where she feels safe and loved at all times to raise a child with me.

"I love it, Jax." She turns to face me, her smile growing bigger as I walk over to join her. "When did you do this?"

"When you were at work earlier. Why do you think I rushed you out the door for the cookout?" I move in behind her and run my lips over her neck, making my way around to her lips. "I wanted something in our home that would make you happy. Something that would remind you of good times. That tire swing meant a lot to us as kids and still means a lot to both of us now. There's no way I was not putting one in our backyard for you and our baby."

"You make me truly happy," she whispers across my lips. "It's always been you, Jax. If it were anyone else pushing me on the swing..." She grabs my face, forcing me to look her in the eyes. "It wouldn't have felt the same. It was and still is you. I love you. I love you more than anything in this world and I never want to imagine a life without you in it. Just the thought of not waking up to you every morning makes everything inside of me feel like it's dying. I never want to live that way again. I can't."

I swallow back my emotions and place my forehead to hers. "You're about the only thing that can make me smile, Lex. You make me happy. I said these words to you thirteen years ago and they're still true to this day. I never stopped needing you. I've loved you since the age of nine when I found you as that pretty little blonde crying that night, and I'm pretty sure I've been in love with you since the moment you kissed me when I was thirteen. You will never have to go a day without waking up to me. Not now that I have you as mine, Lex. I love you so fucking much that it hurts. I'll die if I lose you again. That's how much you mean to me."

She smiles when I wipe my thumb under her wet eye, drying it the best I can. "I'll never get tired of hearing you say those words."

I cup her face in both hands and hover my lips above hers. "I'll never grow tired of saying them." My mouth moves over hers, showing her just how mine she is. I'll never get used to being able to show her, which only makes it certain I'll make sure to everyday. "Now climb in."

"Really?" She laughs when I give her a look, showing her I'm serious. "It's been ages since I've been on a swing."

"I figured that." I grab her hips and lift her legs into the tire. "Hold on tight," I tease, remembering how I used to tell her that as kids.

She grabs onto the rope and laughs as I push her.

Just like when we were kids, we stay out here for hours talking and laughing, except now we talk about the future of our child.

Our child.

Those words squeeze my fucking heart every single time. She's having my child, and one day soon, I plan to make her my wife.

I can't imagine anything better in this world than getting to spend the rest of my life with the only woman that has ever made me feel complete...

BOOKS BY VICTORIA ASHLEY

Standalone Books

Wake Up Call

This regret

Thrust

Hard & Reckless

Strung

Sex Material

Wreck My World

Steal You Away

Walk of Shame Series

Slade

Hemy

Cale

Stone

Styx

Kash

Savage & Ink Series

Royal Savage

Beautiful Savage

Pain Series

Get Off On the Pain

Something For The Pain

Alphachat Series (Co-written with Hilary Storm)

Pay For Play

Two Can Play

Locke Brother Series (Co-written with Jenika Snow)

Damaged Locke

Savage Locke

Twisted Locke

ABOUT THE AUTHOR

Victoria Ashley grew up in Illinois and has had a passion for reading for as long as she can remember. After finding a reading app where it allowed readers to upload their own stories, she gave it a shot and writing became her passion.

She lives for a good romance book with tattooed bad boys that are just highly misunderstood. When she's not reading or writing about bad boys, you can find her watching her favorite shows.

tiktok.com/@victoria.ashley_author
instagram.com/victoriaashley.author
facebook.com/VictoriaAshleyAuthor1

Printed in the USA
CPSIA information can be obtained
at www.ICGtesting.com
LVHW021115051124
795747LV00014B/665